KT BYRD

Raptor Moon

First edition

This book was professionally typeset on Reedsy.
Find out more at reedsy.com

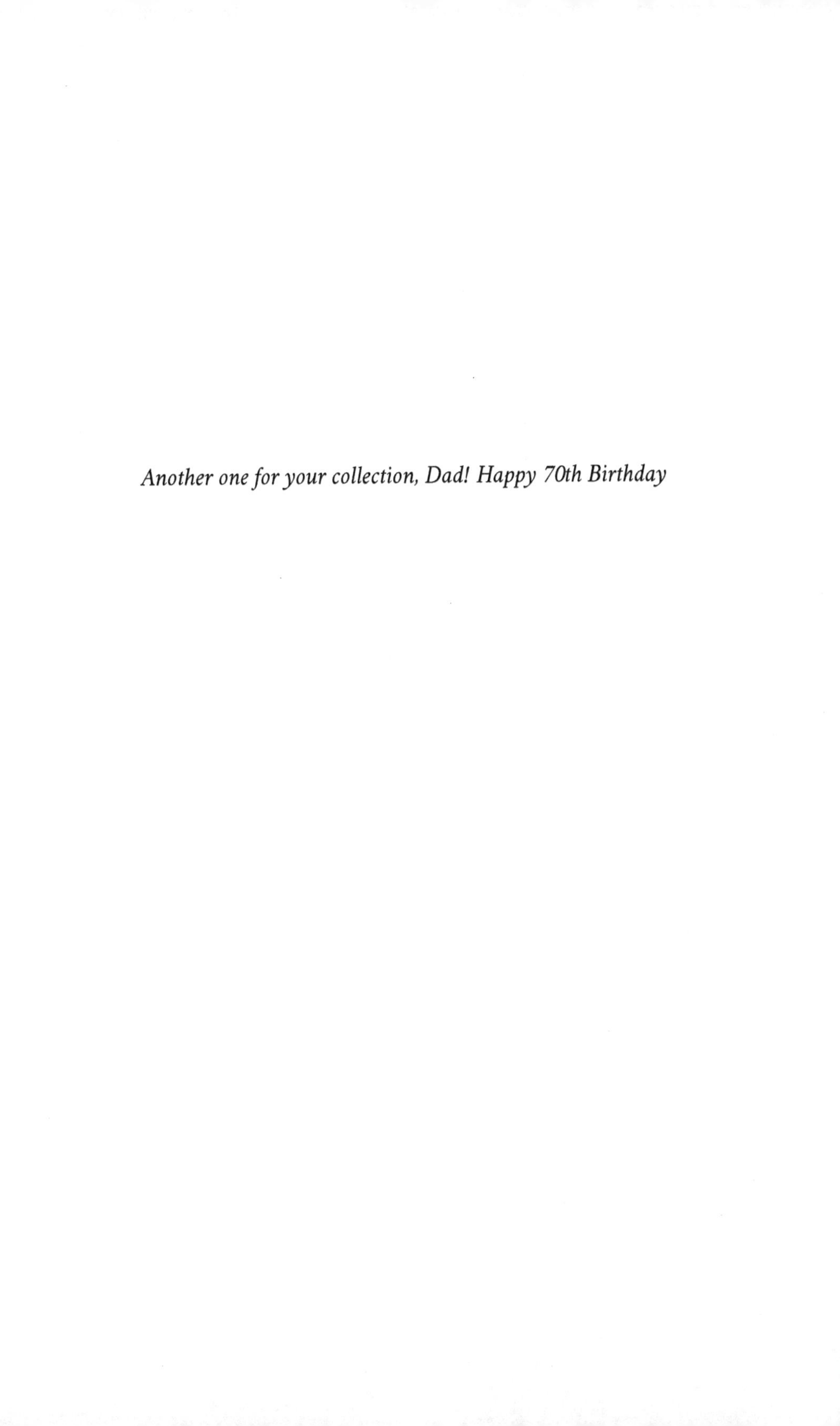

Another one for your collection, Dad! Happy 70th Birthday

Foreword

I thoroughly enjoyed writing and rewriting *Raptor Moon* multiple times over, refining its purpose. I am privileged to present its final form.

The premise morphed over the years. Now, it encompasses the joy of me reuniting with my father after nineteen years of separation. I creatively twist my workplace experience and education of aviation and general safety and health. In the final drafting stages, I chose to use the gas leak underneath Beau Heights as a catalyst for a conversation relevant to an ongoing dilemma in our society. While paying respects to the victims and survivors of the New London school explosion that occurred on March 18, 1937, I briefly use it as a case study driving the events of *Raptor Moon*.

Acknowledgments

I'd like to thank the people who helped me transform from that financially struggling lady who makes pretzels and sells T-shirts at a kiosk in the middle of the mall to a real-deal professional: CAROLYN HAINES, for helping me while I was down, being a friend, and mentor when I was an undergrad trying to figure it all out. ANGELA HULL, for being the best watch supervisor ever at KMFC tower and telling me about "mayo and onion sammiches" that one night we had the midnight shift. Our crew helped me get over the hump in becoming a certified air traffic controller. Also, you are the best for knowing that guy who knows a guy who knew my dad before he retired as an aeronautical analyst for the FAA. You and auntie PAULETTE HORTON helped me reunite with him after he had been out of my life for nearly twenty years. Thank you! I want to thank my team from the safety office I worked at while in the military. Your actions and the education you've provided invented the premise of *Raptor Moon*.

As for the novel, I'd like to thank my editors JESSICA POWERS, JULIE TIBBOT, and SCOTT COLBY. Thanks for helping me clean it up, and saying yes to the ideas that should be yessed and no to the ideas that got tossed into the abyss. Round of applause for cover designer FELIX TINDALL who elevated my vision and also added the 3:17 detail on the clock tower for the approximate time the 1937 New London School Explosion occurred.

Lastly, my husband CHRIS (My inspiration for Isaiah "doggy boy" Marksman comes from him) is deserving of many thanks for his support and listening to my off the wall ideas, refining them and trusting that they'd become interwoven into the coolest story. Turns out he's also a blurb master.

I'm lucky to have him by my side. And he's lucky to have an author for a wife. How many husbands get to say that?

Introduction

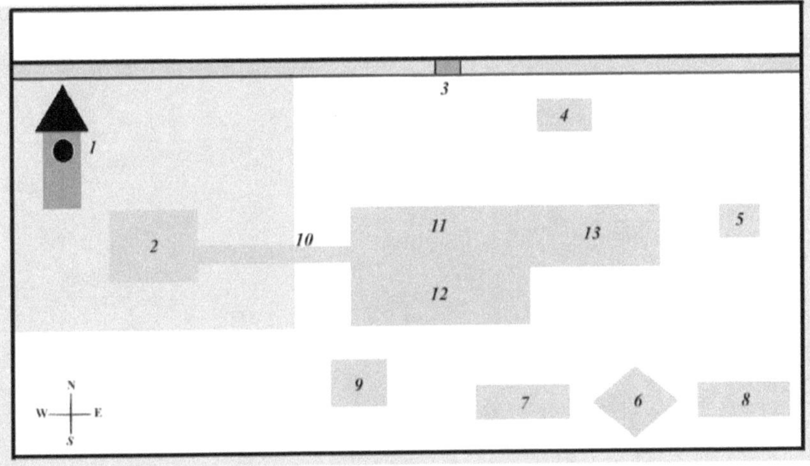

Map of Lynbrook (not to scale)

Lynbrook is 30 acres (think small private airport or 23 football fields)

1. Beau Heights **inside exclusion zone**
2. West Building (classrooms) **inside exclusion zone**
3. North Gate
4. Eric Fowl's Cabin
5. Mail Room
6. Courtyard

7. Male Dorms
8. Female Dorms
9. Supply Office Portable
10. Elevated Breezeway **inside exclusion zone**
11. Upstairs Main Building (library)
12. Downstairs Main Building (Headmaster Kite's office, infirmary, dining hall, cafeteria)
13. Bal-chatri (upstairs only)

I

Friday, November 7

Lunar phase: waxing gibbous
The Raptor Moon

Mikayla Birdwing

4:36 PM

Mikayla hadn't finished a meal in over a month. Food was given to her. She simply didn't have the stomach for all of it. It started October 1, the day of the Great Resignation, the day Lynbrook's teachers and staff went missing. She weighed 120 back then. Now 98 pounds, she stood at a barred window on the upper floor of the library with one arm crossed over her chest, hand clenching her other arm. Her uniform hardly fit the same from when she first got it. Outside, Beau Heights, Lynbrook's clocktower, overlooked the campus, cracked with age but with a colossal grandeur not yet lost. Natural gases leaking beneath it had ruined everyone's life. No one was spared, not even the people who'd created the problem.

The light from the overcast sky barely warmed her face, but she stayed a bit longer. Below, a soaked squirrel bounced and disappeared again in the wet grass in search of acorns after the afternoon storm. A few more days and the grass would sprout higher, littering the once beautiful campus with patches of crabgrass and dandelions. That same squirrel would dig for acorns beneath weeds and dead leaves. Lynbrook's groundskeeper was gone.

She pushed against the windowpane for a closer look at the squirrel. Chipped paint curled underneath her nails as she clenched the windowsill, then she suddenly staggered back. A red-tailed hawk grabbed the squirrel's hindlegs between its talons, and its wings powered upward towards Alabama's Talladega mountains. The squirrel dangled. It would end up like Lynbrook's groundskeeper.

Near the end of September, one teacher in the school's western quadrant mysteriously fainted. Others became nauseated. Sick Lynbrookians complained about headaches and eye irritation. Days later, the Kite Clan declared Lynbrook's entire western quadrant unsafe and uninhabitable. They moved everyone further east on the campus where the smell of gas was nonexistent, believing they'd be far enough away from the problem. The west area was blocked off with yellow caution tape and orange traffic cones. The teachers and staff tried to protest but soon after departed from the campus in white, unmarked vans, never to be seen or heard from again. "The Great Resignation," Lynbrookians called it.

Mikayla took a shaky breath, fingernails digging deep into her skin. Her hand was wrapped around the entirety of her upper arm. She felt bad for the squirrel, but its fate was natural. It was prey surrounded by raptors. The Kite Clan and their Raptor Admins who had taken complete charge of Lynbrook were predators. Students were the new prey, now that teachers and staff were gone. All thirty-nine of them.

Secured with four padlocks and covered in climbing poison ivy vines, the gate on the north side of campus stood as the barrier between many oak trees and an unkempt dirt road. Aside from meal deliveries, mailmen, and van drivers, outsiders were prohibited from visiting. Lynbrookians weren't allowed to leave either. Perhaps it was out of convenience for the Kite Clan not having to deal with the fallout of what was happening to their school. Mikayla wasn't sure. Raptor Admins told them nothing. They answered no questions and protected the interests of the Kite Clan.

Still gripping her arm, Mikayla stepped back from the window in search of another book. Every book shelved floor to ceiling was about airfield maintenance and airfield logistics. Her mother was a lawyer. Atlanta's best environmental prosecutor, in fact. Mikayla wanted to be her mother, not an airport worker.

Mikayla spent last summer in courtrooms, spectating. Something about watching her mother hold the unaccountable accountable gave her hope that the polluted world her generation inherited could be restored. At school, she led a conservationist club for rehoming clothes or belongings classmates didn't want so that they wouldn't go into landfills.

She spent many sleepless nights wondering why her mother sent her to a boarding school that didn't prepare her to become a lawyer. She felt more prepared to patrol an airfield or fix a small jet than file an appeal for court or write an affidavit. The Kite Clan, a trillionaire family in the oil and gas industry, could afford any innovative solution on the planet. And yet they did nothing. They were the exact type of evil corporation her mother would go after. Any environmental prosecutor would condemn this, especially Atlanta's best. Where was she to stand up for the Lynbrookians? There had been no words from her since their goodbye hug. No letters, despite the many Mikayla mailed.

Mikayla hugged the book about aircraft hangar maintenance to her chest and stepped down the spiral staircase. The Lynbrookians were divided in half: the side where the boys sat and the girls to the right of them on the other end of the library. Many of them stared off into the distance, disassociating. Mr. Sparrowhawk, a Raptor Admin, sat on watch front and center. He wore a black tie and matching suspenders over a white button-down. His long, dark hair framed a face reminiscent of someone in mourning.

Book open to a random section, Mikayla took her seat and watched the skinny hand on the clock skate along for twenty minutes. Freedom Hours were near. Her eyes went to Mr. Sparrowhawk. His void-black pupils were unreadable. She turned away, feeling her stare linger too long. Raptor Admins held some sort of militant bearing that made her wonder who they were and where they came from. All seven had that chilling but somehow enthusiastic look, as if they believed in nothing and yet had complete faith in serving the Kite Clan.

Something stuck out of the baseboard between two adjoining bookshelves. A dandelion weed. Crouching down, she wrapped her finger twice around its pale, deformed stem. It reached desperately for the slivers of sunlight filtering through the barred window. Her other palm rested flat on the floor, keeping her balanced.

Back at her seat, she wrote *"Ewed Ogrwing Rthough Lwal ni Blirary"* in the margins lightly with her pencil. Translated, it read *Weed growing through wall in library.* Lynbrookians' writings were encrypted to confuse Raptor Admins in case they were caught passing notes to each other.

Mr. Sparrowhawk approached, moving past her and going directly towards the weed. He pulled it and ate it. Mikayla hid her dropped jaw behind her palms. Mr. Sparrowhawk marched back to his chair where he sat smirking. It was like he had read her mind.

Beau Heights's bells tolled at 5 o'clock. Freedom Hours had begun. Lynbrookians quickly departed the library.

Dinner was yesterday's beef stew. Rations were limited to a first come, first served basis because Raptor Admins had taken the place of cafeteria workers. Mikayla wasn't hungry.

Outside, autumn leaves and pine needles crunched beneath her shoes. The trees shed a ton of leaves, an assortment of red, yellow, brown—far too many for anyone to rake and gather. Chattering students, screaming cicadas, the screeches of vultures circling above—it all assaulted her ears, leaving her unable to think. How nice it would be to act carefree like the Lynbrookians who lounged around wherever, trying to make the best of it.

Mikayla stopped at a small, windowless building. Opening the door, the stench of mold briefly paralyzed her. The evening sunlight shone on scurrying insects as they sought shelter inside mail slots or dark corners. The brass doors of the antique PO boxes were engraved with Celtic knots along the edges. The newer postboxes were cherrywood, older ones cedarwood. Hers was #147, cedarwood covered in cobwebs. Hopefully a letter awaited inside. Dad had sent one for sure. Mother, probably too busy.

Raptor Admins read everything. She'd carefully chosen her words in the letter she wrote last week.

NOVEMBER 1

DAD, YOU HAVE TO COME SEE THIS. LOVE YOU. –MIKA

She knew he would understand. After her parents divorced, that was her way of telling him to come check out something wrong. Worked every time. Last time she said that to him, she showed him the scar from her brain surgery on the back of her shaved head. Her parents argued and screamed at each other about it the entire night. That was when she was twelve, five years ago. Her hair had regrown enough to hide the scar, but extreme shrinkage made her curls appear several inches shorter because they shriveled up like wire coils.

Surprisingly, her dad's request for visitation was approved, scheduled for tomorrow around lunchtime. She noticed her shallow breathing and relaxed. Tomorrow could be the best day of her life—but also maybe the worst. Dad coming was too convenient. It was convenient like how Lynbrookians' lives mattered whereas the teachers' and staff lives did not.

She almost stopped breathing again. Recomposing herself, she turned the postbox's ten-pointed star combination lock clockwise, stopping at the point between A-B. Then, she turned it counterclockwise to I-J and clockwise to H-I. The bottom knob clicked.

She pulled out a yellow envelope addressed by her dad in Oklahoma City. "Yes!"

The yellow envelope's flap had been ripped open and stamped partially shut with the golden wax seal of a swallowtail kite—the official mark of Headmaster Kite's approval. She removed a ripped, taped-back-together sheet of stationery out of the envelope. A pause slowed her fingers down. All the words, front and back, were blacked out with the thick stroke of a marker.

"Censored…again," Mikayla muttered, balling up everything.

The mailroom door opened. A breeze eased through the crack, lifting the cowlicks that stood above her other kinks and coils like butterfly antennas. Sado Swallowtail entered. Her eyes locked onto him until she lost the nerve to gaze at his copper eyes any longer. Because the sides of his hair were tapered and he had trained his dreads to lay forward, two of them stood up like antennas, like her hair.

From New Orleans, he had a passion for Cajun cuisine. He used to talk about opening a late-night restaurant-slash-comedy club on Bourbon Street with his sisters. Swamped in credit card debt, his family didn't save for his college, let alone any post high school opportunity. Debt was the typical Lynbrookian sob story. Even Mikayla's mother struggled with law school bills.

Mikayla scooted to make room for him to stand next to her. The mailroom was no bigger than a walk-in closet.

"Whoa, you actually got a letter?" Sado laughed in disbelief. "Well, wait...I forgot you're the only one who gets mail."

"Yeah, from my dad," she mumbled, showing him that every line was redacted.

"That's a power move." He hesitated. "Sure about goin' through with your plan tomorrow, Mika-Chou?"

He called her Mika-Chou because of her last name. A Birdwing was a type of butterfly, and chou was Japanese for butterfly. To her, the nickname was annoying, but at least he wasn't calling her Mikayla.

She shrugged. Her lips disappeared inside her mouth.

"Dependin' on other parents to respond to your letters is a weakness in your plan. Letters are slow, get what I'm sayin'?"

"Slow but stealthy," Mikayla spoke up. "I can't send anything over a network. I think Headmaster Kite has someone who monitors and deletes everything Lynbrook-related online. It's like this place doesn't exist."

Her mother had sprung Lynbrook on her one night before summer break was over. She hurriedly packed her bags and got to the train station where an unmarked van picked her up. She only had one night to run a quick search about the school online. Results showed nothing. No images. No webpages. Lynbrook was low-tech. There were no computers or cellphones for Lynbrookians to access. After the Great Resignation, she collected classmates' home addresses with a plan to mail tell-all letters once she was back in Oklahoma City with her dad.

Sado crossed his arms. "Couldn't Headmaster Kite nudge somebody at the Oklahoma City post office to *lose* letters with your name and dad's address?"

Mikayla gasped, and her eyes widened. "Then I'll use a pseudonym and get him to rent a PO box. Better yet, I'll get Dad to ask one of his friends to—"

"Mika-Chou, some miracle from above is sendin' your dad here. Go home with him and forget about savin' the rest of us."

"I can't be the only one who gets out. It's the right thing to do."

"The rest of us will get to go one day, whenever the Kites decide movin' us away from the leak ain't safe enough." He got quiet. His lips were in a straight line, making him look softer. "I saw what Mr. Sparrowhawk did. I think they're watchin' you."

Mikayla shrugged, although she was creeped out. She felt like Mr. Sparrowhawk was inside her mind and knew she'd taken interest in the dandelion. The note about the weed was a self-reminder to show her dad proof of Lynbrook's degradation. However, she trusted he wouldn't want her stuck in a place that leaked natural gases and made people "disappear."

Sado continued. "They're not goin' to let you leave knowin' all that's goin' on and whatnot, get what I'm sayin'?"

"My dad gets to come in, so he'll have his cellphone. He'll call the police. It's that easy."

"You see nothin' strange about that? The rest of our parents can't come. They don't even bother to write or reach out."

"But if they did, you know they'd get over here, Sado. Your folks haven't forgotten about you."

"Whatever," he mumbled. "What if it doesn't work out?"

"I don't know."

Her plan made sense. Dad would come, find out about the chaos, and take her home. She honestly had no earthly idea what to do if things went wrong. She couldn't even conceptualize what going wrong would look like.

"Give up. Your plan won't work." He slowly placed his hand on hers. "I don't want you to end up like the teachers."

She pulled her hand away, storming out of the mailroom. He called her name, but she kept trudging through the thick grass. She headed towards maple and oak trees where a cabin was located near Lynbrook's barbed wire gate.

There would be no quitting. Her dad was already on his way to Alabama.

Lorelei Avian

5:14 PM

Inside the cabin, Lorelei leaned against the wall, picking at her sweater. The off-white garment had turned beige over time and was covered in her waist-length, moonlight blonde hair. Bird feathers were stuck in the threading and unknown stains dotted along the sleeves. On her crystal-beaded lariat chain, a tarnished whistle dangled above her bosom like a tassel. She kept it on at all times, even while showering.

From the outside, the cabin was shabby and unwelcoming, much like an abandoned home. Inside, it felt rustic and cozy, resembling a place where a lumberjack rested after a hard day of chopping wood and hunting deer. Last night's downpour flooded the foundation, and water seeped inside through the floorboards. The wood sagged and warped, smelling moldy. Though it wasn't perfect, it was her home during Freedom Hours. Family was nearby. Birds played with her there. No Raptor Admins stood by, watching her every movement. She loved it.

"You think you can snag me a new one before tonight's over with, Uncle Eric?" Lorelei held up the sweater. "Kinda getting annoyed with all the stuff that's stuck on this one."

Her uncle, Eric Fowl, napped on a beat-up recliner with his feet propped onto an overstuffed duffle bag like an ottoman. His chest rose and fell smoothly. He had no need to be alert. No Lynbrookian had ever tried to escape.

Uncle Eric both lived and worked in the cabin as Lynbrook's security guard and sole gatekeeper. He had never been the type to hold down a respectable job. He'd gotten his money partaking in shady activities that got him frequently tied up with provincial police back in Canada. Although he'd stopped doing drugs years ago, he occasionally got drunk. Because he needed a job that would overlook his criminal and drug charges, Headmaster Kite hired him.

A knock pounded the door. Lorelei glanced at her muddy bare feet, embarrassed that whoever was on the other side would see them. Then again, it was her birthday. She could do whatever she wanted. She opened the door, frowning.

"Happy birthday, Lorelei."

It was Mikayla Birdwing, a newer Lynbrookian. Lorelei usually never bothered learning their names, but she liked Mikayla. The girl had grit but in a quiet, spunky way. She never judged her whistle or gave her a headache about her dirty clothes. She was okay to joke around with too. Lorelei gripped the door, pretending to slam it.

Mikayla threw her hands in the way to stop the door's momentum. "I need your help."

Lorelei hid her grin behind her sleeve. She pulled herself together and opened the door wider. "I can't even help myself. Your life is over tomorrow."

"Please?" Mikayla clasped her palms together.

Lorelei had forgotten—a naïve, hopeful girl like Mikayla didn't handle hardship with dark humor like she did. Now eighteen, Lorelei would soon be sent to Meccanicville, an airport owned by Headmaster Kite. Lynbrookians were automatically assigned there after their eighteenth birthdays.

Lorelei softened her tone. "Come in for a sec. I need to grab a different sweater. This one's getting itchy."

Mikayla had never been invited inside the cabin before. She entered and shyly leaned against the closed door.

"What's that say?" Mikayla asked, pointing up.

Above her was a talking fish plaque, and above that was an engraved, handcrafted hook knife.

"This?" Lorelei smacked her palm on the wall next to the knife. She was tall enough to do it effortlessly. "Uncle Eric got it tattooed on 'em too. That's French for 'Rebel Hard, Die Young.' Like it?"

Mikayla's lips curled into a timid, pursed smile. She loved it but was too shy to say so.

Lorelei walked away from the door and spotted a sweater next to an empty bottle of whiskey on an end table. Reaching for it, her foot bumped Uncle Eric's recliner.

He jolted out of his sleep. "Now that's the second time today you done hit my chair, sasquatch."

Lorelei curled her toes and snatched the sweater across his body. The chronic hoarseness of his voice turned Mikayla's head. Uncle Eric sounded like he ate cigarettes back in his day, she thought, picturing a younger version of him smoking three cigarettes between each of his fingers. She couldn't imagine him with anything other than gray hair and liver spots.

Mikayla suddenly stamped the ground as if she were shaking off something. Landon, Lorelei's twin brother, had brushed against her leg as he prowled on all fours. He was born an hour later, the day after Lorelei. They grew up with their mom and dad in a suburban neighborhood in Ontario. At school, they had friends and after-school activities that took up a fair bit of their leisure time. Mom was a loving homemaker. Dad grinded 9 to 5 as a middle manager for a local business. They shared dinner at the table every night. Sundays, they attended the chapel for service and afterward ate at a buffet for lunch. Every week repeated the one before it until their parents were murdered in a home invasion. They were only thirteen, so Uncle Eric took custody. At the time, he had just gotten released from prison for a petty theft. A month later, he found work at Lynbrook in America.

Lorelei chuckled. "Landy, I thought you were still outside."

"No, I was under there." He pointed to a small, circular table on the other side of the cabin.

The hood of his gray pullover hoodie cocooned most of his face, except the tip of his pointy nose. The tightened drawstrings were knotted above his chapped lips, and thick, overgrown bangs covered his eyes. Standing up, he pulled out a plastic jar from underneath the hoodie. The contents inside pulsed. "Lorelei, look at what I got so far. Did I do good? It's what you asked for, right? It's four hundred caterpillars, beetles, dragonflies, crickets, grasshoppers, cicadas, moths, spiders and worms and fleas and some ticks and some—"

"Looks good!" Lorelei cut him off and gave him two thumbs up. "Best birthday gift ever!"

Mikayla flinched. "Why are you shoving them in there like that?"

Landon froze. The only girl he was used to talking to was his sister. A plump, yellow-and-black striped caterpillar circled his wrist and lower forearm before crawling underneath his hoodie's sleeve.

Mikayla shuddered.

Breaking the tension, Lorelei snatched off Landon's hood and ruffled his shaggy hair. "Landy's a big nerd for bugs, Mikayla."

"And antisocial," Uncle Eric added as he shifted his body towards Mikayla. "Birdwing, is it? What brings you here to see Lorelei, besides wishing her happy birthday?"

"Mr. Sparrowhawk ate her flower," Landon said before Mikayla could get a word in.

Lorelei rolled her eyes as she put her arm into the sweater. "Ugh, Sparrowhawk...he's *something*, isn't he?" She motioned for Mikayla to go outside. "She's here to talk to me. I'll be back in a sec, Uncle Eric."

"Sure thing," he said.

Landon waved her off. Lorelei felt bittersweet. Soon, she would leave Lynbrook for good. No more evenings in the cabin.

The sunset warmed her face as she sat cross-legged on a patch of crabgrass. It wasn't too damp beneath her, but nowhere was completely dry. She flexed her toes, dug them through the grass, and lodged them into mud.

Mikayla plopped down beside her. She was more careful and poised. "Why is your brother collecting bugs for your birthday?"

"Admit it," Lorelei began in a tone that let Mikayla know she wasn't in control of the conversation, "you're worried."

Mikayla's eyebrows raised. "Worried about what?"

"How things are going to go tomorrow with your dad," she said.

Mikayla had collected the home addresses of Lynbrookians with intentions to mail tell-all letters once she was back in Oklahoma City with her dad. Lorelei felt bitter that she and Landon were the only two not on her list to save. Mikayla had never asked either for their address, not that it would matter. They had no one back home, although Mikayla didn't know that. It would've been nice to have been considered worth saving.

The stress of her and Landon's fate at Meccanicville came back. She curled into an upright fetal position with her arms hugging her knees, curling her toes deeper into the mud.

Mikayla avoided her eyes and stayed quiet.

"There's something I didn't want to bring up with my uncle and Landon around," Lorelei said. "That's why we're out here."

"What is it?"

Lorelei lifted her head. "You'll see and hear about some weird stuff tomorrow. It'll be weirder than a jar of bugs. I can promise that."

Tight-lipped, Mikayla rested backside down.

Lorelei liked Mikayla's guts to stick it to the Kite Clan. No Lynbrookian had ever tried that before. Having her company was okay. Besides, it had been years since Lorelei stargazed with anyone other than Landon, and Uncle Eric preferred nights alone with a bottle.

"The moonlight makes your gray eyes reflect like sterling silver," Mikayla said. They were the first words spoken in thirty minutes.

"Thanks," Lorelei said.

"Ever noticed the dippers look like kites?" Mikayla asked.

"Kites?"

"Y'know, the Big Dipper and the Little Dipper. They kinda look like kites."

"I hate them," Lorelei grumbled, tightening her fetal position.

"Sorry, wasn't thinking," she mumbled.

Saying diamonds would have been better. It wasn't a secret that Lorelei, Landon, and Uncle Eric were related to the Kite Clan, sharing a grandmother who had two husbands, one Canadian and the other American. Lorelei and Landon were Headmaster Kite's niece and nephew. Unfortunately, he viewed them as assets, no differently than any other Lynbrookian student.

The cicadas and crickets took turns filling the silence. Beside Lorelei, an ant stumbled upon a crumb five times its size and sluggishly carried it to an anthill before it had fallen through a hollow spot. It never reemerged, and that section of the anthill caved in.

"Lorelei," Mikayla whispered, "I think my plan has holes, like it might not work out tomorrow…"

Mikayla explained everything she had done already and everything she planned on doing from start to finish once her dad arrived. She had gathered addresses, and then she was going to send a letter about the natural gas leak and Great Resignation to the families once her dad took her back to Oklahoma City. Not complex, just very naïve and hopeful.

Lorelei sat up straight and fully leaned into Mikayla. "Yup, full of holes, like you said. It doesn't plan for handling Raptor Admins. You have no idea what you're getting into. Look how tiny you are. What are you? Five-foot-one? I've seen twigs thicker than you." Lorelei snickered, then a half beat of silence. She felt bad and changed her tone back to a serious one. "Spend a second thinking about why your dad's visit takes priority over bringing in a plumber to fix our toilets. What makes him more important than maintenance? A doctor? A groundskeeper? We're low on food, mind you! Why does he get to come and not someone who can stop the natural gas leak?"

Mikayla palmed her face. "I know there's something fishy about it. I get that. Everyone picks on me about it, but why not take advantage of the situation? He can get me out of here tomorrow."

"And you think the Raptor Admins are going to let you leave that easily?"

She picked at her brittle fingernails and mumbled, "I still believe it'll work," she said weakly.

"Really?" Lorelei asked skeptically. She knew Mikayla was scrambling to save face. "I have a plan that's better."

"But earlier, you said you couldn't help yourself."

"I lied. Did you really think I was going to sit back and let Headmaster Kite send me to his stupid airport so he can exploit me for the labor?" Lorelei slammed her fist on the grass. "I got a question for you. How come you didn't ask anyone else for help? You got lots of friends."

She sunk her head. "I didn't want to get them in trouble, Lorelei."

Mikayla was the popular girl everyone adored, nothing like the mean girls that used to bully Lorelei back in Ontario. Her close friends were seventeen years old, weeks or months away from turning eighteen. Understandably, she didn't want to risk involving them and seeing them get sent to Meccanicville earlier. Lorelei missed having friends who cared.

"Were you okay with getting me in trouble? Or did you feel like I was a goner anyways?" Lorelei clenched the grass. She couldn't believe she had asked those questions and how they came out like daggers.

Mikayla looked away. "I don't know how to help you and Landon. You're related to the Kite Clan."

Figures, Lorelei grunted. "Eh, I guess I can see why you didn't ask for help. Trusting others to pull their weight is like trusting a cat not to scratch the crap out of you when you rub its belly. I'm the cat that scratches, get what I mean?"

Mikayla didn't laugh.

Lorelei shot up. "I can save my own ass, Mikayla. Don't worry about me. I have a plan Landon and Uncle Eric are clueless about."

"What's your plan?"

Arms spread wide apart, Lorelei shouted *"Mateo, vas!"* at the top of her lungs and blew her whistle. Something a distance away jingled. Soon, a barn owl flew over fast, like a fighter airplane swerving out of a tight one-eighty turn. There was a bell attached to its ankle. It rose above and dove back towards Mikayla again, hooting. Mikayla crouched into a ball, hiding her face as it swooshed around them, quieter than a whisper—then silence. Mikayla lifted her head and watched the owl's tail fluff as it headed back from wherever it came.

Lorelei felt the adrenaline flowing through her. She laughed and clapped her hands. "That's my plan!"

Mikayla sat up straight in disbelief. They simmered in an uncomfortable silence, and then she asked, "What is your plan exactly? I'm a bit confused.

All you did was show me a bird."

Lorelei wanted Mikayla to be confused, but at the same time wanted her to think she and Mateo were cool. She tucked her chain and whistle between her breasts, then pointed beyond the gate. "I'm escaping tonight. I'm not coming back, and tomorrow's going to be crazy because of it."

"Are you kidding me?" Mikayla asked.

"Nope."

"Why now? Why haven't you tried before?"

"Same reason nobody else ever leaves. They're scared."

"Are you still scared?"

Lorelei shrugged.

Trembling and shaking her head, Mikayla stood up. "Okay, I didn't come here for this. Happy birthday. Good luck." She left.

"She always runs away when it gets tough," Lorelei mumbled under her breath.

She called Mateo to come back. The owl returned and let her embrace him. She needed a hug and good luck. After tonight and tomorrow night, her energy would wane on the full moon. Tonight was still the Raptor Moon. Sunday would be the Canine Moon, when the Raptor Moon would turn full.

The details of Lorelei's own plan were just as naïve and hopeful as Mikayla's. Difference was that she had no friends to hash it out with. There would be no quitting. Her bag was already packed, and her mind was made up.

She went back into the cabin. Uncle Eric slept with his feet up. Landon sat at the table, immersed in a book about Cessnas. She put on her boots, grabbed her packed bag and the jar of bugs, and left quietly with her uncle's keys. He had copies in a drawer on his nightstand.

Lynbrook's fence was very tall with barbed wire at the top. She unlocked all the locks, hands shaking, and snuck out without being seen. Mateo followed.

Mikayla Birdwing

5:59 PM

Lorelei became dot-sized as Mikayla walked several minutes south towards the back edge of Lynbrook's perimeter. Her shoulders were stiff, and she caught herself not breathing again. She forced herself to inhale and reminded herself that her plan could and would work.

The campus was thirty acres, with a two-story main building in the center featuring a connected, elevated breezeway that greatly extended east to west, separating the condemned building on the west side. There were plenty of places without people around. Without access to technology, there weren't many ways to unwind from a day of cramming aviation and airfield knowledge. Many of the Lynbrookians lounged three or four deep with their cliques on the north side by the fence. Everyone else socialized in the courtyard between the dormitories on the south side. Hanging out anywhere but west was okay. Of course, faint traces of natural gas reached everywhere, but it was most concentrated far west underneath Beau Heights—the condemned zone.

Cicadas had quieted down with the daylight gone. Something else in the grass continued a faint buzzing. Stars filled the sky above. Miles away from the city, Lynbrook had almost zero light pollution.

Mikayla breathed. She couldn't wait to stargaze from the comfort of her dad's backyard. He had a hammock where she liked to read her astronomy and environment books on months he had custody. She closed her eyes, meditating.

A soft moan came between the intermittently chirping crickets.

"Thought I was alone over here," Mikayla muttered under her breath.

She tip-toed around the tree. Right then, Jericho Kite kissed Naomi Maus hard, mashing her arms against the trunk with his hands completely wrapped around hers like cuffs. The string of saliva connecting his tongue and hers broke. Naomi arched her back and pressed herself against him for another kiss.

"*Ew!*" It slipped out. Mikayla cuffed her mouth.

Smug, Jericho nudged Naomi aside. Naomi looked at the ground, almost as if she were afraid to make eye contact. Jericho was Headmaster Kite's son. Although it sounded ridiculous, he preferred to be addressed as The Honorable Kite. His outfit was reminiscent of a military officer's, except his obsession with orange accessories disrupted the uniformity of it. His orange handkerchief showed his initials stitched in gold threading. The orange cravat neatly tucked beneath his chin, spotless and starched, accented his gray embroidered tailcoat blazer. He wore melo pearl cufflinks and button covers to match. His eyes were silver, same shade as Lorelei's and Landon's. They were cousins.

Jericho walked up to Mikayla. "Hey, Birdwing." He bumped her shoulder. "Goodbye, Birdwing." He left without urgency.

Mikayla waited for him to be gone before closing in on Naomi.

"Why are you kissing that horse-faced Kite boy?"

Naomi wiped her mouth. "He, um…well, he came up to me, and then…" Her voice trailed off, and she clapped her hands together. "Please don't tell anyone. Please."

Mikayla's heart sank. "You were kissing our enemy! And you have a boyfriend."

Nodding, Naomi palmed her entire face, unable to hide the redness rushing to her head. Her complexion was fairer. Mikayla had never been more grateful to have much more melanin to hide behind. She turned away from Naomi, arms crossed. Naomi froze. She wasn't the type of person to say what was on her mind when it came to confrontation.

Naomi's whisper broke their silence. "He came on to me."

"That's not what it looked like."

"You know how he is. He made me feel like I had to do it."

Mikayla felt like she should've known Naomi would say anything to get out of this one. She had known her for a while. Both their mothers were lawyers in Atlanta and had introduced them to each other because of their surgeries. Naomi's surgery was on her uterus, about the same time Mikayla had hers on her brain while they were twelve. They loved volleyball and drawing comics, but that went away in high school when they were sent to Lynbrook. Naomi's eighteenth birthday was in two weeks. She would soon be given a slot for Meccanicville.

"You didn't tell him about my plan, did you?"

"No, Mika. He doesn't know, I swear." Naomi was firm. "Once your dad takes you home with him, you'll arrange for the rest of us to be freed. Then I won't have to deal with Jericho coming on to me. I'll be back in Atlanta, hopefully." She paused as if she were eager to change the topic.

Mikayla crossed her arms. "Why were you kissing Jericho? I know he didn't come on to you. This is *not* the first time I've seen you alone with him."

Naomi opened her mouth to reply, but the sound of howling coyotes along the fence overtook her voice. Mikayla glanced over Naomi's shoulder. Isaiah Marksman headed their way, quickly. He was Naomi's boyfriend. The barking grew louder as if the coyotes wanted his attention. They hopped along the fence, tracking him.

"Not him, not now. He's such a dork," Naomi muttered. "Please don't tell him what happened, okay?"

"Why are you with him if you think he's a dork?"

Naomi's eyes widened as if Mikayla wasn't supposed to have heard that. "Mika, promise me."

Mikayla sighed. "I won't tell him."

Isaiah waved before he got close enough to say hello. His Appalachian twang was thick, but his quiet intensity made Mikayla long for a conversation alone with him. She hadn't spoken to him in a week. He had the warm, rich eyes of a golden retriever. In September, something had been special between them. She still felt that way, and she hoped he did too. They constantly talked about how they would take pictures of the sun and moon every day for a year to track the solar and lunar analemma. He wore a tarnished, bronze, twenty-four-inch chain with an upside down crescent moon pendant. She had one just like it back home.

"The coyotes are cutting up again tonight because nobody's given them a baloney sandwich," he said to Mikayla with a goofy smile before turning to Naomi. "Hey, what's wrong?"

He had a soulful gentleness about him, as if he was always listening, always understanding, always ready to cheer her up. It wasn't fair that Naomi got to have that side of him. She was the tall, gorgeous one, pretty smile. Long, wavy hair. Well-endowed. Mikayla controlled her envy with a neutral face, but she felt her insides boiling.

Naomi uncovered her face, flashing a very convincing smile. "I stubbed my toe on that tree behind us. I'm so clumsy, huh?"

Isaiah leaned into her with his hand out for her to take. "You okay?"

"Yeah, I'm fine. Feeling kinda woozy." Naomi took his hand and fell into his embrace.

"Oh, wow, we're actually hugging. That never happens. Oops, I didn't mean to say that out loud." He chuckled nervously. "I got you. Don't fall down again. That would be really bad, heh."

Naomi pressed her chest against his head and wrapped her finger in his brunette curls. Isaiah's blushing highlighted the freckles on his face. He was shorter than her. Most boys were. Naomi never showed him affection. She seemed to be overdoing it out of guilt to keep him from asking questions. On the outside, they looked like awkward middle schoolers at their first dance. He tightly held the small of Naomi's waist with one hand while his other cupped her face. Naomi grimaced but fixed her smile. Mikayla turned her back on them, bottom lip pouted out.

He should be holding me like that, not her. Her throat ached, and her eyes got watery.

"Hey, Mika. Tomorrow's your big day. Your dad will be happy to see you again," Isaiah said, moving away from Naomi. Her eyes remained on the ground until she felt his hand on her shoulder. "Chin up. Tomorrow might not go as bad as you think. Sometimes, there's help in the background." He winked hard at her, smiling.

Beaming, she covered her blushing cheeks. She liked that he was a bit of a dork.

"No supply office tonight, Isaiah?" Naomi asked.

"Nope. I'm finished with the project, for good."

Naomi's voice became radiant. Now she was acting over the top. "Really? For real this time? Now will you tell us about what you were doing?"

Mikayla looked over her shoulder, curious. She wanted to know too.

"Not yet," he replied. "It's a surprise."

Since October, Isaiah had spent many of his Freedom Hours working in Lynbrook's supply office in a portable building at the back of the campus. One of the Raptor Admins found out he was good at cataloging and assigned him to organize items that were delivered. He regularly skipped dinner for more time there. He claimed he was doing an extra credit project but wouldn't go into detail.

Dealing with the stress of tomorrow weighed on Mikayla enough. Adding Naomi's affairs with a Kite and Isaiah's secret to the mix—bad idea. She walked away.

"Wait, Mika, tonight's a clear night," Isaiah said. "How about you go get Sado and we hang out together one last time?"

"Ugh, don't invite Sado. Are you out of your mind?" Naomi asked.

"Why not? He's going to invite himself anyway."

"No, he's always talking negative about everything, making everyone feel scared all the time," Naomi said.

"I know, but you know how he is. Might as well skip the drama and have fun," Isaiah said, eyeing Mikayla. "Full moon's out tonight."

"No, it's not," Mikayla said.

He grinned. "Ah-ha! That's right. I was seeing if you were paying attention."

Mikayla pretended not to be flattered. "I gotta go. Night, guys."

Though staying sounded like a good idea, the last time the four of them hung out together, it created a tension she would rather forget. It happened on October's full moon, the Hunter's Moon. Sado sat on Mikayla's left, holding her left hand. Naomi sat on the Mikayla's right with Isaiah on her other side. They didn't hold hands. Mikayla and Isaiah, however, were caressing each other's hands behind Naomi's back. Sado caught them. Naomi didn't care, but Sado never got over it. Mikayla looked forward to spending the next full moon at home in Oklahoma without the drama.

She continued south towards the two dormitories. One dormitory was for the males, the other for females. Centered between the dorms was a courtyard filled with weeds and dying flowers in mulch. Wisteria, vines, and ivy wrapped around the columns and climbed upward towards the roofs of both dormitories. Weeds had taken over Mikayla's path on the cobblestones and strangled shrubs and flower beds.

She went inside. Lynbrookians who chose to return to their dorm early from Freedom Hours were not allowed to go back out. But it was better to return an hour early than return one second after the curfew.

The dorms weren't luxurious in the slightest. Cement floors. White brick walls like a prison. Thirty full-sized beds, fifteen on each side—all worn down and old. Plain, scratchy linen. Wall lockers in lieu of a closet. Some of them barely shut, and they all creaked at the hinges. The windows above every other bed were the size of a shoe box, notably not big enough to squeeze through. Nobody was going to run away easily.

Mikayla stood alone in the communal shower for a while without moving. Her body felt heavy and tired. She palmed the wall for balance. With her dad coming, escaping with Lorelei would have made no sense; however, she wondered why nobody else had left after everything that happened after the leak began. Were they that afraid? That cowardly? She wondered why the Kites and their Raptor Admins stayed. What was keeping them there? Fear? Unfaltering loyalty? Her head began spinning. She wished she had eaten something.

Eventually, she plopped into her bed, face in her pillow. Her tears dropped onto the cotton, and the dampness soaked away little by little. She questioned why she wanted to help other Lynbrookians, especially Naomi. Years of friendship in jeopardy. For what? A senseless fling with a Kite?

Like Sado, most Lynbrookians had given up, lounging around waiting for a miracle. They put no thought into helping themselves. They were scared. She understood that, especially after the Great Resignation. But why did she care on their behalf? Why make the sacrifice? Would they appreciate it? Mikayla even worried about Isaiah. It felt like his secret project was something that would backfire on him.

Other girls filtered into the dorm. They began chores, meticulously shaping hospital corners in their respective beds or cleaning. Dorm inspections were common on Friday nights. Seven minutes till eight, Naomi entered. She knelt in Mikayla's zone beside her bed, going over the sloppy hospital corners. Her hair was disheveled and dirtied with grass and petals, and her blouse was partially unbuttoned.

"Huh, Lorelei's not here." Naomi grunted as she tucked sheets underneath the mattress. "We have to do her bed quickly."

"She can do her own stupid bed when she gets back."

"Are you mad at me?"

Mikayla ignored her. There were twenty other girls in the dormitory now. A confrontation would magnetize the gossips. Beau Heights chimed, signaling the end of Freedom Hours.

"I'm sure Lorelei heard Beau and is on her way," Naomi spoke after the seventh ring.

"She has the grace period," Mikayla said, hoping Lorelei was joking earlier about leaving.

The grace period lasted five minutes and cost one infraction—not that it mattered for Lorelei. 8:05 PM came. She never returned.

"Lorelei's going to get disappeared like our airfield teacher," a girl said.

"Maybe not. She's related to *them*," someone replied.

"Pfft, if she had special privileges, then why does she get treated like one of us? Like I said, she's done," the first girl said, dragging her finger across her neck.

At 8:10 PM, a Raptor Admin stormed the dorm, demanding answers on Lorelei's whereabouts. She flipped beds over, kicked storage trunks across the floor, and broke belongings. Mikayla kept her mouth shut. The Raptor Admin left Lorelei's bed untouched as a reminder of why the rest of their beds were in disarray. Mikayla remembered why she cared—why she sacrificed. She would rather risk her life to save everyone from this hellhole than abandon them. Nobody deserved to feel unsafe, without any agency.

Jericho Kite IV

8:50 PM

ootsteps pounded outside of Jericho's private quarters. Shadows of shuffling feet zipped past underneath his door. The shadows flashed by more urgently as time went by. On his nightstand, the 9:07 PM numbers from his clock emitted an annoying red glare against the wall in front of him. Around 9:45 PM, he flipped the clock over and turned towards the wall, covering his ears. The noise outside passed through his palms.

He wondered what was going on out in the bal-chatri tonight. His father called the hallway to his and the Raptor Admins' private quarters the bal-chatri. The bird cage reference wasn't lost on Jericho. His father had always wanted to be a falconer but never committed to the work of becoming one. Controlling his Raptor Admins was the next best thing.

Jericho tossed onto his side, arm dangling, waiting for the shadow of whoever it was lingering outside his door to go away. He flipped the pillow over to the cool side. Thinking of Naomi's adorable face and the kisses they shared earlier relaxed him. He had no idea what more than kissing her would feel like, but it didn't stop him from wondering. He clenched the pillow, closed his eyes, and breathed fast out his nostrils. The racket in the hallway erased Naomi's face.

The two of them exchanged smiles two weeks after her arrival to Lynbrook. In October after the natural gas leak got chaotic, being alone with her and getting to know her became easy. Big, open campus. Less oversight with teachers and staff gone. He loved her giggles and the way she wore two small buns in her hair so that she appeared to have mouse ears. He'd just gotten her into his life; he didn't want to see her go already. Almost eighteen, she was weeks from being shipped to Meccanicville. Before their kiss earlier at the oak tree, Naomi cried about her fate. She begged him to explain Meccanicville. He refused. His father would kill him. Instead, he promised her he would do everything in his power to delay her assignment.

In sight of Talladega Mountain, Lynbrook was in a humid, chilly forest outside Talladega, Alabama. Meccanicville Airport resided far west of San Antonio, Texas, somewhere not encroached by the city. Arid and hot with temperatures into the triple digits, drought conditions encumbered the airfield. Newly transferred Lynbrookians who couldn't acclimate died of heat stroke after working too hard. The ones who lived worked tirelessly to make up for the dead. Meccanicville's mission focused on fixing planes and getting them in the air. The flights supported Kite Express's gas drilling sites and refineries. Kite Express monopolized oil and gas across all the Western countries.

Jericho felt grateful for his wealth but not the cost that came with it. He wanted something money couldn't buy.

He touched the sketch Naomi had drawn for him. It was thumbtacked beside his headboard, a mouse in a tutu with butterfly wings. The shading and smoothness of the mouse was beautifully done. She should sell art, not work for his father's "oil tycoonery." He called it tycoonery when he felt bitter—and he felt bitter about his father constantly.

As Jericho Kite, fourth of his name, Lynbrook and Meccanicville would be his to inherit. There was one more place called Kan, thus completing the Trinity. He wasn't allowed to know much about Kan, but he had already figured that evil things beyond comprehension went on there from overhearing pieces of past conversations. On a spectrum from unethical to evil, the company's holdings were ordered Lynbrook, Meccanicville, then Kan. Unfortunately, he wasn't going to inherit the Trinity soon enough to make it better. His father desired to keep the Trinity the way it was. He got his way.

A Kite wants what they want and gets what they want.

Jericho felt more like a Lynbrookian than like a member of a trillionaire family. Born in Lynbrook's western quadrant years before it became the condemned classrooms of today, he watched his mother grow ill postpartum. She died from complications a week later. His father raised him, barely. The man was busy traveling back and forth from Lynbrook to Meccanicville, occasionally crossing the North Atlantic into the Arctic towards Kan. The Raptor Admins around him did all the work raising Jericho. Back then, there were only three Raptor Admins, not seven, and the group hadn't been officially named yet. They were just three loyal people who highly respected his father and the company. Jericho had no meaningful childhood and no friends. He had never left Lynbrook's campus, not once in his entire life. Now twenty-one, he had nothing to look forward to but inheriting the Trinity.

Rain tapped his windowpane. Light droplets, then heavy pounding. A flash brightened his quarters, then the booming thunder rattled his rings on the nightstand. One ring was a twenty-four-karat gold gothic-style band; another, a diamond encrusted mixture of rare metals and tungsten; and the last, a swallowtail kite sculpted out of stone. Together, all three were worth more than the GDP of most underdeveloped nations combined.

The dreaded knock on his door finally came. He groggily came to a sitting position, turning on a lamp.

"Who's that? What do you want?" He rubbed his eyes.

A man replied, but Jericho could barely make out who he was and what he had said because his message sounded muffled.

"And Osprey," another man added. His voice was also muffled but had enough bass to cut through.

Jericho cursed under his breath and got to his feet. He put on a pair of sweatpants, then wiped sleep out of his eyes as he opened the door. Condor and Osprey greeted him with their heads bowing as far as they could while wearing HAZMAT suits and respirators. Through the face shield, Jericho could see Condor was shaken up by something. This type of thing wasn't what he was hired for.

Condor was Lynbrook's network analyst, a cyber expert. He was the genius who ensured no digital online footprints existed for any facility associated with the Trinity. He was slender, with a brooding appearance much like Sparrowhawk, except he lacked the other man's callousness. In fact, Lynbrookians confused the two from behind, then would exhale when they realized it was just Condor. The man wasn't feared.

Osprey, an older gentleman, was hard of hearing. He'd retired as an airport manager from Mexico with forty years of flightline experience. His hearing had been damaged by years working around Meccanicville's turbojets without ear protection. Jericho felt like Osprey wasn't much of a disciplinarian either because he was a legacy Raptor Admin, one of his father's first hires.

"Was that you two running up and down the bal-chatri like hooligans?" Jericho asked.

"Our apologies, Honorable Kite," Condor's voice trembled.

Jericho became smug. Being called Honorable Kite by both Lynbrookians and Raptor Admins satisfied him. However, his relationship with Condor and Osprey was like an awkward social dance he didn't consent to. Condor and Osprey were two of the three Raptor Admins who'd raised him. Condor was like a nerdy older brother he could go to about academics but not for advice on women. Osprey felt like a laid-back father who wanted his beer, football, and a recliner. The men had changed his diapers, seen him eat disgusting things off the floor, and taught him how to read and write.

"Something you need to know, Honorable Kite," Osprey said seriously. "Lorelei Avian never returned to the female dormitory after Freedom Hours."

"She's gone?"

"Yes, Honorable Kite."

His mouth hung for a bit, then he said, "So after nearly two hours, you decide to tell me this because—" He bit his tongue and paused again. "Obviously no sign of her in the western quadrant or else you wouldn't be dressed like *that*." He gawked at their black rubber boots and HAZMAT suits.

"Not unless she got her hands on one of these suits and managed to hide very well," Osprey replied.

"We haven't checked there yet," Condor added.

"There's no way Lorelei's hiding on the west side. She's crazy, not stupid." Jericho kneaded his forehead. "Are all the HAZMAT suits accounted for in the supply office?"

Condor fumbled through his clipboard and nodded swiftly. Jericho hoped he had accurate numbers. Isaiah Marksman worked in the supply office and very well could have screwed up the inventory, maybe even on purpose. He spent a suspicious amount of time there.

"We tried not to wake you, honestly, but your father is pushing us to have her found as soon as possible," said Condor. "He's making us look everywhere."

"Including places that make no sense," Osprey added bitterly.

"Anybody tried asking Landon or their uncle?" Jericho asked.

"Your father consulted them first, though nothing came of it," said Osprey. "They were surprised she was gone. Your father wants you to be a part of the search."

Jericho pictured Lorelei's dead body on the ground somewhere near Beau Heights. Flat. Pale. Eyes bloodshot. Blood running out of her nose. Although his father had forbidden him from talking to his cousins, he couldn't stomach the thought of that happening to anybody, let alone his half cousin.

"Not interested."

"Not optional," Osprey said. "Don your HAZMAT and get out here."

"In five minutes," Condor added.

"Two minutes is all he gets." Osprey narrowed his eyes at Jericho. "We have to stick to your father's schedule. He wants us to meet him back here in the bal-chatri before 11:30 PM."

"Why put it on?" Jericho asked.

"To double check. Your father requested it, specifically for you to do. He said he wants you to take more initiative."

Jericho closed the door on them and stared at what little he could see of his orange HAZMAT coveralls protruding out of his closet. He sighed and went for the sleeve. Quickly, he inspected the entire suit for punctures, rips, and defects. While sitting on the edge of his bed, he unzipped it and placed both legs through and down into the sewn-in socks. The rubber squeaked and smelled like tires.

His family had the money to stop the natural gas leak and prevent another. It just wasn't a priority. They had their sights on other investments. Since government workers were the only personnel trained in pipeline repairs and hazardous environments, his father let them deal with it. However, major companies had to abide by a three-strike policy.

Lynbrook had its first natural gas leak ten years ago. The government subsidized fixing that, letting Kite Express off with a recommendation to invest in sustainable piping. Strike one.

Three years later, hydrogen sulfide killed someone working in a manhole outside a hangar at Meccanicville. Government stepped in to help with ventilating that area to get rid of the toxic gas. Kite Express was fined, nothing that couldn't be earned back inside a week. Strike two.

Lynbrook's current leak came from the same damaged pipeline. No more chances. Reporting it would lead to heavier fines on Kite Express. Strike three would be publicized and destroy relations with stockholders. Kite Express would go bankrupt, forced to close every gas station in North America. There would be lawsuits, questions, and outrage.

His father had two older brothers who ran Kite Express's other entities, the more public, high-stakes positions outside the profitable cluster of subsidiaries that made up the Trinity. His father redefined the meaning of a family's black sheep. If it came out he couldn't even manage the Trinity correctly, Jericho and his father may become estranged from the rest of the Kite Clan, at best.

One minute left. Jericho rushed to put on his safety boots, zip everything, and adjust all the splash guards. Carrying his mask, respirator, and gloves in hand, he left his room. Condor and Osprey bowed again, seeming pleased he hadn't taken much more than the two minutes.

"Mask," Condor said. "Put on your mask and the rest, Honorable Kite.

That way it's already on."

Jericho cut his eyes at Condor. He wanted to tell him they were in Lynbrook's upstairs eastern quadrant where there was no need to put the suit on so early. In fact, he felt like what they were wearing might be considered overboard. He had to keep in mind they were dealing with a natural gas leak, the invisible threat that drove the Great Resignation. However, he believed the fumes didn't reach where they were staying on the east side. He hated the respirator the most of all. He felt like he couldn't breathe well even while taking bigger breaths than needed.

"You'll make yourself lightheaded, Honorable Kite. We have a long walk ahead of us," said Osprey.

Because the campus was thirty acres and they were on the far east side, it was going to take them well over twenty minutes to cross to the west side building.

Jericho nodded and asked, "Where are the other admins?"

"Beyond the gate, in case she's out there or tries to secretly return," Condor replied.

The three of them walked.

"Keep your ears peeled for her breathing. Might hear it even with all this rain," Osprey said and breathed heavily once through his respirator.

"It's 'keep your eyes peeled and listen out' or 'ears open.' Nobody says keep your ears peeled,' especially not to you," Condor argued.

"Huh? Say that last part again," said Osprey.

Jericho rolled his eyes and walked slowly to linger behind them. The wind pushed against the windowpanes. Lightning lit up the arched stained-glass windows, coloring the glossed enamel a bluish violet hue only seen on stormy nights. The chandeliers hanging below the skylight highlighted all the stained-glass's laser engravings and crystals. He touched the window, watching the ripples of water slew downward from color to color. His father had spared no expense. Each Raptor Admin had a window displaying their respective bird of prey. Condor's was perched tall on a canyon of citrine and bronze enamel, resembling a computer circuit board. Osprey's outstretched wings and talons clenched an airplane. The background was pearl-enameled clouds overlapping topaz crystals for the sky. Jericho hated his. It was placed at the back of the hall, a baby swallowtail kite emerging out of an egg in a nest.

They approached yellow caution tape wrapped around the locked door for the elevated outdoor breezeway leading to the west side. Although the breezeway was covered, the heavy, sideways rain drenched the cement walkway. Before Jericho could reach out to rip away the tape, Condor moved his hand off the door.

"Honorable Kite, wait." Condor showed Jericho an orange device in his hand. "It's a combustible gas detector. See this sensor here? It'll beep when— well, you know—the leak is high in concentration."

Osprey and Condor headed out first, and Jericho got a glimpse of the breezeway before the door shut. Raindrops near the outdoor lantern were white against the black sky. There was a feather on the cobblestone, white as the rain that drenched it. He caught the door with his boot before it closed and leaned near the feather. Condor and Osprey turned around. Rain pebbles on their face shields warped their features.

Jericho pointed at the feather and said "Mateo was here" loud over the thunder. There was no evidence it was Mateo's feather or that the owl had been there at all. It could've belonged to any random bird. The idea Lorelei was nearby made him hope they could get the search over with and call it a night.

Walking along the breezeway felt like an eternity. The dead space reminded him of hallways inside that had no purpose other than to display expensive paintings and photos of their countless oil rigs along the Gulf Coast. The breezeway seemed pointless, other than as a means of showing off how they could afford an aesthetically pleasing yet sturdy structure. However, it came in handy this time, since they didn't have to cross the ground below in the rain.

Inside the western building, visibility was limited by the range of their flashlight. Electricity in those abandoned classrooms and hallways was shut off. There were open books and supplies spread about as if a fire drill had dismissed the class and they were expected to return and pick up where they left off. The search party was able to check most of the classrooms and bathrooms before the device began to beep rapidly.

"We've got to get out!" Osprey shouted.

Their urgency hadn't come soon enough. Condor vomited in his HAZMAT suit. He lost his balance and fell. Osprey pointed at the entrance towards an emergency staircase. He and Jericho, each hoisting a pair of Condor's limbs, carefully stepped down so as not to slip or drop him while heading out of the building. It was safe to assume Lorelei wasn't there *and* alive.

Outside, they helped Condor remove his HAZMAT suit and waited for him to take in fresher air. Afterwards, they quickly walked through the rain, headed east for the main building's central entrance.

Condor cleared his throat and regained his composure. "Well, that wasn't supposed to happen."

"Look." Jericho inspected Condor's suit, tracing his fingers along a tear on the back of the neck seal.

The respirator indicated an expired filter cartridge. Both Condor's and Osprey's eyebrows furrowed. All three of their filters were expired.

A moment of silence came over them before Jericho spoke. "Isaiah Marksman should've discarded these and installed the new ones."

"Marksman is usually trustworthy." There was a hint of denial in Condor's voice. "An oversight, perhaps. We made the same mistake by not inspecting every piece of our gear."

Jericho shook his head. Condor had recommended Isaiah Marksman for the supply office duty. If word about the defect reached his father, Condor would be punished. Something inside of Jericho held back from mentioning it. Condor was already humiliated enough, and Jericho didn't want to aggravate the man any further.

"I will tell Father to investigate Marksman's work. I won't mention this incident."

Osprey shook his head. "Can't let you do that, Honorable Kite. Your father is stressed. There's enough pressure on him as it is. Kite Express is in trouble."

"Yeah, yeah, and I'm fine," Condor stood up. His voice trembled. "See?"

They all removed their HAZMAT suits, shut them in a janitor's closet, and dried off their hair with paper towels in a nearby restroom. Osprey stepped into a stall where he grunted and groaned on the toilet, farting endlessly. Condor splashed water on his face to wash off the remaining vomit. Jericho leaned against the wall, tossing a pack of cigarettes up and down and catching it like a ball.

"Honorable Kite, you're smoking again?" Condor pulled a second paper towel from the dispenser. "Thought you quit and all."

Jericho shrugged. "Started back."

"I believed in you," he said. "Maybe you can try quitting again."

Jericho looked at the packaging. It was a highly sought-after brand, best in the world. He felt like he could quit whenever, but what would be the point in it? Before the campus shut down, he had stocked up on several cartons. He had enough to take him through February, maybe even March.

"Condor, don't you feel like we shouldn't stay here?" Jericho asked. "What happened to you back there…we could've lost you."

Condor nodded. He and Jericho shared an aggrieved glance.

"Why is my father making us stay here? Can't we leave, get it fixed, and come back home?"

"Um…your father is prideful. I think leaving would be him accepting defeat. Think of what your other family would say," said Condor.

Jericho clenched the pack.

"Hey, Honorable Kite, we're getting by just fine—on this side of campus, of course. I think being far away from it justifies staying," Condor said.

"For how much longer though?"

"Listen up. Got a text from the boss," Osprey said before he grunted out a fart.

Jericho lifted his head, now listening.

Condor turned off the faucet. "And?"

The toilet flushed. They waited for the clinking of Osprey's belt buckle to stop.

"Robert Birdwing checked into his flight. He'll fly out of Oklahoma tomorrow morning and be at his layover in Atlanta by 9 AM," Osprey replied.

"Wow, he's actually going to come this time," Condor said.

"I can't believe it either. Boss has been after him for years."

Robert Birdwing had retired as an aeronautical analyst. That was the job title Condor's background search yielded. It meant Robert had spent decades of his life managing databases for airports, their construction, and the airspace above them. He knew a great deal about aviation. That knowledge made him useful for solving problems at Meccanicville. Allowing Robert Birdwing to see his daughter was the leverage Jericho's father exerted to lure him in.

"I'll be outside," Jericho said, opening the pack of cigarettes.

He walked upstairs, crossed the bal-chatri, entered his quarters, and stepped onto the balcony on the other side of his bedroom. Outside, protected by an overhang, he listened to the rain and exhaled, the petrichor in the air calming his nerves. He stared beyond the gates, hoping to see a glimpse of Lorelei's moonlight hair or her owl, Mateo. *She couldn't have gone that far*, he thought, reaching for a third cigarette and his lighter. Avoiding the rain, he pressed against the brick wall, worried for Lorelei, Landon, Naomi, and even Mikayla. Aside from the nice things Naomi told him about her, he didn't know Mikayla well. He felt like she didn't deserve to have her father dangled in front of her. Everyone's damning fate was at the hands of his sonofabitch father. He hated him. If the Trinity were his, things would be different.

The tiny mailroom building below took a beating from the storm. Its roof shingles barely held on. About three weeks ago, Jericho found Naomi crying at her empty post box. Her mother hadn't responded to any of her letters about the natural gas leak. She had told him Mikayla's mother ignored hers too. The girls found it strange because their mothers were bigshot environmental justice warriors in the legal system. They were the type of lawyers who'd come for Kite Express, and yet they did nothing. Jericho knew why, though he couldn't tell Naomi the truth. His father would kill him, just like how he'd ordered some of the Raptor Admins to kill the teachers and staff and bury them in the woods.

He lit his fourth cigarette, shaking and anxious. Mikayla Birdwing and her father, Robert Birdwing, were the only family members allowed to communicate because his sonofabitch father wanted them to.

#

In the bal-chatri, all seven Raptor Admins and Jericho stood in front of their respective stained-glass windows. Four on one side, four on the other. The ones who'd searched for Lorelei beyond the gate were dressed in dry clothes. They had sunken, defeated expressions, mulling over how they were going to explain why they would have no answers for the girl's disappearance. No one spouted so much as a bit of small talk to break the tension.

Jericho's father entered twenty minutes late. He was a tall, middle-aged man with a cynical aura and narrow eyes. His salt and pepper hair was styled with a mauve hue, but his stubble was full gray. He was dressed in black pants, a crisp white button-down shirt, and a black tie.

The Raptor Admins bowed in unison, then snapped to attention as his father assumed his position at the center of the hallway where his stained-glass window was the grandest. It was an onyx kite perched on a golden sun with diamond-encrusted helix nebulae for its eyes and pupils.

"We will have the advantage tomorrow. We will crush Mikayla Birdwing's plan and take her father into our possession. Be prepared for an attack from Lorelei. She's the main threat, our primary target. Lorelei made her move. Now, we make ours. I made a request for two pilots from Meccanicville to fly in with their most fuel-efficient planes. They are skilled reconnaissance fliers too. They'll find her from above." He gazed ahead, a mad look in his eye. "My next instructions will come at dawn. Question nothing!" He paused, staring at the floor. "Return to your quarters. Be here zero six hundred. Night watch is in effect, starting with Condor, then Osprey. Dismissed."

The Raptor Admins walked away from their respective windows, and each disappeared behind the door of their personal quarters. When the seventh door closed and clicked to lock, Jericho's father approached him.

"Boy, you smell like your grandmother Carolyn's ashtray." Jericho completely tilted his head back to look up at his father. The man's eclipsing presence made him feel five years old again. "It's a shame I had to send Condor and Osprey to your quarters. There's no doubt in my mind you heard a commotion and decided to ignore it. I know you, boy. You should've taken some initiative and gone out there to do what it took to drag that witch back!" His father unclenched his balled fist and turned around. "A nuisance covered in her blood is coming tomorrow."

Jericho pursed his lips, unsure what his father meant by *a nuisance covered in her blood*. He had noticed any time blood was mentioned his father's language would become evasive or encrypted. There was something hidden from him.

"When it comes to Lorelei and Landon, you change, boy."

He couldn't argue in the presence of his vengeful, angry father. Accusations about what Isaiah Marksman did would be dismissed. Condor's near death would go unpunished.

"What are you going to do to Lorelei when you find her?" Jericho asked.

His father turned his back, walking away. Jericho had caught a glimpse of the look in his eyes. Things were about to get bad—Great Resignation bad.

Lorelei Avian

11:52 PM

Lorelei's adrenaline wore off, gradually slowing her down. The Raptor Admins gave up chasing her about an hour ago. She combed her way through branches and decaying forestry with a compass in hand. Rain droplets blurred the cardinal points. She was in search of a cellphone buried northwest, according to detailed instructions given to her.

Three miles from the campus, she stumbled upon the mass grave where the teachers and staff were buried. Grass had started growing around the weeds of the disturbed soil. She knew what had happened there.

Later, the moist smell of dirt hit her nose, then rain drenched her, flattening her hair against her face. Mateo sought refuge in a tree. Lorelei joined, climbing halfway up the eighty-foot pine tree to where her owl perched. They settled on a thick branch for the remainder of their sleepless night until the early morning hours.

She climbed down and tried for the cellphone again. Throughout the walk, she thought about Mikayla and hoped her dad would get her out of Lynbrook somehow—though she doubted it would happen. The way Mikayla talked about her dad reminded Lorelei how close she used to be with her own dad before he passed. Mom taught her how to dance; Dad taught her how to fight. Boxing, Muay Thai, Krav Maga, Systema, wrestling. She hated her sasquatch feet but appreciated what they could do.

Within an hour, she uncovered the cellphone's burial site. It was where she was told it would be, near a log and a warped, discarded tractor tire. She was surprised it could turn on and make a call. Only 21% of its battery remained available. The Birmingham Chemical Safety Board's office number was one of two preprogrammed on the contacts list. She called them at 4:23 AM, leaving a voicemail.

"Hello, please send help as soon as possible. I'm a kid who goes to a boarding school in Talladega, Alabama, called Lynbrook. It's owned by Kite Express. It's in the middle of nowhere, near a forest. The school has a very, very big clocktower that's got a gas leak underneath it. Lots of teachers are gone *and one passed out*. That happened last month. Our heads hurt, and we get sick from the fumes. We're very scared. Please, send help today."

Lorelei hung up, grinning. The information she gave was strategically planned word for word. The best part about her mentioning trillionaire corporation Kite Express was that it should alarm anyone reviewing the message. It was a big corporation with a documented history of gas leaks. Who wouldn't jump on the opportunity to bring it down?A part of Lorelei didn't want to leave her cousin, Jericho, behind to deal with the fallout, but he had the means to find his own way. She and Landon didn't. She needed to get them out. Mateo too.

She thought about calling the police but felt like the Chemical Safety Board would ultimately end up doing that anyway once they uncovered the horrors during their investigation.

At 6:00 AM, two dragonfly-shaped airplanes flew overhead. Lorelei dodged and hid inside the wide, hollow log. It wasn't long before she realized they were spy planes searching for her. For the next hour, she continued hiding in the trees and studying their flight paths. She timed them and found it took four minutes and twenty-six seconds on average for the planes to make a full revolution around a five-mile radius. At times the pair circled to check out an area, increasing their average revolution by one minute and forty-eight seconds. They maintained visual flight below the clouds despite the weather. Occasionally, they altered their direction based on the wind. From her readings in the library, she predicted that they would adjust for sun glare after sunrise.

She watched the flowing leaves on the trees and stayed aware of her cardinal position relative to the rising sun. She and Mateo headed in the direction that would put them out of sight behind the pilots. Sooner or later, they would have to give up and leave to refuel.

In her mind, she had done her deed by calling the CSB. At 7:01 AM, she called the number labeled "unknown" in the contacts list, expecting to speak with a trillionaire named Alexander Ravensbourne. He was the man who'd given her the instructions to the buried cellphone. The call went straight to voicemail.

"Hey, Alexander. I did what you told me to do. It's really cold and wet out here. Call me back and let me know you'll have that van ready for me, Landon, and Mateo. We wanna go back home. Don't forget, you promised us a flight to Ontario."

She hung up, the phone's battery nearly drained. 9% left and no charger.

II

Saturday, November 8

Lunar phase: waxing gibbous
The Raptor Moon

Mikayla Birdwing

7:32 AM

Mikayla awakened after what felt like two hours of sleep. Worrying about Dad's arrival and Lorelei's disappearance kept her tossing and turning. All the other girls, fully dressed in their uniforms, were scattered throughout the dorm. They picked up broken glass, hung up clothes, and placed mattresses back onto the box springs. Tidying up from last night's raid was almost complete. Half dressed, Mikayla hurried back and forth between the aisle of beds and girls tucking the comforters back into place. Naomi popped up in front of her and handed her one sock.

"I need two, not one." Mikayla grabbed the sides of her head. "Gawd, why didn't you wake me up earlier?"

"You needed the extra sleep. You were up all night." Naomi had bags under her eyes too. Nobody slept well.

"We have ten minutes to get to breakfast." She wasn't hungry despite not having anything to eat since yesterday's lunch. The consequences of being late scared her.

Mikayla plopped down to put on the sock Naomi gave her, and then she pulled on another one she found. She didn't know whose it was, nor did she care. She added a loose-fitting blouse and her blue neck tab. As the other girls filtered out of the dorm, Naomi tossed Mikayla a pair of pants she'd scavenged from the laundry pile. She was only able to slide them halfway on before Naomi grabbed her hand and yanked her over to where a sky blue notebook lay upside down on the floor. The cover showed baby possums wearing kitten ears in a flower basket. The pages contained every Lynbrookian's home address.

Naomi picked up the notebook and shoved it in Mikayla's face. "Hide this."

"Let me put my pants on all the way first! You almost made me fall and break my neck!"

"What if it was found last night?"

Mikayla shushed Naomi, took the notebook from her, and hid it in a crevice beside her wooden box spring. She went back to getting dressed, not saying anything.

"I think I know why you're mad at me," Naomi said. "It's because Isaiah asked me out. At the time, he thought you and Sado were dating. He said Sado gets very jealous when it comes to you and that he didn't want problems. He said he settled for me instead so he can still be close to you without Sado thinking much of it. I felt bad saying yes, I swear. I know you've always liked Isaiah so much. That's why I never care whenever you two spend time alone."

"Why did you say yes to Isaiah knowing he's not the type of guy you like? You have nothing in common with him."

"Look, I'm gonna break up with him. That way if I leave in two weeks to go to Meccanicville, he can be there for you guilt free."

Mikayla frowned. She'd hoped Naomi would finally acknowledge kissing a Kite was a slap to her face and her efforts to save them. Instead, she'd gotten a word salad on how her problem was everyone else's fault. Jericho Kite would always stay at Lynbrook; therefore, being with him was pointless. She left that part out conveniently.

This was Mikayla's first experience with this side of master manipulator Naomi. She had no idea how to handle it. Perhaps this lying was Naomi's way of handling the immense stress of Meccanicville looming. Mikayla hadn't eaten for almost twenty-four hours, and she wasn't quite herself either. Plus, the thought of Isaiah being free made her blush. Once she helped everyone leave Lynbrook, there were many ways to reconnect with him. They had an analemma to put together.

"It's okay, Naomi. Everyone's going home anyways. I'll make sure of it. It'd all be a bad memory. You're not going to Meccanicville."

Naomi sighed with relief. "Thanks for getting it, Mika. I'm sorry." She reached out for Mikayla's hand. The other girl took it, and they stood quiet for a while.

Like that, the tension dissolved. Naomi's friendship meant so much in these times, even if it was full of silly drama.

Puddles along the route to the cafeteria downstairs in the main building forced Mikayla and Naomi to slow down and lighten their footsteps to avoid splashing mud on their uniforms. Rain soaked through their backpacks as they used them in place of umbrellas. Inside, the silence amplified the squeak of their shoes against the wet tile. The boys were already seated and eating on the opposite side of the cafeteria from the girls. A few boys looked their way but only for long enough to call it an accident in case a Raptor Admin caught their wandering eyes. They weren't allowed to look or talk to a girl until Freedom Hours at 5 o'clock.

Naomi lowered her head, whispering, "We're *soooo* late."

"I didn't hear Beau ringing. We're good," Mikayla said, bumping into somebody's back.

A man wearing a navy blue jacket with reflective, neon yellow letters spelling USCSB turned around. "Excuse me, boy," he said.

Mikayla pulled a curl to show him her hair extended out six inches or so. She let it go, and the curl snapped back into a tight corkscrew.

"My apologies, young *lady*," he said, walking away.

"What a jerk. You look nothing like a boy," Naomi whispered.

"He didn't mean it. He's distracted."

Some days, the shrinkage of Mikayla's hair was more severe than others, when her coils and curls hung long. Other days, it would all stand like a dandelion or a halo, depending on the weather or whether or not she'd used a comb.

"U-S-C-S-B," Naomi spelled out quietly. "What's a USCSB, Mika?"

"Our moms worked with the CSB before. Remember that one case where that business let all that petroleum spill in the Chattahoochee River?" she asked. "Stands for United States Chemical Safety Board. He's a government worker."

The CSB investigated chemical incidents and issued safety recommendations. Their mothers interacted with them occasionally, alongside the Environmental Protection Agency, on cases dealing with businesses who'd committed violations against the environment.

"Oh!" Naomi squealed almost inaudibly. "He's here about the leak. You think our moms finally saw our letters and called them?"

"Maybe." Mikayla smiled.

They couldn't directly write what was happening at Lynbrook with the Raptors screening their mail. Perhaps their mothers had read between the lines and reacted on gut feeling. It was hopeful but not farfetched.

"But...how did he get in here, like through the gates? They're locked."

Mikayla shrugged. "I guess the Kites told Mr. Fowl to let him in."

The Kites had no choice. Government workers outranked trillionaires. They were official enough to pass Lynbrook's gates without dispute or a warrant.

The two girls got their breakfasts and sat beside each other at the first open table they could find on the female side. Mikayla ate her entire plate. She had scrambled eggs, bacon, and a glass of tap water.

#

8:00 AM came. Mikayla slumped in her seat in the library, staring at a random page in a book about airfield management. She couldn't stop thinking about her dad's smile again. She wondered if he still had his goatee.

The man in the USCSB jacket crossed her mind too. The government presence meant the Kites' reign would die soon. She couldn't stop smiling. Who summoned them? Oh, it didn't matter!

The echoing tap of Miss Kestrel's kitten heels came close. The slate blue rhinestones on them sparkled, catching bits of sunlight as she walked by. A lover of bedazzling her possessions, Miss Kestrel was a young, unmarried redhead. She'd singlehandedly destroyed the girls' dorm last night. Barely over five feet tall, even Mikayla had an inch or two on her. She often talked about how Lynbrookians should hate their parents and ever being born. Two days ago, she'd stabbed the point of her heel on Mikayla's hand, twisting it deep until Mikayla collapsed. Torturing Lynbrookians was a pleasure for her.

Mr. Falco, another Raptor Admin, paced the boys' side of the library with his shotgun positioned at port arms. His name was supposed to be Mr. Falcon, but he'd dropped the n for no conceivable reason other than he thought it sounded cooler. He expected everyone to call him Falco, including people he didn't know or like. Only the Kites ignored his request.

Normally, he carried a shotgun for shooting the cardinals he called "sky rats." He wore a bolo tie with red cardinal feathers to show off his feats. His sleeveless vest revealed his large tattoo of the *Mayflower* with *PURE* etched into the sail, showcasing his family pride in centuries of "untainted" White blood.

As Miss Kestrel's and Mr. Falco's steps receded, Mikayla exhaled.

"They're watching," Naomi said under her breath.

Mikayla buried her head in her crossed arms. The intercom buzzed.

"ADMINS ON LIBRARY WATCH, REPORT TO THE BAL-CHATRI IMMEDIATELY!"

Headmaster Kite's voice alerted Mr. Falco and Miss Kestrel to answer the call. His boots pounded the marble, and her heels tapped faster as she followed, converging from opposite sides of the library to confront Mr. Sparrowhawk. The three exchanged words, then rushed for the door. Minutes passed. No one spoke above a whisper, in case one of them returned.

Alone, Landon Avian sat many tables away, head buried in *The Reverie of Night's Pass,* a book about drone wars and cyberattacks on airfields. It was one of the more boring, harder to read books. He appeared stoic as if he wanted to convince everyone in the room that he was unfazed about his twin sister's disappearance. Without his hoodie, his eyes were uncovered today. They were intense and hardened yet gleamed a shade of silver that was even lighter than Lorelei's. Mikayla felt bad that his eighteenth birthday was overshadowed by everything going on.

"Look outside!" someone shouted.

Mikayla heard the whir of propellers. A low-flying plane painted with racecar stripes whirled by the library's window. It was a dragonfly-shaped contraption that looked like a combination of a seaplane and a helicopter, with one pair of fixed wings on top of the body behind the cockpit and a singular propeller installed behind them. A similar plane—this one painted with a checkered pattern—zoomed behind the first, both headed towards a kettle of hawks.

Along with others, Mikayla shot out of her chair and sprinted towards a window. The two airplanes hovered above the forest as low as they could. Their searchlights whitened the sheets of rain, and the force of their propellors parted the tree canopy like a comb on fine hair. Lightning struck, illuminating the horizon for miles. A thunderclap rumbled as the hawks rose above the forest, bolting for the airplanes, their talons elongated like daggers. Dozens more charged for the fixed-winged targets. The airplanes turned swiftly, dodging left then right.

Outside, Mr. Falco, Mr. Sparrowhawk, and Miss Kestrel ran across the grass, armed with rifles. They stood shoulder to shoulder, barrels pointed at the hawks. Mr. Falco readied his aim before pulling the trigger. His muzzle flashed and *kapowed*! The rest fired. Hawks spiraled downward like fallen arrows.

"They're shooting the birds!" Trembling, Naomi pressed her arms against her ears. "I can't! I can't!"

"They're not getting shot. It's blank bullets," Isaiah said, trying to sooth Naomi. "See, no projectiles, so that means those birds are safely controlling their descent. Look closer, Naomi."

"No! I won't look!"

Mikayla side-eyed Isaiah, then gazed outside again. The hawks' wingtips were stiffly tilted. Their noses, beak down. They weren't limp or flopping. A controlled descent, like Isaiah said.

Isaiah held Naomi's shoulders. "Look, please. You won't overcome your fear without understanding."

"I don't care!" She pushed him away.

Burglars had shot and killed Naomi's dad years ago. Everyone dear to her knew how badly she wanted a world free of guns. Isaiah couldn't see it her way. His adoptive father was a weapons master. He'd taught the boy about firearm safety and gifted him the very semi-automatic shotgun Isaiah used to become a certified sharpshooter. He dreamed of becoming an Olympic shooter and owning his own gun range.

Nobody except Mikayla knew soft-spoken Isaiah Marksman was fired up about weapons. It was one of the first secrets he'd told her about himself. Afterward, she'd started liking him *a lot* because he dedicated himself to the things he cared about.

The hawks dispersed like sparks in a fireworks show. The airplanes flew a straight line down the forest, then ascended hundreds of feet higher before turning away, disappearing behind the curtains of rain and clouds. The three Raptor Admins ceased fire and lowered their weapons, once again proving their loyalty to Headmaster Kite. Miss Kestrel, Mr. Sparrowhawk, and Mr. Falco were no doubt the evilest. Everyone knew it.

Sado came over to Isaiah, eyebrows raised. "Whoa, nerd, you knew exactly what was goin' on. None of those birds died."

"Blank bullets release no projectile and therefore should not injure a bird that far away," Isaiah said. His brown eyes were wide with excitement.

He explained how contractors at airports shoot into the sky on the airfield to deter birds from flying near the runway while planes take off and land. He talked about pyrotechnics and other small explosives used to scare off other wildlife at the airport. Mikayla remembered reading about that in her airfield management book. People hired at airports to shoot blanks were important for preventing birds from striking plane engines and to stop planes from crashing into animals like deer or foxes that wandered onto the runway.

Sado leaned into Isaiah. "Why do you know this stuff?"

Isaiah shrugged reluctantly. Sado narrowed his eyes at Isaiah and walked off.

Thirty minutes passed. By then, everyone was back in their seats, quietly waiting. The thunderstorm died down into a light rain. Half the sun cut through the gray clouds, casting a rainbow above Talladega Mountain. Its iridescence shimmered.

Miss Kestrel returned with two men wearing navy USCSB jackets. One was the older, buck-toothed gentleman Mikayla and Naomi had run into earlier. The other was beady-eyed with big ears. He wore a golden pendant, an enameled flower. From where Mikayla sat, it looked like the red spider lily—the death flower.

The older man stepped forward. "Good morning, Lynbrookians. My name is Mr. Edmund Rabbit, and with me is my co-worker in training, Mr. Ren Usagi. We work for the Chemical Safety Board. That means anytime something goes wrong—like a chemical spill or an explosion at a workplace—we step in to find out what happened and why."

The room got quiet. Mr. Rabbit cleared his voice and continued. "Our office in Birmingham received an anonymous phone call early this morning that prompted us to investigate your campus for a gas leak. We're here because we want to talk to you about what happened last month. I understand Lynbrook is going through a major teacher shortage. A teacher fainted and others quit?" Mr. Rabbit nodded as his eyes scanned the library for nods of confirmation. "Good. What we've been told seems to line up."

"Does that mean we get to go home?" a young boy asked, shooting out of his seat with enthusiasm that matched the hope of all his fellow Lynbrookians. He was thirteen and bound to be stuck at Lynbrook for at least another five years before his transition to Meccanicville.

Mr. Rabbit nodded to the boy and continued, briefly telling them about a school explosion that happened in New London, Texas. A spark ignited hazardous natural gas mixtures within the school. It killed almost three hundred students, leading to a movement to add artificial scents to odorless gases. Other safety protocols were created in response as well.

"I'll never forget what happened to those children," Mr. Rabbit pledged with his hand to his heart. "That story was why I became a part of the Chemical Safety Board. Mr. Usagi and I will make sure you get home. Then, we'll conduct a thorough inspection and find out why the gas is leaking, okay?"

The Lynbrookians beamed at one another. It was finally happening: a savior had come to their rescue. Naomi grabbed Mikayla's hand and held it tight. Mikayla couldn't help but smile. That anonymous call had to have been one of their mothers. Thank goodness.

"Mr. Rabbit, *darling*, I'm afraid none of that will be happening."

Miss Kestrel snatched the end of Mr. Rabbit's necktie, tugged him towards her, and wrapped the tie around her hand. Mr. Rabbit slipped his hands underneath his tie, gasping.

"Hey! Let him go!" Mr. Usagi shouted. "Let us do our job! We meant it when we told your headmaster nobody's under arrest. We have no power to detain anybody. We're not police."

"No, but you're gonna wish you were." Miss Kestrel reached underneath her blouse for a slate blue pistol—bedazzled, of course. She loaded a full magazine inside it and sent a bullet into the chamber. The click of the pistol's disengaged safety lever echoed.

Mikayla's palms became sweaty, but she and Naomi still held each other tightly. Her mouth had become so dry that it hurt to swallow. This was the tomorrow Lorelei warned would happen, and soon her dad would be intertwined with the danger. He was well on his way.

Jericho Kite IV

8:44 AM

Fifty feet up, a shared patio on the balcony outside the bal-chatri gave Jericho an unrestricted view of Lynbrook's south side, the dormitories, and the courtyard. The air was humid, but he didn't mind. He finished a cigarette and glared at the forest beyond the campus, hoping to see a flicker of Lorelei's golden hair through the trees.

He reached into his pocket for Mateo's white feather. A light brown streak went diagonally across the end of the tip. He twirled it around his fingertips, fixated on the stripe. Lorelei wasn't a smiler, but she had been that day she'd introduced him to Mateo—their little secret. She showed him how she could summon him with the single blow of her whistle. It was like magic how she had total command over that barn owl.

After putting the feather away gently so it wouldn't bend, he lit another cigarette. A breeze ran through his hair, and strands fell above his brows. It was too quiet and peaceful to last forever. The CSB's arrival changed everything, putting Kite Express in jeopardy of strike three. The government workers would discover the leak coming from the pipeline underground.

The CSB had already spoken to him and his father over mugs of black coffee earlier that morning. They mentioned Kite Express's past infractions and fines from previous incidents. They also explained that they weren't unlike the EPA and other government agencies, but that they couldn't issue fines themselves and needed to recommend such punishments against Kite

Express to other federal entities. The tension in the room grew when they demanded the schematics of Lynbrook.

Little did they know, there would be no investigation.

His father assigned Kestrel to let the CSB believe they were going to perform witness interviews with the students in the library. Kestrel was a human trafficking specialist, and he wanted her to eventually lead the investigators into isolation and poison them. She liked doing that kind of stuff. She'd shot half the teachers last month, alongside Falcon, in a race to see who had the fastest trigger finger and reloading speed.

There were already measures in place to conceal the CSB investigators' deaths so no one from their office in Birmingham would suspect Lynbrook was involved. Their families would receive millions in hush money, and nothing would come of it once all the right people were paid to forget. Same procedures as with the teachers and staff. Rinse, recycle, and repeat. His father had become a sick psycho, a shell of who he once was.

Jericho was shaken to his core. Trembling, his teeth accidentally ground his cigarette into shreds. He spat over the balcony's edge and put out the cigarette.

Bam!

His father was on the other side of the sliding doors, fist balled to bang the door again. Jericho cursed under his breath, hoping the headmaster hadn't seen him smoking. He unlocked the sliding doors and tried to look indifferent.

"Is this where you've been? Chain smoking?"

Jericho's eyes shifted away, then snapped back. He couldn't show weakness before a predator like Headmaster Kite. "I'm thinking about what the CSB told us, Father."

His father firmly gripped Jericho's shoulder. "Why don't you take some initiative, boy?"

Jericho glanced at his father and saw his approval to speak more freely. "I think Lorelei called the CSB."

It was no coincidence they arrived the morning after her disappearance. What he couldn't make sense of was how she knew who to contact and what she'd used to place the call. She didn't have a cellphone, and it wasn't normal for a teenager to know about the Chemical Safety Board. Jericho only knew about them because of his family's dealings with oil and gas regulations.

"I also think she called them, and I think I know who helped her," his father said.

"I don't think her uncle helped," Jericho replied.

"No, Eric knows not to cross me." He took his hand off Jericho's shoulder. "I'm afraid it was someone else."

Jericho spun around. Afraid wasn't a word his father typically used. Headmaster Kite carried himself as a man who feared nothing.

"Who do you think helped her?" Jericho asked.

"I want the CSB dealt with before Robert Birdwing's arrival. Kestrel works fast and can do what she did last time."

Jericho winced and softly said, "No, Father, is there a way without killing more people?"

The headmaster paused to consider. "I need the CSB gone. Those bunny boys should've found a different rabbit hole to jump in." Jericho opened his mouth to respond, but his father continued. "When you take my place as headmaster and leader of the Trinity, you'll find yourself doing anything to avoid disgracing the Kite name."

Falcon and Sparrowhawk approached the sliding doors. Falcon, a retired military policeman and detective, had been hired to be his father's professional bodyguard. Sparrowhawk's past and reason for employment were mysterious, but Jericho knew he had an extensive knowledge of eugenics. Seemed out of place for an oil and gas tycoon. He had been hired five years ago, right around when his father's demeanor turned darker, more morally questionable.

"Boss, I walked by the library and saw Kestrel. Things got out of hand in there." Falcon whipped out his cellphone and showed an image of Kestrel pointing her gun at the CSB. In the background, horrified Lynbrookians cowered underneath tables. "She messed up."

"Inevitably," Sparrowhawk added.

"Goddamn that woman's temper," his father grumbled. "Why didn't she handle them quietly, like last time?"

"Respectfully, sir, it's 'cause she is a bimbo with a brain the size of a chicken nugget. I'll fix Kestrel's mess up." Falcon patted his pistol. "Depend on me."

"May I?" Sparrowhawk elegantly lifted his hand. He waited for both father and son to acknowledge him. "I have an idea that'll put the leverage back on our side. Send Honorable Kite down the hall into the library to discredit the CSB." Sparrowhawk looked at Jericho. "Accuse them of being felons, posing as government officials. Word it right, and you'll make Kestrel look like she's protecting the Lynbrookians from strange men."

"I like it, Sparrowhawk." Jericho's father clapped once. "That's what taking initiative looks like."

Falcon laughed. "I like it too. It'll be a good chance for the kid to practice bein' Lynbrook's next headmaster. Like father, like son." Falcon turned to Jericho. "Right now, the Lynbrookians just see ya as a spoiled Kite boy. This is yer chance to show them ya got nuts."

Jericho hesitated but somehow pulled off a nod and a smirk.

"Robert Birdwing is expected to arrive soon," the headmaster said. "Sparrowhawk, Falcon, go downstairs to the dining hall and get the area set up. When he gets here, I want the two of you to escort Mikayla to the dining hall and monitor their conversation. Make sure she's unable to speak with him about anything that's happened in the last month."

Falcon snickered. "She's gonna be too scared to try with us there."

"I concur," Sparrowhawk said. "Mikayla is a very shy girl who's got a lot on her mind. I will ensure she says nothing pertinent."

Jericho scratched his head. His father wanted Robert Birdwing for work at Meccanicville and had planned to capture him. Why allow him to see his daughter? He understood using Mikayla as an incentive to get him onto the campus. Letting them have lunch and leading them to believe they could be together again was cruel.

"And let me be clear: I'm not worried about that girl. Focus on Robert. He will put up a fight, but he may hold back with his little girl there." The elder Kite smirked. "Do all within your *power*, Sparrowhawk."

"Yes, sir, with pleasure," Sparrowhawk replied before shifting his eyes to

Jericho.

The two of them had a brief stare down that made Jericho feel like nobody else was on the balcony. Sparrowhawk had undermined him, proving to his father once again that he was the more loyal Raptor Admin. At twenty-three years old, Sparrowhawk wanted the Trinity to be willed to him. Jericho felt Sparrowhawk's unspoken desire through his intentions. His behavior was a language unto itself.

Breaking eye contact, Jericho said, "I will go handle the CSB and Kestrel."

Swiftly, he left the balcony and went out into the bal-chatri. Falcon's stained glass window depicted his namesake perched on an emerald-colored cactus wielding two pistols. Kestrel's featured her bird standing upon a tombstone in a graveyard, lots of sapphires, topazes, and turquoise. Sparrowhawk's was the second most expensive. The backdrop was a night sky colored with black diamonds ranging from jet black to smoky gray in color. A ruby blood moon cast a shadow upon a small hawk with red eyes. Falcon, Kestrel, and Sparrowhawk were his father's death dealers—his loyal combatants.

Jericho felt his chest tighten. He clenched his cravat and breathed shallowly. Until now, he had no idea his desire to prove he wasn't too weak to fix the Trinity put this much pressure on himself. If he was ever going to have the chance to change the organization for the better, he needed to prove himself worthy of inheriting it. For now, he had to do his father's devilish work. He had to act like a sick psycho, and he had to be better at it than Sparrowhawk.

His body knew its descent into total darkness was imminent and necessary for his father's respect. "I am a man. I can do this," he told himself, looking at his shaking hands.

He made a fist and punched the wall, frustrated. Those investigators did not deserve what they had coming. They were men there, doing their job. His father was the careless one who didn't invest in properly fixing Lynbrook's underground pipeline. Jericho was eleven when the government came. It was not fair this had come back on him.

He had never played a direct or indirect role in someone's demise before.

He clenched his hands harder to stop the shaking. Sparrowhawk's test wouldn't get to him. He wouldn't let it.

He practiced his most stern, hardened expression every chance he got as he passed mirrors or reflective windows on the way to the library. The students there needed to fear him—yet also believe him more than ever.

But Naomi Maus was among them. Jericho cursed under his breath, knowing he had no choice but to continue. He could beg for her forgiveness later.

At the library doors, he fixed the collar on his blazer and combed his hair back. He fixed his expression as practiced and entered. His shoes had titanium plates bolted to the soles like horseshoes, and every step he took clicked. He felt powerful. He felt in control. All eyes were on him.

Kestrel released Edmund Rabbit, lowered her gun, and removed the magazine. She had a bored look on her face, as if Jericho had ruined her fun.

"Thank you, Kestrel, for stopping them!" Jericho pointed at the CSB. "You two lied to us! We confirmed that you are *not* registered investigators of the Chemical Safety Board. You have a criminal record a mile long, pretending you are government officials to extort money!"

Ren Usagi shook his head. "No way! We don't do that!"

"We showed you and your father our credentials this morning!" Edmund Rabbit argued.

"They were inauthentic!" Jericho bellowed.

The Lynbrookians gasped.

Edmund Rabbit clenched his fist. "You're out of your mind, kid! This boarding school is absurd! This woman harassed me and my colleague!" He pointed at Kestrel. "She assaulted me! And now the headmaster sends his son in here, talking nonsense? What a joke! Return my phone to me! I'm calling the police!"

Jericho acknowledged this with a smug smile. "Kestrel, escort them out."

She nodded once before handcuffing Ren Usagi with zip ties from her back pocket. Edmund Rabbit resisted when she came for him. "We are real investigators for the CSB! Call the Birmingham office to validate my ID!"

Kestrel cuffed Edmund Rabbit's mouth and manhandled him. She was very skilled and used to dealing with men twice her size. As she escorted the investigators out, the Lynbrookians were silent.

Jericho stalked up the spiral staircase to the second floor of the library, then leaned over the iron railing like a prince above his subjects. The students below slowly came out from hiding underneath tables or behind bookshelves. He couldn't believe he had done it.

He clicked his heels together to gather the attention of all fifty-five students. Half were crying, including Naomi. He had to look away from her or else he would lose his composure. He needed his father to know he could do this, start to finish.

"Those supposed CSB men were imposters," Jericho declared. "We ran a background check on them and discovered the previous criminal charges against them. Kestrel did what she had to do to protect you all. They will be dealt with."

Naomi dabbed her cheeks with her sleeve. He desperately wanted to pull her aside and explain the sick psycho that she witnessed was an act for a long game to win over the Trinity.

There was one second of processing before the flurry of questions echoed throughout the library. With all the Lynbrookians talking over one another, he felt like an official bombarded at a press conference.

He gritted his teeth and lost it. "Be quiet!" A pause. "Everyone needs to stay calm."

"Honorable Kite." A girl stood up, stealing the floor. Her sweet East Tennessee accent quivered. "Will we be going home anyway?"

A hush fell over the room. That was all they wanted to know. After what happened to Condor last night, Jericho felt like nobody should be there either. He didn't know the reason why the gas leak was concentrated acres away on the west side. A part of him wished the investigators would get a chance to do their job so what happened to Condor wouldn't happen to anyone else. What if the leak would get worse and move east into the safe zone?

Unfortunately, he had no answers he could share without inducing the wrath of his father. It was their parents who'd forsaken these kids. He had no way to explain it without facing dire consequences.

Jericho leaned over the iron railing. "Lynbrook is my home—and yours." He spotted Mikayla Birdwing in the crowd, glaring. He pitied her. She was about to rue her life, and her dad would suffer alongside her. He felt conflicted about it. Things were getting out of hand, and the circumstances at Lynbrook had reached a point of no return.

It was going to be like the Great Resignation all over again...

Mikayla Birdwing

10:55 AM

Mikayla went for the bookcase near the window. She lingered around it, pretending to choose another book, but her eyes were more drawn to the dirt road. She bit her fingernails, tearing at the brittle edges of the tips and cuticles. Any minute now, she'd have her shot at leaving.

Jericho Kite remained in the library, not doing anything differently than what the Raptor Admins would've on a normal day—if being crammed in a library because a gas leak shut down the classroom portion of the campus was considered normal. He sat in the chair at the center watching the students, occasionally getting up to pace the room. He walked by Naomi once, raking his fingers gently across the side of the desk beside her hand. It was as if he wanted to touch her but had the wherewithal to restrain himself. Everyone else quietly buried their defeated, unenthusiastic faces in aviation books. They gave up.

Mikayla refused to quit. She was going home that day, whether the CSB could help or not.

Someone had called them, and she wholeheartedly believed it was either her mother or Naomi's. Jericho Kite had lied. Mr. Rabbit and his co-worker Mr. Usagi were honest men who cared about chemical safety. Her mother had taught her about the New London explosion years ago while in law school, writing a case study on the dismissed lawsuits. An imposter posing as a government official wouldn't have invested time in researching that disaster, let alone in bothering to collect witness statements from the Lynbrookians. They would've focused on how to extort as much money out of the Kites as possible before being discovered as scammers. The Kites were scheming to do anything to hide the leak but not fix it. Mikayla's mother told her companies tend to prioritize profits over safety and the lives of people.

Outside, a white van struck a deep puddle as it drove up the dirt road. Rust-orange mud splattered on the front bumper, then slid off as the van slowed to a stop at the gate beside the CSB's black SUV. Running on idle, dark fumes sputtered from the van's exhaust pipe. Mr. Fowl, Lynbrook's gatekeeper, unlocked the chains and four padlocks, each with different keys, before sliding the gate open.

"Yes!" Mikayla whispered underneath her breath.

The van sped through and parked on the grass near the entrance to the main building. Her dad stepped out, hugging a marble chessboard case. Mr. Fowl escorted him inside.

Beau Heights rang ten times and then the double doors of the library opened on the eleventh chime. Mr. Falco arrived, strutting down the aisle towards Mikayla. His shoulders were broad, making his buff arms look bigger. Trailing behind him was Mr. Sparrowhawk, exhibiting his signature, soulless stare. His eyes were arrows, and Mikayla was his target.

She bit her lips, realizing how powerful her heartbeat thumped. Each beat reminded her she was alive, at least for now.

Her eyes trailed down to Mr. Falco's pistol. She gulped quietly so that Mr. Sparrowhawk, who stood on her left side, wouldn't react. He side-eyed her through his long, stringy hair. She walked down the stairs to the first floor of the library, ready.

"Birdwing, we got some things you gotta do before seein' yer dad," said Mr. Falco.

Mikayla nodded. "Yes, sir."

"Empty all yer pockets and turn in place." Mr. Falco licked his top lip. "I wanna see all of ya. Twirl like a ballerina for this security check. Real nice 'n slow, got it?"

Shuddering, Mikayla turned her pockets inside out. A ball of lint tumbled to the floor. More lint stuck to her sweaty palms. When she started her turn, she caught a glimpse of concerned faces. She made sure the other students saw optimism twinkling in her eyes and not fear.

During her second turn, Mr. Sparrowhawk searched her before giving a thumbs up. She had no written notes, pens, or blank paper, assuming they would look for it.

Mr. Falco smacked her behind. It echoed. "All done!"

Grabbing her butt, Mikayla whimpered a little and breathed sharply to make herself calm down. In the hallway, she stayed two steps behind the men, walking with her hands subtly covering her backside. She couldn't read Mr. Sparrowhawk's facial expression; it was hardened and unwavering. Mr. Falco occasionally bit back a smirk or appeared to be contemplating something.

Mr. Falco spoke quietly. "Sparrowhawk, notice somethin' wrong with that ammo we shot a few hours ago? My rifle kept malfunctionin'."

"I did notice," Sparrowhawk replied.

"Imma launch my own investigation on it after the day is over with."

"Finding Lorelei is our priority."

"Yeah, yeah, I get that, but findin' out why the weapon was screwed up, that's *my* priority. I think that bird-chested boy Condor picked to work in the supply office messed with the ammo."

"Don't let Boss know."

"I ain't. I'll still do what he wants, but I'll be doin' my investigation on the side, even if it takes all night."

Mikayla bit her lip, hoping Isaiah hadn't done something throughout his time in the supply office that would backfire.

They went downstairs to the center of the main building. At the private dining hall's double doors, each of her escorts opened one, revealing her dad's smile. The dining room had the capacity to seat at least two hundred guests, but it was only furnished with one table fully set with stainless steel utensils and porcelain dishes centered underneath a crystal chandelier.

Everything else, except for an occasional plant or a few paintings, had been taken out. The carpet was a crisp maroon that could pass for burgundy on a brighter day. The walls were light gray, and the ceiling was at least twenty feet high.

Tears freely falling, Mikayla's heart fluttered. She ran for her father's embrace.

"Careful, baby girl. I'm an old guy." Her dad bent his knee back and forth slightly. It crackled each time. "Heard that? Bone rubs together."

She wrapped her arms around him and rested her head on his chest. His voice, his goatee, his cologne, his smile—they were all the same. She didn't care that he was getting old.

"Mika, your eyes...so wide." He touched her face. "My beautiful girl, you have your mother's eyes, I swear. Look how big and round they are. Hey...you've lost weight, a lot of it."

"I've missed you, Dad. How was your trip?" Mikayla asked to get his mind off what this place had done to her.

"A bit unusual." Her dad nodded once to acknowledge Mr. Falco and Mr. Sparrowhawk, then turned back to Mikayla. "A van picked me up from Atlanta about two hours ago."

"Please seat yourselves and allow me to serve you," Mr. Sparrowhawk said.

"You're a handsome young fellow. What's your name?"

"Sparrowhawk."

"Is that your last name?"

"No, it's my entire name," he answered smugly, walking away.

Mikayla knew her dad was just being nice, but she wished he would read the room.

"Yeah, allow Sparrowhawk to serve y'all," Mr. Falco said, opening a bag of pork rinds he pulled from his pocket. The smell of barbeque seasoning filled the immediate area. "Don't mind me." He stuffed a handful into his mouth, then licked crumbs off his fingers. He headed towards one of two suede armchairs, one at each end of the dining hall, for himself and Mr. Sparrowhawk.

"You got quiet, Mika. Still surprised I'm here?" Her dad pulled her chair out, inviting her to sit.

Overwhelmed, Mikayla nodded and faked a smile. As she sat, Mr. Sparrowhawk pushed open the kitchen's swinging door with his backside, turning to reveal a silver platter. He came to Mikayla's right and lifted the lid. A lobster with red sauce on kale and lemon stared back at her through beady, black eyes. Along with it was fresh Caesar dressing on spinach leaves, croutons, and shredded parmesan cheese. He also set cheese biscuits and seasoned corn on the cob on the table. In four separate small bowls were butter and cocktail sauce topped with a pinch of basil.

Meanwhile, Mr. Falco continued crunching on his pork rinds, sitting in the suede armchair where he could see Robert Birdwing's face. The way he sat reminded Mikayla of the way birds of prey perched on tree branches awaiting mice or rabbits.

Mr. Sparrowhawk went for his armchair at the opposite end. Once he got comfortable, he draped an amazonite rosary around his middle finger leaving enough chain for the diamond crucifix to swing like a pendulum. He was known to do that out of boredom, and neither he nor none of the other Raptor Admins appeared particularly religious.

Her dad, unaware this was happening behind him, clapped his hands together, excited to eat. He loaded his fork with whatever food touched it first.

"It's a beautiful campus. Lawn looks like crap. What a shame," he added mid-chew.

Mikayla's heart dropped. It would've been the perfect opportunity to mention what happened to the groundskeeper and the dandelion growing through the baseboard in the library. She glanced at Mr. Sparrowhawk before her eyes shifted. "Yeah, it's annoying. Sometimes when we sit in the grass, chiggers dig into our skin."

"It's that bad?" Her dad paused, swallowing. "Teachers any good?"

"The teachers *were* okay." Mikayla dragged her fingers down her face, distorting it. She needed her dad to pick up on Lynbrook's diminished circumstances and her stress.

"*Were?*" He looked intently into her eyes.

Mikayla nodded.

"What are they today?" he asked.

"Gone."

"Okay…I understand," he said, tugging gently on his goatee. He did that whenever he was contemplating. "You can't explain with *them* here watching."

Nodding, Mikayla let out a sigh of relief.

He chewed a mouthful of spinach and swallowed. "No hard feelings, baby girl. I can tell something is bothering you. I'm lucky I was able to shut down my chess kiosk for the weekend. Now, here I am, eating this wonderful meal. Growing up, I ate mayo and onion sammiches, and I was happy if I had sliced cheese to add on it. Do y'all eat like this all the time? This is the Deep South. No greens. No cornbread. I wouldn't even trust this chef to clean chitlins right, let alone fry a chicken."

The chef and his crew were victims of the Great Resignation, buried six feet under somewhere beyond the gate. Mikayla opened her mouth to say something about it, but her eyes locked onto Mr. Sparrowhawk. She sighed, and her dad got quiet. He finished his entire plate while Mikayla had only eaten a quarter of hers. The red sauce underneath the lobster tasted like blood, salty and somewhat metallic.

Mr. Sparrowhawk got up and went into the kitchen area again, leaving Mr. Falco to watch. When he returned, he poured water into each of their glasses from a pitcher. The water was crystal clear, not a pale yellow like what Lynbrookians usually drank. Mikayla savored a sip. It was purified and smooth, washing away the blood taste.

"Mika, I have to ask. Are you mad at your mom?" her dad asked.

Mikayla thought for a bit and said, "Dunno. I don't want to be mad at her, but at the same time, I hate this school. All we ever read about is airplanes and airports. There's no math, science, not even history unless it can relate back to aviation."

Laughing, he broke a cheese biscuit in half. "For the record, I never wanted you here."

"Really?"

He nodded. "Because she's got primary custody of you and the legal leverage, I didn't get a vote."

"You knew she was sending me here?"

"She gave me a heads up at the very end of August. Like I said, she'd already had her mind made up."

"Haven't gotten a letter from her since I've gotten here."

His eyebrows hopped. "Maybe she's busy building up a bigger law firm with Ms. Maus."

"Mom and Ms. Maus are legitimizing their partnership?"

"Yup. All of a sudden, they're not smalltime lawyers anymore. I think they've sold out to the devil. I told Samara: you and Olivia got the huge law firm in Atlanta you've always wanted, but you paid too much for it." Her dad paused, realizing. "I'm sorry, Mika. I shouldn't talk like that about your mom in front of you. The problem I have with her has nothing to do with you."

He hesitated for a bit, and then he said, "She won't talk to me either. The only reason why I know about her firm is because of ads. It's like she kept my last name so she can make their brand cutesy, but that's neither here nor there." He angrily mumbled, "Birdwing and Maus Law Group."

Mikayla sighed. A guilt-ridden expression covered his face, and he seemed lost for words to explain it. The crunch of Mr. Falco's teeth grinding against a pork rind interrupted the silence.

Her dad made direct eye contact with Mr. Falco. "Sir?"

"Dad, don't talk to them, please," Mikayla whispered sharply.

Her dad held up his pointer finger, signaling for her to hush.

Mr. Falco was mid-chew. He swallowed and replied, "Whatcha want, Robert?"

"Excuse my manners."

"Yer fine. Call me Falco," he said, relaxing his hardened face. "I ain't no prude about manners. We're two men talkin'."

"Well, a man tells another man why his phone was taken away."

Mr. Falco smirked. "You were briefed by that driver of yers, right? It's for security reasons, to protect the Kite family."

"Kite family?" Her dad chuckled crankily. "That makes them sound down to earth. The Kite *Clan* owns Kite Express gas stations, a bunch of oil rigs, and lots of other companies. They are one of the two trillionaire families on this side of the planet involved in energy production, them and Ravensbourne."

"You've done some diggin'?" Mr. Falco asked.

"Yeah, I tried this place too. Found nothing, except a picture of that clocktower out there."

Mikayla smirked. She was impressed that her dad found online images of Beau Heights. Lynbrook had no trace online when she'd checked before leaving Atlanta.

"You sayin' you found a picture of the clocktower online?" Mr. Falco stood up.

Mr. Sparrowhawk yanked the rosary chain into his palm and perked up, suddenly alert. He slyly reached into his jacket for his cellphone and began scrolling quietly.

"Yeah, Beau Heights," her dad replied.

Mr. Falco and Mr. Sparrowhawk glared at her father. He wasn't supposed to know the name of the clock tower either.

"Hey, one last thing you gotta tell me. Why are all y'all's names bird names? Get what I'm asking? Like, he's Sparrowhawk and you're Falcon without the n, I'm assumin'. What's with that?"

The vein in Mr. Falco's forearm jerked. "We were paid to change our names," he replied ominously. "A Kite wants what they want and gets what they want—or *who* they want. The Kite Clan can buy everyone in this room a thousand and one times."

Mr. Sparrowhawk put his phone away, then gave Mr. Falco a hand signal. Mr. Falco nodded and suddenly left the dining hall. He returned for his pork rinds a moment later, then left again. Mr. Sparrowhawk pulled out his phone once more and became immersed, scrolling slowly, mouth agape.

"Dad, how did you find a picture of the clocktower?" Mikayla whispered.

"They're making a big deal out of it." His tone shifted. "I don't get it."

"I don't think you were supposed to be able to find that."

"I don't care what I'm not supposed to find when it comes to you, baby girl." A sliver of hatred reached his eyes. "I see the way they look at you. They stressed you out so much, you don't even eat anymore. I'll fight them, every last one of them. They're not buying anyone in here."

"The tall, skinny one stares at me all the time." She leaned in, whispering. "I think they killed all the teachers. The school has a gas leak near the tower." She got quieter, gripping the bottom of her chair and channeling all her frustration into her knuckles. "They're trying to hide it. Two CSB investigators are here, but I think they're trying to kill them too."

Robert reached across the table for Mikayla's hand. "I saw their SUV. It's the Kite Clan. They have a shady track record when it comes to all of their oil rigs and facilities. I knew what I was getting into coming here. I have a plan. For now, act like you haven't said any of that stuff to me, okay?"

She nodded as he reached for his chessboard.

"Wanna play?"

Lorelei Avian

11:28 AM

Lorelei hadn't moved in the hours since she heard the gunshots. She had a feeling that whoever was shooting had their aim at the hawks flying too close to the planes. With Mateo wrapped in her arms, she hid inside a hollow tree. She groped underneath the tattered sleeves of her potato-sack-turned-cloak. The shovel was still tucked in a concealed compartment she had stitched into her sleeve weeks prior. She found she needed to touch it now and then to reassure herself. That shovel meant everything to her, and she couldn't afford it to go missing. It was a tool for digging, a means of capturing rainwater—and a weapon, if need be. Same for her jar of bugs. In fact, her bugs were equally weaponizable.

Without his bewits and bronze bells, Mateo was nearly weightless. She kissed the top of his head and whispered loving phrases in French. She had fallen deeply in love with falconry at a Renaissance faire when she was twelve, living in Ontario before her parents were murdered. The hawk at the faire was attached to a leather jess wrapped around the fingers of a lanky woman wearing men's medieval attire. Lorelei remembered them clearly. Their vest was adorned in golden, upside down crosses and dove-shaped charms. They named their show The Holy Birds of Pray and named themselves Lorde of Lanner, Lanner being the name of their falcon. The bond Lorde shared with Lanner was magical, and Lorelei felt it in her heart. Their falcon obeyed and flew beautifully above the cheering crowd, following commands Lorelei thought were impossible for birds of prey to obey.

A day later, Lorelei tried to capture her own raptor, a small merlin. It pecked her arm and flew off, taking a chunk of skin with it. She reached out, begging for the merlin to come back. It returned, looked her in the eyes, and hovered, awaiting her next command. She looked at the gash in her arm, then at the blood on its beak, then at her arm again. Doubtful, she pointed to a random bush behind her and told it to grab three berries. It flew to the exact bush, collected berries, and dropped three at her feet. Her power had been activated. It happened in the first quarter of the lunar phase, the Raptor Moon. It was the beginning of her learning that her blood bent the laws of falconry.

That very merlin became her sidekick that perched beside the window near her school desk and at her window every night before bed. The merlin was obedient whenever the two of them went hunting. It would perch upon her gauntlet and stay there without Lorelei needing to hold the jess firmly. Her feeder pouch back then was a handmade leather bag with short fringes so her raptors wouldn't mistake them for rat entrails. The bag was her favorite, as it was decorated with amethyst, fluorite, and sodalite stitched onto the flap. Inside, she always carried rodent entrails soaked in her own blood in case the merlin's bond to her wore off.

Despite passing written exams on the history of raptors, their biology, captive care, and methods of handling with perfect scores, no sponsor in Ontario with access to the birds took her seriously. It wasn't her devotion to falconry that alarmed these experts, but her methods of controlling them. They felt like she took the term "bloodsport" too literally, and they blacklisted her from joining any falconry program in the country.

Her parents were too religious to be accepting of what looked like dark magic. Nobody at school would get it. She had friends, but they already thought she was weird enough. She didn't want them to find out how her merlin became her "pet" and lose them. The pastor would've treated her like she was destined for eternal damnation in Hell and possibly ostracize her from the church. Even Lorde of Lanner heard about Lorelei's methods through the falconer community and called them satanic and sacrilegious.

Lorelei kept her power a secret between herself and Landon after that. He was nonchalant about it.

The origins of her power were unknown until Uncle Eric sat her and Landon down a week after their parents' funeral. He explained that their power was called Pure Blood Leash and that they got it from their ancestors who were subjected to hundreds of years of eugenics. Their ancestors, surname Trembley, were poor farmers in Quebec. Trembley's were great hunters widely known for their falconry, horsemanship, and dog handling skills. The family's blood possessed special abilities. It was a genetic advantage, not magic. However, their strengths were connected to the lunar phases. The power emerged in members of the Trembley bloodline every third generation.

Lorelei was no doubt the Falconer. It was unclear what Landon was, but she didn't doubt there was something mythical about him. He and dogs shared a mutual indifference to each other. Horses were aggressive towards him, and raptors ignored him. Lorelei and her Uncle Eric assumed Landon could be the Handler but had no evidence to prove it. They settled on believing Landon's activation with canines was delayed, like a late blooming child eventually entering puberty.

Uncle Eric also revealed that their cousin, Jericho, was the Equestrian. However, Jericho's Pure Blood Leash power to control horses was dormant because there were no such animals at Lynbrook to form a connection with.

By the time Lorelei and Landon arrived at Lynbrook, they were knowledgeable about Blood Leash. Jericho knew absolutely nothing. Therefore, Lorelei and Landon were prohibited from talking about their lineage around him. They obeyed in fear of Headmaster Kite's wrath.

Lorelei felt her Blood Leash power weakening. First quarter was long gone, and the waxing gibbous phase was coming to an end. On the full moon tomorrow, the Handler's power would dominate, the Falconer's becoming weaker as the Raptor Moon turned. That would make her vulnerable.

The cellphone's battery had 6% remaining. She redialed the number for trillionaire Alexander Ravensbourne, but it went to voicemail again.

"Hey, it's me again. Lorelei. Still out here, waiting. My battery is running out. You didn't charge it enough. Anyway, I called the CSB this morning. I have no way of knowing, but I'm sure they sent someone out to the school. Call me back soon so I can know to go get my brother. I'm counting on you now. What I did, you could've easily done yourself. The least you can do is hold up your end of the deal. We'd really love to go back home to Ontario. Okay…gotta go."

The call drained 2% of the remaining battery.

Mikayla Birdwing

11:31 AM

Mikayla's dad unfastened the clips of the marble chessboard case. The brass hinges creaked as he flipped it open like a briefcase, revealing thirty-two chess pieces embedded in their respective red velvet slots. As an aeronautical analyst turned jeweler, he customized chess sets. His hired craftsman carved the wooden chessboards.

Her dad set up the board. All the white gold pieces were diamond encrusted with rose gold trimming that detailed the facial features and clothing of the royal court. The opponent's pieces were onyx and abalone with yellow gold trimming. All four knights, sculpted to look majestic like unicorns yet mighty like stallions, had ruby gems for eyes. The iridescence of the abalone shimmered like the rainbow cloud Mikayla had seen above the mountain.

"This chessboard is my latest bestseller. Folks love the sturdy leather handle and the marble case."

"Whoa," Mikayla gasped. She tried her best to keep their conversation natural and unassuming. "How much do you charge?"

Her dad leaned in, eyes shimmering. "A fortune."

"Why not bring a cheaper one?"

He paused. "Thought you'd want to see something beautiful besides yourself."

That wasn't his true intention, but Mikayla blushed anyway. Her dad was a salesman at heart. He didn't have to explain his plan to her. She had a feeling he was going to trade the chess set for her life. It wasn't a bad idea.

"Okay, okay, I'll stop picking on you. You look like you're about to explode. See that?" He held up an onyx pawn with a grin. "This set has a defect. The pawn is smiling."

Mikayla marveled at the piece's crooked smile. "I love it."

"I'll give you a set better than this when you're a chess master like your old man."

Putting his phone aside, Mr. Sparrowhawk rose out of his chair and walked their way. "This set is the nicest I've ever seen. Will it be trouble if I play a game?"

Her dad was a good actor. "Take a seat."

Mikayla stood up halfway.

"Actually, Mr. Birdwing," Mr. Sparrowhawk said before Mikayla could step away. "I want to play with your daughter."

Her dad's nostrils flared as if Mr. Sparrowhawk's wording and tone didn't sit well with him. Nevertheless, he shrugged. "I don't see why not." He stood behind her with his hands on both shoulders. "Don't worry, Mika. You learn a ton from new opponents. I'm here for you."

She felt his grip tighten and his heart racing through the back of her blouse, and yet he carried on without showing a hint of anxiety. She wished she could be as cordial and collected.

Mr. Sparrowhawk took a seat in front of the onyx pieces. He twisted the board around so that the white gold pieces were on his side, putting Mikayla in control of the onyx set.

"Now, I'm moving first. I'm white and you're black."

Mikayla felt her dad's nails slightly dig into her shoulder a bit. She too couldn't help but wonder if Mr. Sparrowhawk's comment was only about the pieces and not their skin color.

He moved the middle pawn forward two spaces to E4. "Nineteen years ago, taught myself chess when I was four. I associated the pieces with people. And then I made the pieces move like a story. I had *vision*," he said without breaking eye contact with Mikayla.

She swished her lips left and right, wondering why he said vision in a weird tone. The throbbing sensation of a migraine caught her off guard. Miss Kestrel popped into her mind, and Mikayla saw her standing beside her bed, dangling her possum notebook between her long, blue fingernails. It seemed as if Miss Kestrel was there in real time, but Mikayla couldn't feel anything. She snapped out of it and stared wide-eyed at the chessboard. It took her a moment to realize she was in the dining hall, not the dorm. The hallucination was more vivid than a dream.

"Relax, sweetheart." Her dad massaged her shoulders. "I'm here."

Trembling, Mikayla picked the pawn across from Mr. Sparrowhawk's. She knew it was the wrong move to play, but she involuntarily moved it two spaces to E5 to block his.

No, I don't want that! Why is my body moving on its own, making this stupid move? She grabbed her wrist and squeezed it.

"*Tsk, tsk.*" Mr. Sparrowhawk shook his head, swiftly moving his queen diagonally to H5, near her territory. "Check."

There was nowhere for her king to go, but she moved it forward to E7 anyway. A move even a rookie wouldn't make. She had no control of her body at that point.

Mr. Sparrowhawk snatched her king. "*Checkmate.*"

Her dad cleared his voice for Mr. Sparrowhawk's attention. "That didn't look right to me. Mika has been playing this game for years. She would never play so carelessly."

Mr. Sparrowhawk leaned closer to Mikayla, disregarding her dad. Behind the blur of her tears, Mr. Sparrowhawk taunted her with the onyx king. She blinked angrily, determined not to cry. A tear slipped away.

Her dad patted her shoulder. "Alright. That's enough. I'll take things from here."

Mr. Sparrowhawk stood up. "What do you mean by that?"

"You know. You're a smart man." Her dad slowly walked around the table and directly approached Mr. Sparrowhawk. "I shouldn't have called you a man. A man doesn't take pride in making a little girl cry. A man doesn't work for an evil company that kills people."

Mr. Sparrowhawk smirked. "Boxer?"

"Back in the day. What gave it away?"

"Your eyes, Mr. Birdwing." Mr. Sparrowhawk smirked and twisted two fingers together. *"Bond."*

Both of her dad's arms contorted behind his back like he was being handcuffed by an invisible force. Completely restricted, his entire body stiffened, under a paralysis spell. He fell to his knees. Mikayla screamed and jumped out of her chair. Her dad shuddered in pain on the floor as Mr. Sparrowhawk slowly approached.

Mikayla darted in front of her dad, shielding him. "Back off!"

Mr. Sparrowhawk collapsed to his knees, grabbing his head, thrashing about. Mikayla gasped and embraced her trembling dad. She asked him if he was okay. He nodded, able to move on his own again.

Mr. Falco and Miss Kestrel stormed into the dining hall. Miss Kestrel shouted Mr. Sparrowhawk's name and seized Mikayla. Mr. Falco grabbed her dad. Robert tried lunging at Miss Kestrel, but Mr. Falco kicked his knee. He collapsed, face forward.

"Daddy!" Mikayla screamed.

Mr. Sparrowhawk rose halfway, hair disheveled in his face. He pointed at Mikayla. "She's activated! She's Capable!"

Everyone paused. For some reason the Raptor Admins were wary of her, not the other way around.

Miss Kestrel tightened her grip on Mikayla. "Falco, Sparrowhawk, take Robert Birdwing upstairs! Then, get to the boss's office. He wants to see all of us and Condor. I'll handle her."

"Careful, Kestrel! She's Capable!" Sparrowhawk shouted.

"I heard you the first time!" Miss Kestrel screamed, clenching harder. "It's probably something you did, Sparrowhawk!"

"I did what I was told!"

Mikayla winced. Activated? Capable? She had no idea what she was capable of or what had activated.

"Mika!" Her dad's voice was shrill as he struggled to break away from Mr. Falco's hold on him. "Stay strong! I'll be okay! Stay strong, baby girl."

Mr. Falco restrained his arms behind his back.

"Let him go! Please, Mr. Falco!" Mikayla sobbed. "Please don't hurt my daddy! Let him go!"

Mr. Falco covered her dad's mouth while forcing him out of the room. Before Mikayla could let out a scream, Miss Kestrel grabbed her face. Her fingernails dug deep into her cheek. Mikayla could barely breathe.

"You little cunt. What did you do to Sparrowhawk?" Miss Kestrel took her hand off slightly.

"I didn't do anything. I didn't. I didn't I swear!" Mikayla cried. "Mr. Sparrowhawk did something weird to us, to my mind. He made my hands do whatever he wanted them to." She shuddered.

Miss Kestrel dug deeper. "You're lying."

"I'm not! He got into my head and made me see things; then, he did something to make my dad go paralyzed for a split second. Dad tried to go after him, and then he fell down cussing about his head hurting. I don't know what else to tell you."

Mikayla couldn't think of other words to describe the experience. It was like Sparrowhawk possessed mind control abilities or power over their bodies. Maybe both. It was the same feeling in her brain she got yesterday after he ate the dandelion. She felt like he was inside her head.

Miss Kestrel let her go. "What did Sparrowhawk make you see?"

Mikayla bit her bottom lip. She didn't want to admit Mr. Sparrowhawk showed her a hallucination of Miss Kestrel taking her possum notebook. It made no sense.

"What is Mr. Sparrowhawk?" Mikayla asked.

Miss Kestrel grimaced. "You know what? We're going to the headmaster now. If you bring up what happened, I'll cut your tongue out."

Mikayla turned around to take one last look at her dad's chessboard. She snagged the smiling pawn and saw the gemstones of the other pieces twinkling through her tears. The red sauce from the lobster that stained the tablecloth had turned brown, like oxidized blood.

It was a short walk to Headmaster Kite's office. Mikayla straightened her posture once Miss Kestrel pressed a button beside an intercom.

"Headmaster Kite, I have Mikayla Birdwing as requested."

"Come in now," Headmaster Kite replied. His voice was grave and full of frustration.

"Stop crying." Miss Kestrel waited three seconds, then slapped Mikayla across her face. "I said, stop crying!"

Mikayla nodded, wiping a string of snot on her tear-dampened sleeve.

Miss Kestrel opened the door without warning. The bay window in the headmaster's office stretched floor to ceiling. It wasn't barred like every other window at Lynbrook. Also exclusive to his office was the quality of his carpet, which was much denser and softer against her flats. Massive bookshelves framed his centered desk where he leaned forward in his throne-like chair.

Mikayla bowed her head slightly to give Headmaster Kite a respectful nod. She extended her right foot behind her left and bent her knees to curtsy.

With penetrating eyes, Headmaster Kite stood up, slowly. The tails on his blazer were much longer than his son's, and the v-cut was much deeper, extending upward from his waist.

Mikayla reported in. "Headmaster Kite, Mikayla Birdwing here as ordered."

Mikayla couldn't budge from that submissive pose until Headmaster Kite gave permission. Two more silent minutes passed, and her legs began to tremble. The thought of what Miss Kestrel would do if she collapsed kept her balanced.

"Stand at ease," Headmaster Kite finally said. "I like to see my ladies curtsy like swans and my men bow strong like eagles. You managed to do both very well."

Mikayla exhaled and thanked him solely out of obligation.

"Sir, heads up. She's activated and Capable," Kestrel said.

Mikayla gulped, unsure how to respond.

"I know. Falcon and Sparrowhawk stopped by and told me before you buzzed in." Headmaster Kite shifted in his seat. "Birdwing, were you friends with Lorelei?"

Mikayla cleared her throat. "We weren't close, sir."

Headmaster Kite walked towards Mikayla and looked down at her. "You were seen talking to her last night. What were you two talking about?"

Unnerved, Mikayla thought carefully about how she would answer. "Nothing much, sir. We talked about the Big Dipper and other stuff like that."

Headmaster Kite pondered for a moment, massaging his beard. He paced back to his desk, where he opened her sky blue possum notebook. Her eyes widened. Perhaps the hallucination hadn't been a hallucination, but a vision. Mikayla grimaced at the absurdity of it all.

He aggressively thumbed through the notebook, bending the pages. "What's the purpose of all the home addresses written in here? Was this Lorelei's idea?"

"No, sir." She stammered, "I t-thought one day I'll g-g-get to go home and write everyone."

"Why write to their home addresses if they're here at Lynbrook?"

She felt like her heart had leapt through her chest. "I don't know."

"How often did you and Lorelei talk about what your mothers did for a living?"

"Never came up," Mikayla replied, unsure where his questions were leading. She just wanted to know what they were going to do to her dad.

"Birdwing, I am going to be frank with you." He steepled his hands. "I've been trying for years to get your dad to work at Meccanicville for me. I knew you had a plan, so I used you to lure him here."

"When my mom finds out, she'll end Kite Express. She's an environmental lawyer. She can take you down, she and Naomi's mom."

He laughed. Kestrel laughed harder.

"They already know what goes on here," Headmaster Kite said.

"Of course she does. That's why she called the CSB to have them investigate the gas—"

"I can guarantee you your mother didn't call the CSB," he interrupted her.

Mikayla lost her confidence. "Naomi's mom?"

"No, neither of your mothers called. They want nothing to do with you two. This conversation is over unless you have information on what Lorelei

Avian is doing." He pointed to Miss Kestrel. "Take punitive action, however you see fit, Kestrel."

"Yes, sir," she replied.

"And Kestrel," Headmaster Kite said as if he had almost forgotten something important, "don't harm Mikayla Birdwing, or *his* price will be high."

"Price will be high. I know, sir," she muttered, yanking Mikayla out of the office.

They rushed down the hallway faster than Mikayla's trembling legs could handle. Miss Kestrel opened a backdoor facing the south side of campus and pointed to the muddy area near the fence. The rain came down hard and slanted with the cold wind. Every droplet felt like ice.

"Where's my dad? He's not going to agree to work for you people!" Mikayla cried, crossing her arms.

A flash of lightning and subsequent thunder muted Miss Kestrel's response. Mikayla repeated her question. Miss Kestrel shoved her down and closed the door.

Mikayla got up and tried opening the door, but it was locked. Rain and tears impeded her eyesight. She reached into her pocket for the smiling pawn and squeezed it tightly, hoping her dad wouldn't end up being taken to Meccanicville.

She also hoped Headmaster Kite was lying about her mother. She cared about being Atlanta's best environmental prosecutor more than anything else. There was no way her mother had turned evil. Right? Mikayla clenched her shoulders and scrunched into a ball, crying.

Lorelei Avian

11:56 AM

Mateo flew circles around Lorelei. She smiled, gripping the owl's fallen feathers into her palms. It was cold and miserable, but at least the pilots hadn't spotted them. She sat down again and rubbed her hands together to keep warm.

She didn't know much about the CSB, other than they were a government agency with experts who'd investigate the leak. Relying on help—trusting others to do their part—she hadn't ever been comfortable with any of that.

She called Mateo over. He came to her and let her hug him like a stuffed bear.

"Mateo, I should've forced Mikayla to leave last night. I knew all along she wasn't going to be let go of that easily." She caressed her finger across the owl's head, thinking of Mikayla's surgical scar. "She's one of the Capable ones. If or when she becomes activated, it's going to get bad."

Mikayla Birdwing's power was worth so much money it was disgusting. However, she was dormant and unaware, like Jericho. Lorelei knew this all along but couldn't share that knowledge with Mikayla. She feared what Headmaster Kite would do if she opened her mouth about it.

Billionaires became trillionaires off Blood Leash. When eugenics became normalized, scientists funded by wealthy investors experimented on Pure Blood Leash subjects to engineer Blood Leash Capable people through surgeries. After countless deaths, scientists pinpointed three procedures that successfully produced results: brain, heart, and uterus. Unfortunately, the outcomes were unpredictable, but they were intensely sought after nonetheless. There was lots of money in Blood Leash experimentation for the few not afraid of the risks. While most adults were understandably reluctant, they were quick to offer up their children—as Mikayla's mother had.

Sparrowhawk was the only Raptor Admin who'd consented to brain surgery eight years ago to become Blood Leash Capable. He rarely used his abilities, but when he did, he read his victim's thoughts while accessing the prefrontal cortex and hippocampus once his blood was in their body. He could control their nervous system too. Supposedly, Mikayla's brain surgery was a more optimized version of his. Her value trumped his umpteen times.

Conveniently Trembley descendants, the Kite Clan exploited Blood Leash experimentation, hitting two birds with one stone. They indoctrinated Lynbrookians with airfield knowledge, used them for labor to support airfield operations at Meccanicville, then experimented on them at Kan. The only reason Lorelei knew these things was because Uncle Eric had loose lips while he was drinking. Feeling powerless against the Kite Clan, she and Landon kept quiet about it.

A van was supposed to have been there by then to take her, Landon, and Mateo to the airport. She wanted them out of the Trinity for good. Alexander Ravensbourne had promised her that favor in exchange for her running away to call the CSB. Anxious, she took a deep breath and reached into her backpack for the cellphone. Three percent battery life. She dialed the unknown number and waited for the ring. Someone answered.

"Confirmation number." The voice was snarky.

"Code zero-zero-two-seventeen-six," Lorelei replied.

"Say request."

"Put Alexander on the phone."

"Unable."

"Why?"

"Unavailable. Leave a message."

"I don't have the time for that! Put Alexander on the phone now!"

A prerecorded message took over. *"Thanks for calling Alexander's Electric Company, where we value your static satisfaction! Sorry we've missed you. We're nocturnal. Our business hours are from 7 PM until 7 AM, seven days of the week. Standby. Processing request. You are on hold. Standby. Processing request..."*

Lorelei pulled away from the looping message, barely able to hear it as she checked the battery life again. Two percent remaining. She bit her fingernails for the entire five minutes. Suddenly, movement and breathing on the other side interrupted the looping recording.

Lorelei pressed the phone up to her ear. "Hello? Is this you, Alexander?"

"No," an unfamiliar new voice replied.

"I don't care who the hell you are at this point."

"Please don't swear. It's not ladylike. Swearing is bad."

"Tell Alexander I did my part. The CSB will do their inspection, find the gas leak, and end Lynbrook. Tell Alexander to hold up his end of the deal. He promised me a flight to Ontario. Landon and I can't stay here anymore." Lorelei cupped her mouth, on the verge of tears. Her voice cracked. "Where's our ride that's supposed to take us to the airport?"

"There won't be one. You can't put an owl on an airplane."

"What do you mean? Mateo can go in a cage."

"Owls can't fly first class."

"Then put us in economy! Stop kidding around with me. Put Alexander on the phone."

There was complete silence for twenty seconds.

The voice laughed and said, "You don't get it, do you?"

"Tell Alexander he stabbed me in the back! I knew he would! Well, I was hoping he wouldn't, but fine! I have a backup plan that'll—"

The person on the other end hung up. Lorelei looked at the phone and found it barely powering the screen's backlight more than a few seconds at a time. One percent remaining.

"Fuck!" She clenched the phone, wishing she could break it in half.

A kettle of startled, screeching hawks flew out from the treetops. She reached her hands up, and from her perspective, she saw herself grasping eight of them. Smaller birds, hundreds of them, began flying away.

"A Kite wants what they want and gets what they want, eh? Then the same goes for Ravensbourne! They're no different! I'll show you not to mess with me! You're not taking Lynbrook if that's what you want. I'll destroy it before you can get to it!"

She opened the jar of bugs, reached for her shovel, and sliced her wrist deep with the edge of it. As she balled her fist, the pressure pushed out a stream of blood into the jar. The blood covered her hand so she could make what she called her Gauntlet of Fury. She raised her bloody hand to the sky, releasing her scent, and blew her whistle. All eight hawks swooped down to her in submission. Three perched up on her arm. The others ate her bugs.

Blood Leashers relied on their blood entering their target in one or more routes of exposure, like a toxin: dermal absorption through torn skin, eye absorption, inhalation, ingestion, and injection. The most effective route was inhalation, but getting raptors to inhale blood was no easy task. The second-best option was ingestion. Now, with her blood in their stomachs, the hawks were leashed for control. The skies were plentiful with more birds, and she had revenge-fueled stamina.

Jericho Kite IV

12:26 PM

Still in the library, Jericho nodded off. He awakened after a split second and repositioned himself. The chair felt like a cement brick at that point. How Kestrel, Sparrowhawk, or Falcon managed to endure this level of boredom and discomfort while on watch was beyond him.

Osprey entered the library. He greeted the Lynbrookians with a nod and went directly towards the front. Jericho stood up and adjusted his suit, wiping away the wrinkles.

"Honorable Kite, your father is requesting you come to his office."

Jericho managed to keep an unemotional demeanor. "You happen to know why he wants to see me?"

Osprey didn't hear Jericho the first time, so Jericho repeated himself.

"It's about a lot of things, young Kite." He patted Jericho's back and looked at him with the kindness of a father, obviously downplaying the severity of the situation. "I was instructed to take over the watch until Freedom Hours."

"Guess I'm not coming back then." Jericho glanced at Naomi one last time as he left the library. She nibbled nervously on an eraser.

I'll figure out how to get you out of this place, my mouse, he thought to himself.

Jericho took a deep breath and pressed the button next to the intercom at his father's door. "Father, it's me."

The lock clicked. Jericho entered, immediately flabbergasted. The aura in his father's office was grim and sinister. Sparrowhawk, Kestrel, and Falcon stood bunched together to the headmaster's left. They looked relaxed and in their element. On the other side stood Condor, looking worried and out of place, especially when he gave Jericho a shy smile and wave. Jericho acknowledged Condor first, then his father.

The elder Kite spoke. "In case you were wondering, the mission to capture Robert Birdwing was successful, though it did not go according to plan."

Jericho hadn't been wondering at all. He felt bad for Mikayla and didn't want to think about what was possibly going on in the dining hall. "When will Robert Birdwing be sent to Meccanicville?"

"Tonight. I have a helicopter on its way here. The leaders at Meccanicville will show him the way. He'll get the hang of the job in no time." His father smirked.

Jericho shook his head and looked at his shoes. *Is this all he wanted to say? He called me here just to rub how he ruined another man's life in my face?*

"Look up," his father said firmly. Jericho quickly raised his head. "I have a test for you. Imagine this: I am dead, and you inherit the Trinity." Jericho pursed his lips to keep from smiling. "My Raptor Admins are still here, serving you, prepared to do whatever it takes to maintain the status quo. One shows you this image. What would you initially think?"

Sparrowhawk raised up his cellphone. Jericho walked closer to get a look. On the screen was a picture of Beau Heights against an overcast morning sky. His mouth dropped.

"No way," he whispered. He asked his next question more loudly. "Is this online?"

"I am dead," his father said, showing his hands to his Raptor Admins. "Talk to them."

Jericho gulped. He became shaky. "Is this online? Like, is this a real—I mean, is this happening now?"

"It is," Sparrowhawk replied. "This image was uploaded a few hours ago."

Jericho took the phone from Sparrowhawk and studied the image. Whoever had taken the picture was able to get the entire clocktower in frame. Beau was tall but not so tall that an identifiable picture of it could be taken from a distance. The only way to capture this clear of a shot was to be on Lynbrook's campus.

He gave the phone back to Sparrowhawk and looked at his father. The man glared back at him, arms crossed, silently judging.

Jericho felt dryness in his throat. "Who took this picture? How is this possible?" He paused to gather his thoughts. "What time was it uploaded?"

"A quarter after seven this morning, when the CSB arrived," Sparrowhawk replied.

"How did you know about this?"

"Robert Birdwing mentioned it during the luncheon."

"Why was Mr. Birdwing looking for this?"

"Based on our conversation, I think he was researchin' Lynbrook before he got here, and that image showed up in his results," Falcon interjected.

Jericho pointed to Condor, the cyber specialist. "Pinpoint the coordinates of when and where the photo was t—"

"Done," said Condor. He was confident.

Jericho sighed in relief. "Remove it off the internet?"

"Done. What Sparrowhawk showed you was a screenshot. The photo, otherwise, is completely erased from the internet."

"You were supposed to make him think it's still posted, Condork. That's part of the test," Kestrel said.

"Nerd ruined our fun," Falcon snickered.

Jericho ignored them and continued. "And make sure it's inaccessible—"

"Done," Condor whispered. "Sparrowhawk forwarded the image to me, so I researched the photo's metadata and did a reverse image search. Found out it was taken early this morning, to be exact." He nervously cleared his throat.

"Don't tell me Lorelei took the picture," Jericho said.

"And what if she did?" Kestrel asked, leaning forward. Jericho looked away. "What if she did break our no photo policy, Kite Boy? You wouldn't let it slide because she's your cousin, would you?"

"The image's data is linked to the social media account of Ren Usagi, one of the CSB investigators," said Sparrowhawk.

"Well, well, Kite Boy," Falcon snickered. "What are we gonna do 'bout it? That Usagi guy violated our cellphone policy."

"Let me think." Jericho paced back and forth. The adrenaline in his body was incomprehensible. Though he understood the significance of the violation, he had no idea what a fitting consequence would be. Government workers punished corporations, not the other way around.

"Can I see the picture again?" Jericho asked, folding up his handkerchief. He was starting to sweat. His father's eyes were on him.

"With pleasure," said Sparrowhawk, holding out the cellphone.

Jericho scrolled down and saw Ren Usagi's uploaded post underneath the image.

GUYS, WISH ME LUCK. I'M GOING ON MY FIRST INVESTIGATION AT THIS SCHOOL. THIS MAY BE A BIG ONE. DEALING WITH A BIG COMPANY. CAN'T SAY WHO, BUT YOU CAN GUESS IT. MORE TO COME. BY THE WAY, THE NAME OF THIS CLOCK TOWER IS BEAU HEIGHTS. IT'S AN OUTSTANDING FEAT OF WHAT ARCHITECTURE MEETS JEWELRY WOULD LOOK LIKE.

The first and only commenter wrote: *Go get 'em, Ren! Get them Kite jerks locked up. All of em!*

Jericho covered his mouth and looked at his father's furrowed eyebrows. The elder Kite motioned for his son to continue leading.

"I thought all phones were supposed to be confiscated at the gate. Where's Eric Fowl? What did he have to say about this?" Jericho asked.

Kestrel, Sparrowhawk, and Falcon glared at Jericho. Shrugging, Condor seemed sincerely unable to answer the question. Everyone else suddenly smirked, withholding the information purposely. Jericho breathed fast through his nose and sighed. He felt like the only person in the room on his side, Condor, was also being excluded.

"I've seen enough." His father stood up. "Condor, go upstairs and bring me Edmund Rabbit out of captivity."

"You want Usagi as well, sir?" Condor asked with a puzzled face.

"Did I misspeak?"

"No, sir, I'll take care of it right away."

"Sparrowhawk, help him."

Sparrowhawk nodded. "With pleasure."

Jericho felt Condor's brotherly touch as he brushed past him and whispered, "Stay true to yourself. Things are about to get bad like last month… maybe worse."

The two Raptor Admins left the room promptly. As soon as the door closed, Falcon grunted. "Freakin' Condork."

"Right? He ruined the test," Kestrel added.

"Falcon, Kestrel, silence. Now," the headmaster ordered.

Falcon remembered his place and got quiet. Kestrel pouted her lip and *hmphed*. Jericho looked at his father.

"I already had these guys confront Eric," the headmaster said. "Turns out he only confiscated three phones this morning. One from Edmund Rabbit, the head investigator. One from Ren Usagi. And one from Robert Birdwing. Condor tracked down the device Usagi used. The man had two phones but only surrendered one at the gate. I imagine he gave up the work phone, then kept the personal one hidden. It was Eric's job to search for them and confiscate all electronics. We have Usagi's second phone now."

Lorelei would be distraught if something happened to her Uncle Eric during that confrontation. "Oversights can be forgiven," Jericho said.

His father's palms completely covered his face, kneading his worry lines. "You're not ready to lead."

Kestrel cleared her voice. "Quick, let's talk about what Sparrowhawk did before he gets back."

Jericho's eyes widened. Sparrowhawk was the star Raptor Admin, his father's favorite. What could he have done?

"Yes, please fill me in—and Kestrel, mind the boy as you speak."

Kestrel glanced at Jericho and nodded. "Yes, sir. I was putting chains on the CSB upstairs when Falco came in as I was finishing. He told me that Robert had found a picture of Beau Heights online. We looked up the picture, then got Condor to fix the situation. Then, Falco and I went back down to the dining hall to get more info out of Robert."

Falcon inserted himself. "That's when we saw Sparrowhawk grabbing his head, screamin' his guts out. He was on the floor, losin' his freakin' mind. Looked like a demon had gotten to him, git what I'm sayin'? The girl was standin' in front of her dad. He was on the floor."

"She's not a demon," Kestrel interjected. "She's activated, but she doesn't know what she's doing. That's why I threw her outside in the rain. Wasn't sure how to punish her. I don't want to go through what Sparrowhawk went through."

"I'm thinkin' Sparrowhawk don't even know what he's doing either," Falcon added. "Ain't no tellin' what he thinkin' sometimes. All this Capable stuff is still new to all of us."

"I think he activated her by accident when he got into her head, Boss," Kestrel said.

Jericho had no idea what they were talking about. He hoped if he continued listening that it would make sense.

"This is bad news. I knew she had the surgery, but there were zero indications, zero warning signs that her activation was imminent," the headmaster said.

"That's why I believe Sparrowhawk triggered her. She was so stressed out that I believe her nervous system reacted, fight or flight. She chose fight."

"That theory is plausible, Kestrel." The headmaster turned around and looked out the window. "This poses a very serious problem for us. I should send the Capables and Pures directly to Kan."

"That ain't a bad idea, 'cept—" Falcon cut himself off. His eyes darted to Jericho, then averted.

"Not all the Pures, obviously. The two that'll make me some money," the elder Kite said.

Kestrel shook her head. "Kan is still developing. They need one more year."

"They said that last year and the year before. We can't wait another year." His father pounded the desk. "Her activation specifically is troublesome. Samara elected to do a very risky surgery on her. She could activate others."

"I think the only reason she got Sparrowhawk was because he established a Link. She doesn't know what she's doing," Kestrel said.

Jericho still had no clue who or what they were talking about.

His father palmed his forehead. "Okay, for now, avoid mentioning what happened. I stand by my decision about Kan. I already have helicopters coming out for Robert and Edmund. What's hiring another two? The Pures and Capables are worth more money at Kan anyway. Kan's infrastructure is good enough to start using them. They can make room for four more." He sat down and spun his chair around to face his desk. "First, we need to focus on finding Lorelei and getting rid of Usagi. I want these tasks completed tonight."

"What's the pilots' update on Lorelei?" Falcon asked.

"They can't find her and are now complaining about high bird activity. They're having a hard time avoiding bird strikes."

"Can't they just fly higher?" Kestrel asked.

"No, they'll fly into controlled airspace and garner the attention of air traffic controllers. They're flying illegally, without detection turned on. Controllers report that stuff."

"She's out there runnin' amok," Falcon said. "You wanna send us back out there?"

"No. She has gotten too dangerous, and I need you all here. I'd rather send other people. For your awareness, Alexander Ravensbourne called me fifteen minutes ago. He had somehow managed to contact Lorelei. Turns out he was the one who told her to call the CSB. We exchanged a few unpleasant words."

"What did he want?" Falcon asked.

"In a nutshell, he was calling to brag about how he subverted Lynbrook from within using Lorelei."

"That was all he wanted?"

"That was all I care to recall. You know how unpleasant speaking to him can be."

The Ravensbourne family's advancements in electricity directly competed with the Kite Clan's oil and gas company. They were the top two leaders in energy production in the Western hemisphere. Ravensbourne were in the lead. For generations, their family had singlehandedly improved the nation's electrical infrastructure. The Kites didn't have much longer in the energy business, maybe fifty more years at best. To the Kite Clan, investing in eugenics at Kan was better than caving in and investing in electricity or solar power. If that transition succeeded, the Kite Express gas stations could fail quietly.

"Alexander's timing couldn't have been more impeccable," Kestrel said.

"When it rains, it pours," Falcon added, opening a bag of pork crackling strips.

Kestrel glared at him in disgust. "That pork stuff you eat is bad for you. It'll make you stink when you sweat."

Falcon shrugged and began chewing obnoxiously. "I don't give a crap. Not everybody wants to have a child's body like you."

Jericho covered his mouth to keep from laughing. Kestrel was often mistaken for a twelve-year-old girl, and it didn't help that she had a youthful voice and sense of fashion.

One of her eyes twitched. "You know, Falcon, it's your fault we're in this mess and have Alexander coming after us."

"It ain't my fault! The Ravensbourne have always had a big, fat target on us."

"You made it worse calling Alexander what you called him in Denver at the energy convention."

"I wasn't wrong, was I? He don't even try to hide it."

"Why should he hide it, jerk? It's who he is. Your big mouth screwed us!"

"This ain't my fault, Kestrel!"

"Enough, you two," the headmaster spoke out. "I'm making use of the CSB. That's why I have Edmund coming in here. It would be advantageous for us to gather data on how much natural gas is leaking. It'll be useful data we can take to Meccanicville as well."

It got quiet. Jericho took out a cigarette and announced he would be stepping outside for a moment. He went out the backdoor then down the hallway and stood underneath the vestibule, leaning against the brick. The rain came down hard, sounding like white noise but with occasional thunder. Hundreds of small birds frantically flew above the campus.

He closed his eyes after lighting his cigarette. "I want this day to end."

He looked over his shoulder and saw Mikayla standing in the rain. Normally, she wore loose clothing, but she was so soaked, her clothes stuck to her skin. Thin and delicate, she shivered as a streak of lightning stretched across the sky over her head like a thorned halo. Naomi wouldn't like that he was a passive participant in her best friend's torture.

He turned around and exhaled. Then, it dawned on him—Mikayla was out in the rain because Kestrel put her there. She was who they were talking about, the Capable one Sparrowhawk activated. It made sense. Naomi had mentioned Mikayla had brain surgery around the same time she did.

Jericho threw his cigarette on the ground, stomped on it, and ran back to his father's office. He had questions, lots of them.

Edmund Rabbit was already there. Condor had left, but Sparrowhawk remained.

"Make him kneel," the headmaster demanded.

Falcon pushed down on Edmund's shoulder. Jericho let out a slow sigh and fought to maintain his tough expression.

"What do you want? I'll do anything," Edmund pleaded. "Tell me what you want. Please release me and my coworker. Please! This visit will all be swept under the rug. Nobody will know about today. I have that power. I know people who'll make the CSB look the other way. Let me go, please! I have grandkids. They're starting college soon."

"Wow." Jericho shuddered under his breath. He could barely breathe. He had never seen a man beg his father for mercy before, only heard the stories.

His father crouched down to Edmund. "You have a methane detector in that van?"

"Yes, yes." Edmund wiped the sweat above his brow.

"I want you to test the methane levels in the western section of my school and in the clocktower. It's too far away to walk to in the rain. Drive us there."

"Sure thing. Is that all you want? I can get that done in no time. But if we're going to those places, we'll need protective gear because methane is an asphyxiant. I have respirators."

"We have our own."

Jericho remembered last night. "Father," he spoke up. "Our respirators are no good."

His father grunted as if he were restraining himself from saying more. "There will be five of us then. Myself, Sparrowhawk, Falcon, and my son."

Jericho's heart dropped. He had never been chosen for anything that important, let alone tasked to accompany his father's most trusted admins. He held his arm against himself to keep it from trembling. It was another test.

"Alright. Well, gentlemen, if you'd show me out to my van, I'll grab those respirators, then we'll be on our way to those buildings you want me to check out."

As the five of them left the office, Edmund turned to Jericho and his father. He clapped his palms together and held them as if praying. "Please, reassure me this is all you want, and Ren and I will be set free. Like I said, I know people who'll dismiss this investigation and wipe it off the face of the earth. That anonymous phone call, the recording of that young lady who called this morning, that'll be gone, not archived. Gone!"

Jericho looked to his father, knowing he would be the man to make the final decision. The headmaster placed his hand on Edmund's shoulder and smiled with his eyes closed.

"The people you know are erasers. The people I know are paper shredders. This is what you get for entering the Trinity rabbit hole. I hope you like Texas."

Edmund's mouth dropped, and he stopped in place. His father continued walking. Sparrowhawk and Falcon each grabbed one of Edmund's shoulders and nudged him to walk forward.

Jericho whispered "Sorry" to Edmund and followed his father's footsteps.

Mikayla Birdwing

1:45 PM

Still outside, Mikayla felt weighed to the ground in the very spot she hadn't moved from since Miss Kestrel left her. The rain pitter-pattered into a drizzle that calmed her scattered mind. Although she couldn't predict when and where the next raindrop would fall, at least she knew it would land somewhere. On her face. On her arm. On her pants. On the grass. On her dad's onyx pawn. On a dandelion's white seeds.

She rested stomach down in a puddle and watched droplets roll off her nose. Another rolled off. Then another. And another...

Watching the droplets kept her mind off Headmaster Kite's hurtful words. She refused to believe her mother wanted nothing to do with her. Sure, she wasn't a mother who always paid attention, but she wasn't heartless. Was she?

Another drop rolled. And another...

It wasn't raindrops.

The buzz of propellers woke her.

The race-striped, dragonfly-shaped plane zoomed a few hundred feet over her. Seconds passed, and its checkered wingman coasted by at a lower altitude. They both had white letters painted along the side of their fuselages, VH-KCRKMV and VH-KCUKMV, respectively.

When the sharp crescendo of the airplanes' turbine blades lessened with distance, Mikayla heard footsteps, then felt a gentle hand pat her forehead. It was Sado. She knew his earthy scent; it reminded her of cedarwood. Instead of looking at him, she watched the planes become dots, disappearing behind the clouds. They were leaving Lynbrook.

"Mika-Chou, ya okay?"

"Uh, I'm not feeling so good, Sado." Her voice sounded like a soft cry.

"Maybe yer gettin' sick from bein' out here in the cold rain for hours. Brought a tea for ya. It's good to drink now."

Mikayla felt Sado positioning her hands to receive a mug warm enough to shock feeling back into her numb fingers. Her first sip was so satisfying it brought tears to her eyes.

She took another sip. "Well…if you're here, that means Freedom Hours started, but I didn't hear Beau ring."

"Huh? Now that ya say it, I ain't heard it neither. Wait…looks like Beau's hands are stuck. Stopped workin' around 3:17 PM."

Mikayla paused to digest the fact that she had been left outside for over five hours. Above her, thousands of small birds blackened the sky.

"There're so many birds up there." She was awestruck.

"Oh, yeah, it's been like that since lunchtime. It started out small, at first. Then it grew into hundreds, and then this." He kneeled. "Where's yer dad?"

"I don't know." Her body tensed at the sight of the birds.

"What happened today?"

She shook her head, not saying anything.

"Well, I told ya it wasn't goin' to work out."

Mikayla nudged him away. Sado, ignoring her gesture, made himself comfortable sitting next to her. Too tired to object, she let him stay. He began complaining about everything that had happened, spouting out one negative thing after another. Everything was doom and gloom, some of it baseless. Mikayla paid no attention to most of it. She wanted him to stop touching her, so she got up and began walking towards the dorms. Sado followed her, not missing a beat in what he was complaining about.

On the south side, the rattling fence interrupted his rant. Behind them, four coyotes stood on their hindlegs, pawing at the fence. Their barking and howling grew louder, more aggressive.

"I hate dogs. Had one bite me when I was a kid," Sado mumbled, shrinking back at the sight of their fangs.

"Those aren't dogs, silly," Mikayla said. "They're coyotes."

"Whatever. They carry mange and fleas, smellin' like doo-doo. That makes 'em dog enough for me to hate 'em." He walked his fingers onto her hand and held it. "What's wrong with nature today? A thousand birds. Rabid dogs."

Mikayla moved her hand away from Sado. Wishing the coyotes' barking and birds' cawing would end, she kneaded the side of her head. She loved dogs, just not when they barked while she had a headache.

"They'll go away if you give them a bologna sandwich," Isaiah said from behind them.

"I didn't hear ya come up," Sado said.

"Wonder why," Isaiah said with a smirk, looking at the coyotes and the birds.

"Yer a sneaky snake in the grass, that's why. Menace," Sado muttered and cut his eyes away.

Isaiah ignored Sado. "Hey, Mika, I'm here checking in. You okay?"

"I'm fine."

"She's feelin' sick, Isaiah. I'm gonna walk her to the dorms so she can get some rest somewhere warm."

"Maybe I can talk to her for a second first?"

"Nah, you can leave," Sado said, blocking her from Isaiah's view. "You already got a girlfriend."

"Not anymore." Isaiah stepped to the side. "Mika? Can we talk?"

Shivering, Mikayla lifted her head and shook it. She wanted nothing to do with either of the boys. They were pointless. Everyone was pointless. Everything was pointless.

"Not now, both of you. If you see Naomi, tell her I went to bed early." She walked away.

"That's who I wanted to talk to you about," Isaiah said loudly. "Naomi broke up with me and went off with Headmaster Kite's son…again. She went off with him last night too."

Mikayla paused mid-step. "When last night?"

"A few minutes after you left us. Jericho came up, said something to her, and they were gone."

Last night, Naomi returned to the dorm with her hair disheveled, blouse half unbuttoned. *All along, it wasn't Isaiah she'd made out with, but Jericho Kite! The nerve! What was wrong with Naomi? Why did she choose a Kite? Why?*

Mikayla had been through enough crap for the day. She stormed off, hearing bits and pieces of Isaiah and Sado arguing.

Inside the dorm, her tears blurred the destruction Miss Kestrel made while raiding her area for the possum notebook. Her mattress was on the floor, leaning against the wall. All of her belongings were either scattered elsewhere, lost, or damaged. Her books, shredded. Her trinkets, shattered. Her clothes, missing. She stepped over the mess and went to the shower, where she stood until the hot water turned cold. She went to sleep on the mattress afterward.

#

Her mother sizzled sunny side up eggs and turkey bacon on the stovetop, using her laptop as a skillet. Mikayla waited at the breakfast nook, dressed in her old uniform from when she went to school in Atlanta.

Her mother served breakfast on a stack of file folders instead of a plate. Mikayla stabbed her fork into her egg. The yolk crumbled into dark chunks that looked like coal. The bacon disappeared, then reappeared on the floor. Mikayla reached for it, but the bacon hopped up and clung to the ceiling like putty. She couldn't get her mother's attention.

Her mother, aloof to what was happening, sat across the table, her shoulder cradling her cellphone. Talking, she sat inside of a tub of coffee with her head buried in a high pile of casework. She dipped her mug inside of her tub to drink from it. Mikayla waved in desperation for her mother's attention, but she began to shrink in her chair until she became the size of a caterpillar. She had to burrow up through her clothes until she surfaced at the top. Her mother pinched her fingers like tweezers to pick up Mikayla so she could drop her inside of a dark briefcase.

The chandelier in the briefcase shined above Mikayla like a spotlight.

Antennas, four more legs, and a pair of blue birdwing butterfly wings sprouted out of her. Sado, flying with tiger swallowtail wings, emerged from the darkness. He too had six legs and feelers that twitched when he laid eyes on Mikayla. Behind him was a field mouse that turned around and had Naomi's face. Isaiah trotted up and sat beside her, panting, wearing a dog's body. Mikayla glanced at her wings, at her friends, and then at the chessboard underneath her legs.

An invisible force pulled her forward two spaces to E5, where she stood face to face with a kestrel she couldn't run from. A sparrowhawk flew diagonally towards her and landed on H5, near Mikayla. Every one of her legs felt like they were glued to the chessboard. Raptors flew over her head.

She turned around and saw a lump in a swallowtail kite's throat and the last of Sado's tiger swallowtail wings being swept inside with the bird's lashing tongue. A vulture had its claws on Naomi's tail while an osprey pecked a hole through her skull. Mikayla locked her eyes shut to block the blood spatter.

A falcon flew over the chessboard with its claw on a rifle's trigger. Bullets and brass casings rained upon them. One by one, they exploded in a bloody heap of feathers and guts.

She screamed, "Stop!"

Everything blackened. She had her normal body again, but she was alone, floating in the middle of nothingness. The black void remained until stars sprinkled all around her. The crescent moon materialized behind her and tilted, sweeping her off her feet. She slid down its curvature to rest on it like a hammock. Above, Lorelei and Naomi sat cross-legged at the top of the moon. Jericho had his legs wrapped around the top part, and he hung upside down with his face in hers. Isaiah snuggled beside her, holding her hand. She tried to ask them how they got there, but no words came out. They all started laughing and talking but it was silent. They understood one another through their hearts.

Confused, Mikayla woke up at 7:00 PM. Nobody was there. There was one Freedom Hour left. Her dreams felt real, and for the first time, she was able to control parts of them. She had never had a lucid dream before.

Hugging her pillow up to her face, Mikayla closed her eyes again. She dreamed up what could've been, had her mom called the CSB and her dad saved her.

Awakening ten minutes later, she felt like it was her best dream ever. A smile curled across her face. She drifted back into slumber, reviving the exact same wonderful dream.

Jericho Kite IV

5:07 PM

Freedom Hours resumed as usual to keep the Lynbrookians unaware of the ongoing chaos, like Rome's bread and circuses. While students got together to gossip about the crazy stuff that went on or be with their friends without supervision, the headmaster and the Raptor Admins had time to convene in his office. Jericho wanted no part of their meeting after they had finished using Edmund Rabbit and put him back into captivity.

He stood on the shared patio on the balcony outside the bal-chatri, smoking a cigarette. Below, Naomi walked side by side with Isaiah Marksman. The two of them weren't holding hands or looking at each other. Isaiah was a fake boyfriend to keep around as a front in case anyone accused her of her real relationship with Jericho, but seeing the pair together still rubbed Jericho the wrong way.

"Why is she hanging out with that dork?" he muttered, jamming the butt of the cigarette against the pillar.

He had a lot on his mind after the inspection of the clocktower. Some of it, he had to share with Naomi. First, he had to get her away from Isaiah. He turned away and went back inside to put on his blazer. There were a few breath mints in his pocket. He grabbed them to mask the stench. Naomi hated his smoking.

Downstairs in his father's office, all seven Raptor Admins gathered tightly around the desk, hiding the headmaster from view. Jericho clenched his fist and quickly left the building from the south door, glad he wasn't seen. He

105

felt like he was supposed to be in there, proving he deserved inheriting the Trinity. However, after the inspection, he wanted space from his father.

He took his time approaching Naomi and Isaiah. The last thing he wanted was to be spotted practically running across campus to ambush the couple. Beau Heights caught his eye. Stuck at 3:17, its hands reminded him of the exact moment Edmund Rabbit told them to shut the clocktower down. It was barely two hours ago. Time dragged on so slowly, it felt like weeks.

Wearing a respirator inside Beau Heights had triggered unpleasant memories of what almost happened to Condor last night. Jericho tried to stay nostalgic, thinking of the good times Beau brought. There was a day years ago he climbed the stairs inside too fast and almost fell down. Landon was with him and had reflexes fast enough to catch his hand, halting his fall. Lorelei was there too, ready to help him regain his footing. Together, one hundred and thirty feet up, the three of them stood on top of Beau Heights, wind flowing through their hair. The sunlight made the trio's silver eyes glimmer. The Talladega Mountains blocked the world Jericho wasn't allowed to explore. He wanted to see that world more than anything. Inheriting the Trinity and changing it for the better was the second-best thing he could hope for. He needed to be strong enough to defend and manage it. Though Beau Heights was a small piece of his inheritance, it was his favorite.

Because of the natural gas leak, Beau Heights had become a dangerous place Edmund Rabbit declared a "prohibited space approaching the upper explosive limit within the flammable range—an environment that poses immediate danger to life and health." Jericho had no idea what any of that meant because it sounded too technical. All he knew was the methane detector had measured Beau's methane levels at 11% by volume, which was 9.6% higher than the levels in the classroom he, Condor, and Osprey had searched the night prior. Edmund warned them an air sample was needed and would be more accurate, but it would take weeks to return from a lab. He was able to confirm oxygen levels measured deficient at 17.8%. He explained further that the methane vapors could burn, given heat and an ignition source. Because of this, Edmund urged them to stay away from the west side. He also terminated Beau Heights's electricity because the entire clocktower was made of flammable materials and he was afraid the moving mechanical gears or the lights inside would generate a spark. Igniting the methane vapors could cause a series of fires and explosions across Lynbrook, killing many.

Seeing the clock's gears stop had brought tears into Jericho's eyes. Luckily, his respirator mask shielded him. Had his father seen those tears, it would've been bad. He wasn't allowed to cry.

Jericho lingered behind a tree to watch Naomi and Isaiah, unable to make out their words. Isaiah had his arms crossed, still looking away from her. She spoke to him, but her tone didn't seem pleasant.

This was it. She was breaking up with him.

A minute went by. Isaiah hadn't moved. Naomi kept on talking. Isaiah suddenly let out a yawn. Naomi went ballistic. Isaiah glanced at his watch, then put his hands on his hips.

Jericho pushed off the tree and approached. "Naomi, I need to speak with you." Her mouth hung open, and Isaiah backed away. "You need to come with me."

"Okay," she replied.

Jericho and Naomi walked off and turned onto a secluded path. She followed his lead, not questioning him. Jericho guided her through a side door to a staircase that would lead them directly upstairs to the bal-chatri.

She cleared her throat. "I broke up with him."

"Finally," he replied.

"I've never kissed him, in case you've been wondering."

Jericho looked at her skeptically. "You've been fake dating him for weeks. You expect me to believe you didn't entertain him with one kiss?"

"I didn't! I swear."

"*Pfft!*"

"You're jealous for no reason. The whole thing was a sham. You knew that."

"Yeah, it was working until Mikayla poked her nose in our business last night."

"Uh, once again, we were out in the open. Not her fault." She shrugged. "Look, if it helps you feel better, Isaiah actually likes Mika a lot."

Jericho paused at the absurdity of it all. "Why didn't he ask *her* out then?"

"Because they're nervous dorks around each other. And Sado gets really jealous about Mika because he's in a relationship with her in his head. He's never asked her out. He just decided one day that Mika is his, and she goes along with it because she's too scared to tell him to go away. Sado is a bully. He takes advantage of her niceness. I tell Mika she needs to sucker punch him right in the teeth…"

She continued rambling. Jericho tuned her out. He didn't care about that petty drama. Less than two hours ago, a man named Edmund Rabbit had saved Lynbrook from potential destruction. Now he was held captive, locked up somewhere for doing the right thing for the wrong people. Love triangles were child's play. Jericho grew up watching the drama of Lynbrookians dating and breaking up with each other. It never made sense to him. Then again, he had the big picture of what would happen to them and why. They didn't.

Naomi's voice shifted to a higher pitch. She had asked a question.

"I'm sorry, my mouse. I didn't catch that," Jericho said, stopping on the first landing of the stairs.

"I asked if you were even listening. I'm trying to explain why it took me so long to break up with Isaiah."

Oops, he thought. He forgot that when you're talking to girls, you're not supposed to make it obvious when you're ignoring them.

"I was. You're saying all these names, and I don't know who these people are."

"*Mika and Sado*," she repeated with emphasis, as if it would get her point across.

Jericho knew who Mikayla Birdwing was. In fact, he had questions about her. Who Sado was didn't matter; he was another damned Lynbrookian. "Oh, I remember them now," Jericho replied simply.

Nobody was in the bal-chatri. Good. Jericho took Naomi's hand and rushed her down the hallway. Naomi tried keeping up with him but was distracted. The sunset glistened through the gemstones of the stained glass facing north. Jericho paused to marvel at the sight. Thousands of birds on the horizon looked like black specks against the sun. He squeezed her hand, urging her to follow. They went into his room. Jericho locked the door and sighed in relief. Having her in his bedroom was a dangerous game for a young man already on eggshells with his father.

"Jericho, why are there so many birds flying around outside?"

"I don't know."

"Everyone's been talking about it. Does it have something to do with the planes that have been flying around?"

Jericho shrugged. He wasn't in the mood to explain they were searching for Lorelei. Everything was falling apart, and he wanted some answers before it was too late. He didn't want to be a bystander like during the Great Resignation.

Naomi began wandering throughout his bedroom as if she'd forgotten she'd asked a question. "Oh, wow, your room is really big. It's like the size of my mom's apartment."

"This is the smallest room up here. The Raptor Admins and Father get the bigger ones," he mumbled.

She giggled and ran into his bathroom. He heard her turning the sink on and off repeatedly.

"First time in a bathroom?" he asked.

"Your water comes out clear."

"Yeah," he said, laughing under his breath.

She sprinted out of the bathroom, plopped face down on his bed, and began rolling around, taking his silk sheets into her hands.

"Oh, wow, your bed is the best. Our beds in the dorm are terrible. Even my bed back home wasn't this nice."

Smiling, Jericho pressed against the wall. He couldn't believe what he was seeing. *How does a girl have a day like today and still act happy-go-lucky?* That was what he absolutely loved about Naomi. But at the same time, she seemed like the type of girl who'd been in a boy's bedroom many times before. He didn't want to ask how many. Some things were better left unasked.

A lighthearted, beautiful girl. He felt lucky and still got butterflies in his stomach around her.

"Your pillow kinda smells like a cigarette."

"I apologize."

"I hate that you smoke. Why do you smoke so much?"

"I don't know."

He knew why. He didn't want to admit that he was stressed out from the secrets he was forced to keep.

She composed herself and sat up. "Where are your family pictures or some art? The walls are *bleh*, boring."

"Pictures of my family? On the wall?" This concept sounded foreign to Jericho.

"It's what us normal poor people do," she said facetiously. "We also put up pictures of our pets and vacations spots."

"Vacation," Jericho muttered.

He had heard the word before but couldn't remember what it meant. He relaxed his shoulders, figuring Naomi needed some time to warm up before he could have a more serious conversation with her. "I have your picture here." He climbed across his bed and pulled the winged mouse in the tutu she drew for him off the wall.

Naomi gasped. "Oh!"

"Shh," he said softly. "We can't be loud in here. All those doors we passed in the hallway are the bedrooms of the Raptor Admins."

Naomi's eyes widened. She shot to her feet. "And you brought me *here*."

Jericho put his hands on her shoulder and gently got her to sit again. "They're in a meeting with my father downstairs in his office. They've been talking for hours. They're not coming up anytime soon, but if they do, it needs to sound like nobody's in here."

She nodded and quietly said, "Your room's boring."

"My father's secretary designed it."

"And how much of a choice did you have? Like, did you even get to pick your clothes? I bet not," she said, tugging on his cravat. "Your haircut is like military style. So boring. Calling yourself Honorable Kite. So cringey."

He laughed it off. He had no idea how to respond to that, so he cut to the important stuff. "I brought you in here to talk about something serious."

Naomi tensed up, making herself look small. "But we always joke around and have fun. You're the only one I can be myself with. I mean, I have Mika, but she's been uptight for weeks. She's actually really silly and goofy. I guess calling her uptight was mean with everything going on. Not counting what happened to her today, she's been sad that she couldn't have Isaiah. She likes him a lot. But Sado clings to her. He's kinda obsessed with her, and that's why Isaiah couldn't ask her out. But now I feel wrong for saying yes to Isaiah because I used him to hide me and you. I should've told him no and helped them be together."

Sighing, Jericho wanted to tell Naomi that he couldn't care less about that love triangle stuff. Then again, he realized that maybe she couldn't handle thinking about the more serious things going on. Normally, he would comfort her or give advice, but he barely was able to cope himself.

He cuddled up to her and put his finger on her chin. "Don't look so sad, my mouse. You know, I like the way we can be ourselves, but there's a lot going on. I need to talk to you. I brought you in here because I can't talk out there."

"Okaaaaay," she said. She slumped against his shoulder and buried her head in his chest. "I'm listening."

He smiled, feeling lucky to have a pretty girlfriend. "I need you to help me remember something."

"Okay."

"You and Mikayla had surgeries, right?"

"Yeah. When we were twelve. That was forever ago."

"I know. What was yours for?"

Naomi wrapped her arms around her stomach. "Why do you want to know?"

"I've been thinking about it. What was Mikayla's surgery?"

"Her brain."

"Was something wrong with her that required that surgery?"

"Why are you asking me this stuff? You didn't care this much when I mentioned it before."

Jericho took a deep breath. "Something strange happened to Mikayla today. My father and his Raptors were talking about it."

Naomi picked her head up off his chest. "I know she's having a hard time. I feel bad for her. She's in trouble, isn't she? That's why she never came back. Can you tell your dad not to punish her too hard?"

"Naomi, I need you to think really, really hard." Depending on her answer, she was possibly one of the four his father intended on sending to Kan. "Did you and Mikayla feel like you had some kind of newfound power or supernatural energy after your surgeries?"

"My period cramps stopped killing me every month. I'm not sure what you want me to say. You're weirding me out. Is Mika in trouble or not?"

"I can't answer that."

They sat in silence for a while. While she raked her fingers through her hair, stress and guilt ate him up. He thought about the secret he had been hiding from her—why her mother never mailed her. That was too risky to mention. His father would kill him. Instead, he felt like she could at least know the truth about what had happened that morning.

"I lied in the library," he said.

"About Mr. Rabbit and Mr. Usagi being imposters. I know."

He turned to her. "How'd you know?"

"Mika reminded me that our moms used to work with guys like that, and the more I thought about it, the more I realized they were real. The clothes. The words they used. The way they acted. They were real CSB."

"You're not mad at me?"

"I was earlier, then I remembered." She spread her arms out and looked around his bedroom. "You don't have a choice. Whatever your father wants, he gets."

Jericho opened his mouth to say something, and then he swallowed hard. His throat felt dry.

"I know *he* makes it so you can't answer all our questions. The way you, Landon, and Lorelei act. It's obvious all of you are hiding something from us."

"Yeah," Jericho mumbled. He felt like Landon and Lorelei hid stuff from him too.

"Why can't we leave?"

"Because Father feels like the gas leak is far enough away on the west side of the campus not to be a big deal."

"But it does matter. My mom has seen cases like this where the problem gets ignored and pushed off until—"

"A point of no return."

"That's not what I was going to say, but yeah, a point of no return. When people get hurt or it's too hard to fix it or someone gets caught." She got quiet for a while, and then she asked, "Did the Raptor Admins kill the teachers?"

"Naomi, I've told you a million times I can't answer that."

"Literally everyone thinks that's what happened. I think your dad didn't want them to be whistleblowers, or whatever it's called."

"Just stop."

"Are we next? Is he going to come after us next? You didn't hear this from me, but there are some working up the nerve to leave like Lorelei did. I'm just bringing it up because I don't want to see or hear them get shot. Maybe you can beg your father to let us go home."

"I can't. Stop talking. It's—just stop, okay?"

"You said you wanted to be serious."

"Now I don't."

Naomi got quiet again. Jericho went to the drawer where he kept his cigarettes. He repeatedly pulled one out and slid it back in until he felt her touching his shoulder.

"All you've ever wanted was to get out of this place."

He shook his head. "Yeah."

"But he keeps you cooped up here."

Naomi understood the gist of what was happening in his life. Jericho always kept it vague when talking to her about it. She didn't need to know the details.

He held her hand. "Naomi, I want to save you so bad. You don't have a clue."

She pulled his face in and gave him a long, slow kiss. "It's time you do whatever you want, Jericho."

"Whatever I want?" he whispered before another kiss. He felt like he was ensnared in her lovely spell.

"Yeah," she said, pushing away slightly. She batted her pretty green eyes. "You're very, very strong and have lots of power and money. And yet you're not using it. You keep worrying about what *he* thinks, what *he'll* do. Kick him to the curb."

Jericho's eyes widened as she stood up and skipped towards his closed balcony door. She leaned against it with a sultry look, teasing the knobs with the tips of her fingers. "There's a whole world out there, Jericho, and you're so rich you can do whatever you want. He cooped you up in this place your whole life because he doesn't want you to live up to your full potential. He is willing to take you down with him. Remember what they say: a Kite wants what they want."

"And gets it," he said softly.

"You're a Kite. Don't forget that. Look at you. You're young, handsome, bigger than him. He knows you can take his place easy." Jericho looked at his reflection in the mirror as she kept talking. He put the cigarette down. "You don't even have the slightest clue how rich and capable you are because you've never been anywhere before!"

Jericho felt his heart racing. Caught up in excitement, he had forgotten to tell Naomi to quiet down. He stood up and went to her. She pulled on the collar of his blazer and brought his ear down to her lips.

She spoke very softly, letting her lips caress his earlobe. "If you really, really want to save me, you'll make me yours, and then we'll both be Kites. Then we'll both get whatever we want, right?"

"Yeah! I think so!" He grabbed her and kissed her. "I love you, my mouse."

"I love you too," she whispered, catching her breath.

They hugged for a while longer, and then he told her she had to go. She didn't want to leave. He grabbed her hand, walked her downstairs, and guided her out of the building. She left reluctantly.

He went back upstairs to his room and sat on the edge of his bed, fighting to calm down.

"That was so close. What was that? I almost lost it," he muttered.

At the same time, he wished he had done it. If Naomi was one of the four, he would never have her. She was going to Kan.

He got to his feet and paced the room. There had to be something he could do to stop his father from taking her away from him. He felt like if he thought hard enough, he'd find a way to save everyone. Although, that would result in an unbearable fight against his father and his Raptor Admins.

Only one of the Kites would get what he wanted.

Mikayla Birdwing

11:19 PM

Mr. Falco's voice from outside woke Mikayla, and she began coughing uncontrollably. She pressed her pillow against her face to muffle the sound in an effort not to wake the girls who slept around her. She turned left on her side so she could breathe out one nostril easier. He began yelling louder, and she stood up to look out the window to see what was happening.

She focused on a red flatbed truck that slowly reversed between her dorm and the males'. Meanwhile, Mr. Falco and Miss Kestrel stood side by side, loudly guiding Mr. Sparrowhawk, who cut the truck's wheel, angling the back towards the supply office door. There were about a dozen shovels stacked on top of one another in the flatbed. What lay underneath the flatbed's tarp was strapped down. Round bulges here and there made it difficult to figure out what was being concealed. Mr. Falco, gripping a gas can in one hand, passed by the truck. The brakes screeched as it eased to a halt. A minute later, the door to the flatbed clanked open, and then there were metallic banging and rustling sounds.

Mikayla ducked back onto her mattress quickly. *Is that Lorelei? Is she sealed in a body bag underneath that tarp?* As her eyes drifted away from Lorelei's empty bed, her mind went to the unthinkable. *Dad, I hope it's not you, or the CSB men.*

Naomi crawled up to her and patted her back. "You okay, Mika? I heard you wake up."

Flinching, Mikayla couldn't begin to explain what she saw. She barely had the will to tell Naomi about what happened after she had left the library to see her dad. It would upset her. She tensed up, remembering Naomi had chosen Jericho Kite.

"Did you eat dinner at least? I didn't see you come to the cafeteria," Naomi said.

"Wasn't hungry." Mikayla coughed. "My throat hurts."

Naomi touched Mikayla's shoulder. "We're all getting worried about you."

"I said I wasn't hungry."

"Okay, okay, it's just that I haven't seen you eat a decent meal in weeks."

Mikayla nudged Naomi's hand away and turned around. She planted her bare feet onto the chilly floor. She had no idea where she thought she was going. A part of her wanted to search the campus, rip it apart in search of her dad. The other part of her knew that couldn't happen.

Naomi guided her to take a seat on the mattress. "Mika, please…you need to rest."

A cone of light hit them.

Mikayla clenched her eyelids shut. It was Ximena Gecko on entry control duty, alongside Fahima Robin, her assigned partner. Every fifteen minutes of their two-hour shift, they were to peruse the dorm in search of nighttime violations. Lynbrookians could use the bathroom after hours, but otherwise, they were supposed to be asleep or at least quiet. The Raptor Admins had created entry control duty for the purpose of suicide prevention and surveillance. Most Lynbrookian girls were like Ximena and Fahima—scared to the bone. Scared to take risks. They had to keep things in line. It was their interpretation of survival.

Ximena pointed the light directly at Mikayla. "You okay?"

Mikayla nodded. Ximena walked away.

"Like I said, we're all worried about you. Even Sado took the time to ask about you," Naomi whispered.

Mikayla crossed her arms.

She sighed. "When did you speak to Sado?"

"Around seven thirty or so. He told me he brought you a tea, but you didn't want to talk, not even to Isaiah. That made me worried."

"I was outside for a little while before I came here," Mikayla muttered, wondering why Naomi hadn't once bothered to come see her.

"I know," Naomi nervously replied. Her voice cracked. "I guess that was around when I spoke to Isaiah to break up with him."

Mikayla clenched her blanket. "How did he take it?"

"He didn't seem like he cared."

Mikayla gulped, preparing to test Naomi's honesty. "What happened after you and Isaiah broke up? What were you doing between that and when you spoke to Sado?"

"You were asleep in here, so I did nothing much."

"Did you go anywhere?"

Naomi clutched the torn lace trimming on her gown. She chuckled. "Like where would I go, Mika? We're stuck on this campus."

Mikayla looked Naomi in the eye. "Did you go see Jericho Kite again?"

Naomi didn't blink, nor take her eyes off Mikayla. "Is that what Isaiah said happened?"

"Yes," Mikayla said. It came out like a hiss. She felt her chest becoming tight.

"He came on to me, like, yesterday."

"I think you're lying to me."

"What? Why? He did."

"Then why did Isaiah tell me you willingly went with him yesterday after I left and again today?"

"Mika, it's Isaiah saying this. He's going to make me sound bad."

"Isaiah has been nothing but nice to you, Naomi. Even though you guys went together like oil and water, he was still nice."

"Wow." Naomi rolled her eyes. "I don't get why you're accusing me of this right now. We should get back to sleep before Fahima and Ximena come back around."

"I don't care about the rules." Mikayla balled her fist. "I tried my best to stay hopeful for weeks. I had a plan to help us, and yet you're out there, choosing *them* instead."

"Who's them?"

"The Kites!" Mikayla hissed.

A girl across the room shushed them. Another yelled, "Shut up!"

Naomi shook her head. She whispered, "Isaiah's trying to make me look bad. Jericho came onto me and made me go with him. What was I supposed to do?"

Mikayla palmed her face. She wanted to scream, but instead she blurted out, "I think when Isaiah asked you out, you said yes so you can play your word salad games if anyone brings up you and Jericho."

Naomi froze. "Me saying yes to him gave him a chance for you and him to talk alone without Sado harassing you both."

"That's not why you said yes, knowing I liked him."

"I should've said no, okay?"

"Why didn't you?"

Naomi pursed her lips. They sat in silence for several minutes.

Mikayla broke the silence. "The Kites took my dad. The Kites took the CSB guys. The Kites made Mr. Sparrowhawk do something weird to me and my dad. Why are you choosing the Kites over me, Naomi? We've been friends for over five years. I can't believe you're doing this."

Naomi's facial expression switched. "Mr. Sparrowhawk did something?"

"Yeah, it felt like he was inside my head, and he made my dad lose control of his body. He hurt us, Naomi. Kestrel and Falco hurt us too." She sniffled.

She got quiet, placing her hand on top of Mikayla's, interlocking their fingers.

Mikayla quietly cried. "I'm going to talk to Headmaster Kite in the morning after breakfast."

Naomi gasped. "About what?"

"He's a businessman. Maybe I can negotiate a way to get him to set my dad free. I have to do something. I would rather fail again than have done nothing at all."

"Don't do that, Mika," Naomi whispered. A pause. "I think I know who can help us."

"Who?"

Hesitating, she looked away. She spoke just above a whisper, "Jericho."

Mikayla snatched her hand. "Are you kidding me?"

"He isn't like his father."

Mikayla scoffed. "I'm going back to sleep."

"If you can't beat them, join them." Naomi got back into her own bed.

Mikayla threw the blanket and pillow over her head. She wondered if Naomi's answer would have been different if she had mentioned what Headmaster Kite said about their mothers wanting nothing to do with them. She drifted back to sleep, sniffling.

In her dream, a grand hall was decorated like no other. Dozens of men dressed in armor adorned with achievement medals guarded a staircase, each upon a horse. Protected at the top of the staircase, Naomi wore a flowing empire waist dress, cradling a baby. The diamond on her engagement ring was larger than her knuckle. Her unbraided hair cascaded down to her waist, silky like waves of satin. She wore fire opal and melo pearls that were orange like a blossom. All her natural features were enhanced, and the glow of her caramel complexion was hidden underneath makeup. Standing at thigh height on each side of her were a set of twins tugging the ruffles on her dress. Looming behind them, Jericho sat on the largest horse. His hair ran down his back like a stallion's mane.

Mikayla's eyes split open. She sat up and stared at Naomi, who was sound asleep.

III

Sunday, November 9

Lunar phase: full moon
The Canine Moon

Jericho Kite IV

1:24 AM

Jericho had puffed through two packs of cigarettes since Freedom Hours ended. Distracted in deep thought, he didn't hear his father entering his quarters. He shut the door and looked Jericho in the eye.

"Ren Usagi is dead." There was no emotion, no remorse.

Jericho had to watch his words. He couldn't outright admit he didn't believe Edmund Rabbit deserved to be held captive. He didn't believe Ren Usagi deserved to be executed for taking a photo of Beau. He was tired of his father murdering people over nothing and even more fed up with the mistreatment of his cousins, Lorelei and Landon. The other secret he couldn't mention to the Lynbrookians ate him up inside.

"He had to go for what he did," Jericho replied as firmly as he could. He managed to look smug and nonchalant, but his stomach churned in objection to those haunting words.

"Kestrel, Sparrowhawk, and Falcon could've used your help."

"They are competent on their own."

"This is true. However, the Trinity is in crisis. It's time you take some initiative and step up into a more active role."

Fixing the gas pipelines ten years ago would have been taking initiative. Not letting the Trinity become a series of complex and corrupt investments would've been even better. Jericho wanted the Trinity, but only if he could run it his way.

"Alexander Ravensbourne proved he can subvert us from within when he gave Lorelei the confidence to escape and call the CSB on us. How Alexander found out about our leak, I can't figure out. I do know this: the Ravensbourne are opportunists and will come after the Trinity."

Jericho nodded along, badly wanting another cigarette. "I understand."

"We don't know the nature of Lorelei's relationship with Alexander."

"This is true," Jericho agreed, pacing back and forth. "That's why she needs to be captured."

"I think she's friends with Mikayla Birdwing."

Jericho shrugged half-heartedly. He knew Lorelei got along with Mikayla only because Mikayla was too sweet to *not* get along with. Even a loner like Lorelei found herself liking Mikayla's company.

"Lorelei told me she slept in the bed beside Mikayla's," Jericho said.

"Then I might use Mikayla and her friend, Naomi Maus, to go after Lorelei to stop her from doing whatever else Alexander has planned. Maybe I'll send them out tomorrow."

Jericho paused mid-step. "You're going to send Naomi Maus out there into the forest?"

"Maybe. The Raptors and I came up with this plan during our meeting. Theoretically, it could work because I don't think the girls would attack each other. It's important they come back unharmed."

Jericho turned to his father. "That makes no sense. Why would Mikayla Birdwing and Naomi Maus successfully bring her back when nobody else can? I thought you were going to send them to Kan."

Jericho bit his lip. He had unintentionally admitted to decoding his father's conversation with Falcon and Kestrel earlier. The headmaster kneaded his forehead. Perhaps he was too tired to realize Jericho had caught on and knew more than he should.

"My reconnaissance pilots left the area around 5 o'clock and advised against helicopter inbounds. They said there are too many birds flying in the area. Their radar detected three thousand birds. Nobody wants to fly in. I couldn't send Edmund and Robert to Meccanicville, and I can't send anyone to Kan."

"I've never seen anything like it before. Why are there thousands of birds?"

"Lorelei is a witch. She's doing it."

Jericho doubted this. His father sounded delirious.

"That doesn't mean I can't force one more trick I have up my sleeve," the headmaster said. "Last night, I made a phone call to Kan, ordering them to fly in their strongest bounty hunter. He'll be dropping in soon." Jericho waited for an explanation of the "trick." His snickering father straightened his blazer and continued, "I came here to warn you to do your part in saving the Trinity. I am going to have another meeting at 8 AM, right out there in the bal-chatri."

Jericho's nostrils flared. His father's poorly thought-out plans were desperate and impulsive. Not that Jericho cared, but it played into what the Ravensbourne family wanted. What he cared about was Naomi's undeserved entanglement.

Jericho waited until his father left, donned his blazer, and stormed out of the room. He passed a stained glass depiction of a vulture perched upon a column, claws clenching olive branches and arrows. He knocked on the corresponding door and waited.

Vulture opened the door and bowed his head. He had fleshy, hooded eyes. "Good evening, Honorable Kite." He yawned. "What's the emergency this late?"

"I need legal assistance."

"I figured as much, but Boss is the one who pays my retainer."

Vulture, another Raptor Admin who worked behind the scenes, had been his father's in-house lawyer for twelve years. The bags under his eyes were the result of years of court proceedings and legal business involving the Trinity. He was in his early sixties but could pass for eighty considering the gray hair and wrinkles.

"Vulture, I need you to help me review my contract you and Father wrote five years ago."

"The one from back when you were sixteen? Ah, yes, I remember that one. I think I can help," he said, wandering throughout his quarters, leaving the door open. He found his bifocals on his nightstand and motioned for

Jericho to enter and follow him to a cocobolo desk on the opposite side of his quarters. Soft classical music played. In the glow of the desk lamp, his half empty bottle of scotch cast a long shadow.

"Give me some time to find that document. You understand how it is here."

Jericho's Lynbrookian contract was a series of three hundred laminated pages in a binder shelved somewhere among Vulture's small library. He pulled a step ladder out from a crevice and climbed five steps to search the top shelf.

"Vulture, do you believe the Ravensbourne family is coming for the Trinity after all these years?" Jericho asked.

"Like I believe the sun will rise again." Vulture looked over his shoulder. "You've been warned this day would come, young Kite. Your family's company is the last entity they have to flick off before they have total control of energy production. Then the people won't have any other option. Ravensbourne will be able to raise their costs, maximizing their profits." He pulled a book off the shelf, looked at it, then shelved it again. "I fight tooth and nail, day and night to keep that from happening. There is still a place for oil and gas in this world."

"I've heard Falcon said something that triggered Alexander to come after us."

Vulture paused. "Don't remind me. I'd rather not talk about what he said."

Jericho glanced away and nodded. In the same moment, Vulture pulled out a dusty binder and began climbing down.

"Alexander will be a challenge for years to come, in my opinion. He's young like you—same age, in fact." Vulture blew the dust away.

"I don't know much about him. Can you tell me something?"

"Heh," Vulture scoffed. He looked somewhat dumbfounded. "I don't know where to begin."

Jericho leaned in. "You can start with telling me if he's good, bad, evil, or—"

"He's complex."

Jericho waited for an explanation. "That's all?"

"That about sums him up, young Kite. There are advantages you have that go beyond his capabilities."

"I'm not a bad, *complex* person. That's the advantage," Jericho muttered.

"There is no such thing as a good or bad person." Vulture blew the thicker dust off. "Morality is a spectrum. Live by that, and you can't be disappointed by anyone. Even Sparrowhawk has good in him, depending on who you ask."

Jericho had had enough of what Vulture was saying. He didn't care about dissecting what it meant. Calling Sparrowhawk good made no sense to him.

"Is that the one?" he asked, flattening the sides of his blazer.

"Definitely," Vulture said, opening the binder. "What is it you're looking for, exactly?"

"Clauses on marriage."

Vulture lowered his head, letting his bifocals slip to the tip of his nose. He looked over the rims. "Marriage? That's what you're concerned about? It's like you didn't process anything I said about Alexander." He mumbled and turned the pages faster. "Oh, this binder is so dense."

"Try section two-hundred, paragraph seven."

"Oddly specific, but I'll take the lead, especially this late." Vulture placed the binder on his desk and went exactly to the section Jericho spoke of. "Huh, you dedicated this to memory."

MY SON, JERICHO KITE IV, MAY WED ANY LYNBROOKIAN OF HIS CHOICE ONCE HE IS AT LEAST AGE EIGHTEEN, GIVEN HE HAS MY (JERICHO KITE III) APPROVAL.

Vulture looked confused. "Who is it you intend on marrying?"

"Naomi Maus."

"You can't."

"Why not?"

"Are you serious right now? You met her nine weeks ago. Even adults don't move that damn fast."

"I am an adult."

Vulture scoffed. "There is the Romeo and Juliet law, but you're too much older than her for that to be applicable." He took his glasses off. "Let me be straight with you. You're twenty-one, and that girl is sixteen."

Jericho crossed his arms. "Actually, she'll be eighteen in less than two weeks. If she's old enough to work on a flightline or go to Kan, she's old enough to be my wife."

Vulture put the tip of his glasses in his mouth and sat quietly for a moment before he said, "I warned your father this would happen. He's sheltered you."

"Naomi's almost eighteen. She loves me, and I love her. What's the big deal?"

"There's no reasoning with you." He took a sip of scotch. "I've advised your father that when you're ready to get married—which you're not—you'd need an older woman. She would have to be more experienced to make up for what you're lacking."

"The contract says I get to choose."

"That was written years ago. I doubt he'd take this seriously today. If you're going to involve me in this, then you owe me an explanation."

"Naomi's refreshing, peaceful. I can tell her anything, and it'll never leave her. I trust her. Can you do it tomorrow?"

"I'm not an ordained minister. Let's see, the age of marital consent in this state is eighteen. However, sixteen- and seventeen-year-olds can get married with guardian consent. Because Naomi's mother gave up custody of her to Kite Express, that means the company is her guardian." He shuffled some papers around on his desk. "All we need is your birth certificate and hers. We've got both, so that won't be a problem at all. I've got a judge who's a friend of a friend. He'll sign off on damn near anything if you butter him up. In fact, I'll find out his rate and give him a call when these Lorelei shenanigans blow over. Of course, Boss has to agree, which he may not."

"I don't care what my father wants."

Vulture raised his eyebrows. "If you help us capture Lorelei, you'll be in your father's good graces. He'll be more likely to *approve* of this marriage like the contract reads. Boss has plans for tomorrow, so I can't let this marriage stuff get in his way."

"Vulture, I've seen you do much harder things in a shorter amount of time. You expect me to believe you can't call around and make this happen?"

He kneaded his forehead. "I lied to you just now, young Kite."

"So that means you can do it, right?"

"No, I can't, and I won't." He pointed to the chair across from his desk. "Sit." Jericho sat. Vulture opened his desk to retrieve a document. "These are the four Lynbrookians your father intends on sending to Kan when the birds clear out and pilots can fly in."

The notarized document was dated November 8. Jericho skipped the narrative and legal boilerplate and looked for the names.

1. **Mikayla Birdwing 2. Naomi Maus 3. Lorelei Avian 4. Landon Avian**

Jericho's eyes glued to Naomi's name, then his cousins'.

Vulture waited for his attention and said, "These four are under our watch here but no longer belong to us per se. They belong to the Victor of Kan now."

"Why?"

"You didn't read the damned thing, did you?" Vulture snatched the document. "Mikayla Birdwing was activated yesterday morning, and because she was activated, your father notified the Victor of Kan. The Victor wants all the Capable and Pures sent to him. He also demanded ownership of them be transferred directly to him immediately."

"There're those words again. Activation, Capable, Pure. What do they mean?"

"I can't tell you what it means, young Kite. That's a conversation your father owes you."

Jericho sighed. "When did that transfer order arrive?"

Vulture's long fingernail pointed to the date at the top. The order was issued at 5:45 PM, right around the time when Jericho had brought Naomi into his room while his father conferred with the Raptor Admins.

Whenever Jericho heard about the Victor of Kan, he always imagined the shadowy silhouette of a burly brute. He had never met the man and didn't know his name. The Victor lived on the Arctic Ocean at Kan, where he managed the evilest segment of the Trinity on behalf of the Kite Clan.

Jericho's stomach turned again at the thought. *Naomi, thousands of miles away, surrounded by evil. No, not happening.*

"If you want to marry Naomi Maus, you must make that request with the Victor of Kan. He *will* say no."

"Thanks for helping me, Vulture." Jericho shot up and started for the door, then turned around. "Out of all the Admins, you're the only one who pulls through, except for me."

"There's a misunderstanding here, young Kite. I'm never helping you sabotage the man who pays me."

"I want what I want, and I'll get someone to do it."

Vulture gave Jericho a look of understanding and skepticism, then bowed. "It's my pleasure to serve you and your father any time, but I would feel more accomplished if I knew how to eliminate every moronic, impulsive idea that occurred to both of you."

Jericho let the door slam. He passed the stained glass window of a secretary bird flying above the orange rising sun, glittering with citrine and fire opals. He thought about knocking on Secretarybird's door, but he continued along instead to smoke outside on the shared patio.

After a while, his tired body slumped against a pillar. His shaking hands lit his next cigarette with the bottom of an almost finished butt. He was running out of ideas and precious time.

"Jericho, what are you doing up?" a sweet voice asked. Jericho lifted his cigarette to answer her question. She laughed and said, "I didn't ask you what your hobby is."

He looked left. Secretarybird, dressed in a translucent, peach-colored robe, stepped beside him. She gently placed her hand on his shoulder. She was one of his father's first Raptor Admins, back before the group had gotten its name. A highly skilled concierge, Secretarybird was like Vulture: she worked in the background managing Lynbrook. Alongside Condor and Osprey, she'd helped care for and raise Jericho. He could always speak freely with Secretarybird, and he trusted her with his innermost insecurities and thoughts. She was firm but not judgmental. She made him think like his mother would've if she were alive.

Secretarybird put her hand out. "Give me one of those cigarettes, will ya?"

"Here. It's my last one."

They laughed, knowing it wasn't true. Jericho reached into his blazer for a lighter.

"I tried to quit smoking when I was in my early forties," she said. "Gave up after two or three days. Couldn't get over that initial hump. I was proud of you for trying."

"I can give it up again. I feel like if I weren't here, I could do it."

"I think you're strong enough to quit, regardless of where you are."

They got quiet. Jericho glared at his cigarette. He wasn't enjoying it.

"I heard Vulture's door slam," she said. "Went to check on him. He told me what the two of you talked about."

He tensed his shoulders a bit. "It feels like I'm not going to get the legacy I was promised. It feels like I wasn't prepared for the legacy I'm going to get. Father is trying to put out wildfires he created before he hands off the scorched earth to me when he dies. Alexander's trying to take it before it's ruined."

"You finally see," Secretarybird whispered.

"I asked Vulture to tell me about Alexander."

"What did he say?"

"He's complex," Jericho said, mocking Vulture's stoic, haughty voice.

"That's one way to describe Alexander." Secretarybird giggled. Jericho rarely heard her laugh like that.

"C'mon, tell me what I'm dealing with here? Who is he? I know his family is our competition businesswise, but what is he beyond that?"

She shook her head. "I met him once, years ago, when he was eighteen. He left an impression, that's for sure. Here's the obvious stuff: he's a spoiled brat, flamboyant with his image. Very flirty, but domineering. The two of you are like ice and fire. You're the ice, and he's the fire."

Jericho sighed. "So, what's the not-obvious stuff?"

"He's a lot like you. He wants to make a difference but isn't sure how to go about it."

"*Hmm,*" Jericho muttered.

"But I know you and Vulture discussed more than Alexander. It's okay if you don't want to talk about it."

They were quiet for a while. Jericho listened to the nearby cicadas and the indiscriminate sounds of the other wildlife beyond the fence. The sky was clear. No more rain was forecasted, but the temperature had dropped significantly.

"Sometimes I dream of being out there in a wide-open grassland or trotting across fine white sand on a beach, but then I realize I can't conceptualize it. All I know is what I've seen on a screen." He pointed beyond the forest, pausing for emphasis. "I haven't been able to *feel* my entire life."

"Never had to, since the day you were born. Everything you needed was here until the Great Resignation, so you wanted for nothing. Tell me, Jericho," she said, turning to him with a light smile, "if you could live anywhere else, where would that be?"

Jericho grinned. He had waited his entire life for this question. "You first."

Secretarybird swished her lips, then said, "Northen Europe, somewhere cold. Not as cold as Kan. I've had enough of the humidity and hot summers here in Alabama."

Jericho nodded. "The place I want to live hasn't been created yet."

"You've been thinking and realizing things. I can tell."

Jericho nodded again. "Yeah."

"I'm sorry you can't have Naomi Maus."

"I'm going to get her one way or another."

"How so?" She jammed the end of the finished cigarette against the cement railing and crushed the fallen embers with the bottom of her slipper. "Naomi Maus is property of the Victor of Kan now. Whenever the skies clear up and helicopters can fly through, she'll be gone. It might happen tomorrow afternoon. Maybe Monday, at the latest."

Jericho crossed his arms. "If Naomi and her friend are property of the Victor of Kan, why would Father send them out to go after Lorelei?"

She chuckled nervously. "Trust me. We advised that sending those girls out would be a foolish idea, given how unsure we are of what Lorelei is capable of. He was probably tired and not thinking straight when he told you that."

"He was. He said something about a bounty hunter from Kan."

"That's right. A plane will fly over, and a hunter will parachute out of it. I told your father not to waste the resources on obsessing over Lorelei's capture, but here we are. There's no telling what's going on in his mind these days."

Jericho felt conflicted. If the hunter captured Lorelei, Naomi and her friend wouldn't have to be sent into the forest. However, he didn't want Lorelei captured. He hoped she had managed to get far away.

"Your father," she began firmly before pausing to gather her thoughts. "Jericho, I'm afraid he's not well in the head, so getting through to him will be a challenge."

"For you?" His father always used to confide in Secretarybird before anyone else.

"His declining mental health makes his decision-making...dangerous," she finally said, lacking a gentler word.

"I see it too. Why can't we leave? We have the money to relocate, fix the leak, and then come back."

"Your father doesn't want the rest of your family seeing his failure."

Jericho may have been projecting, but he felt she was dreading the announcement for the morning meeting. He had sensed the weight of his father being the black sheep in the Kite Clan. He didn't realize the pressures of upholding the Trinity were completely breaking the man. Despite it all, it wasn't fair his ego and pride were risking the lives of everyone on campus.

"Should I be worried for the Lynbrookians' lives?" he asked, looking down at the dormitories.

She put her hand on his shoulder and gave him a look. He didn't bother questioning it. The answer was yes.

"You know, you remind me of your father when he and I were much younger. Back when he first got the Trinity." Secretarybird cuffed the side of her mouth, hiding a smile. "He really loved your mom."

His mother had brunette hair and a pretty smile anyone could trust. The pictures of her locked in his nightstand didn't tell much of a story. His father refused to talk about her.

"I need you to help me save Naomi," Jericho said. "It's not safe here. You're the only one who gets why I love her."

She sighed. "I'm not even sure what to do."

"There's no need for a plan. Tomorrow morning, get her from the dorm and bring her here upstairs to the bal-chatri."

"You want to hide her?"

"No." Jericho blew smoke out his nose. "I want Father to see plainly that I'm taking her for myself. He's so stressed out about Lorelei and Alexander that me taking Naomi will fall to the wayside. It'll give me more time to think about a more permanent way of getting her out of this. Things are changing fast around here. A sliver of opportunity is bound to come up."

Her eyes widened. "Don't drag that girl into our lives."

"I'll take care of her!" he snapped. He looked Secretarybird dead in her eyes, passionately. "I'll take her out of the Trinity. I don't know any other way but by marrying her."

"Okay, I'll get her after I finish my breakfast duty in the cafeteria, but I'm not involving myself any further. Your father has no discretion right now. He'll come after anyone who interferes with that contract he made with the Victor of Kan."

"Tell him I made you do it. Tell him I forced you. I'll take the blame. I'll be the bad guy. He won't touch me," Jericho said, even though he doubted this.

"That is true, but it's not because he loves you," Secretarybird said. Jericho swiftly turned his head. "Your blood is worth more than a cave full of gold."

"Why?"

"It's complicated." She sauntered away, sweetly wishing him a good night.

Mouth agape, he wondered how his gold ring was worth less than his blood.

Lorelei Avian

3:35 AM

Awakening from a nap, Lorelei stretched and yawned. She used her power, Bird's Eye View, to navigate through the darkness with Mateo's eyes. Her body followed the owl, moving like a mindless drone using minimal energy. While using Bird's Eye View, most of the calories she burned were expended on transferring her consciousness and sight into her owl. Mateo's point of view allowed her to see past the foothills and over farmlands miles away. It was how she easily confirmed if anyone was in her vicinity; however, she couldn't travel far without hitting a wall of extended fatigue. Daylight savings would bring the sunrise an hour earlier around 6 AM. She looked forward to seeing its rise through her own eyes again.

Birds in the vicinity of the Talladega Mountains traveled their territory daily. They flew up the mountain around sunrise in search of food and back down to roost in trees around sunset. Lorelei took advantage of their flight pattern yesterday afternoon. She sent her eight hawks after smaller birds, flushing them out of trees or resting spots. She continuously did that until every bird in the entire forest was disturbed. Thousands of birds dispersed and swarmed the air for hours until Lorelei ran out of energy and fainted to sleep around 12 AM. Hundreds of displaced birds remained airborne, zipping back and forth.

Lorelei felt terrible about what she had done, but the outcome benefited her. She planned on resuming at the crack of dawn so she wouldn't have to worry about spy pilots. Plus, using the hawks to flush out birds had drained half the energy Bird's Eye View required. Bird's Eye View required a lot of resources, but it worked well as long as the raptors were within reasonable vicinity and maintained a Link with her. Unfortunately, she had no idea how long her Links would last. Sometimes they'd end much sooner than she expected.

She packed up everything—including her empty food cans, so as not to leave a trace of trash behind—and hiked away. There was a small highway not far from her position, but she was reluctant. Leaving Landon behind wasn't an option, but going back wasn't either. Alexander's refusal to help her put her in a conundrum. She was stuck and tired.

Mateo hooted, asking her which direction they should go. She collapsed.

"Sorry, Mateo. I'm so exhausted," she said, rubbing her trembling legs and the soles of her aching feet. "I guess I should go back to Lynbrook."

Hoot!

"It's not like I want to. It's a shorter hike there than getting to a highway."

Lynbrook was within five miles. The highway was much farther away—an impossible distance in her condition.

Hoot.

"I'll get to see Landy again. I miss him. What do you think he was doing all day?"

Hoot.

"Yeah, I think he was reading all day too."

Tears fell from her eyes as she transferred from Mateo's point of view back to her own. She couldn't bear any more of this. Mateo flew into her arms.

"Damn it, I want to leave so bad. But I can't let Landy get sent to Meccanicville alone."

Hoot.

"Right, I know. He's not good at talking to people anymore. He'd get steamrolled out there. He's such a twerp." She tried laughing but cried in her hands instead. She loved her twerp brother to the bone. Although she'd left him behind so that he wouldn't have to go through the risk and struggle of being in the forest, she wished he was there.

Hoot! Hoot! Hoot!

Mateo had a bright idea. He told her to use him to deliver a message asking for help.

"That's not a bad idea, but I'm so tired, Mateo. If I do Bird's Eye View again, it won't last more than a minute or two."

Hoot.

"Well, you should've told me that idea before I did what I did."

Hoooooot!

"You did? I guess I wasn't listening."

She had let her anger and desire for revenge get the better of her.

Hoot!

"What's up there?" she asked, cocking her neck back as far as it could go.

Hoot!

Thousands of feet above, a small plane circled the area. It would be impossible for a pilot to spot her from that altitude without special equipment. Just in case, she crouched down and crawled into bushes, where she watched it circle two more times. Something dropped from the plane before it departed northbound. A parachute deployed. Then another shape plummeted from the plane, soon slowed by its own chute.

"There's a less than one percent chance that's a care package for me." Lorelei activated Bird's Eye View and stayed in position at the bush.

Mateo swooped from her arms and soared upward, aiming straight for the parachutes. Cold air wisped through the owl's feathers as it ascended two thousand feet up. A burly man with weapons in his holster was attached to one parachute. The other was attached to a strange-looking pony in a harness. It looked like they were going to land half a mile south of Lorelei's position.

Shocked, Lorelei snapped back into her own point of view, gasping. She staggered onto her feet, grabbed her bag, and sprinted east. Mateo swiftly dove down, reconvening with her.

She cursed under her breath. Sharp pain shot through her legs and feet as she carried forward along a trail of tire marks embedded in the dirt. There was less gravel, and it was flatter opposed to the ground around it. A stench reeking of burning metal suddenly stuck to her nostrils, overlapped by a rotten odor. She gagged and began throwing up.

A twig snapped. She spun around. Her hand grazed something gritty, like sand, flaky and corrugated. Black ashes covered her palm, and she stood back up to take in what looked like the remains of a scorched SUV. There was no glass on the window, and the vehicle's body, warped and crinkled, had lost its metallic shine. Wires and fuel lines underneath the hood were melted against all the other inner workings.

Lorelei shielded her nose with part of the potato sack, which barely masked the stench from the vehicle. Leaning closer, she realized it smelled like pounds of expired meat. Gnats and bigger flies swarmed at her for disturbing their feast upon a charred human body handcuffed to the steering wheel. The flesh was pale and splotched with curdled blood and exploded organs. Its clothes had burned through its skin and fused into the flesh beneath. A red spider lily pendant was embedded in its chest. Parts of the yellow letters USCSB on the jacket were blackened.

"They killed the CSB?" Lorelei asked as she bent down to her hands and knees, crying, throwing up, then continuing to dry heave.

Her mom and dad crossed her mind. The smell of death reminded her of them. The last meal they'd had together was chicken and vegetable pot pie and butter tarts. Landon didn't feel like eating because he wanted to keep playing video games, but he ate a little to keep Mom happy. Lorelei scarfed down the rest of his portion.

She saw a flash of two coroners zipping her parents' body bags, then the distorted voice of a homicide detective asking her and Landon how many gunshots they heard in the night. She struggled to remember what happened. Landon never could fill the gap in her memory either. He had forgotten everything too.

She felt terrible about not knowing someone had been murdered in the very forest she had been trekking for hours. The questions made her head spin. When did it happen? Where was she? Who did it? How did they do it so quietly?

She cried, wishing she had someone by her side to grieve with. She hated being alone in her endeavor.

"I don't think I can go back there. I can't. I can't."

Hoot.

A branch snapped. Behind her stood the greasy-haired, burly man and his pony. The man sweated profusely, drenched as if he'd dived into a pool with his clothes on. The pony had goat horns. It was stocky but muscular like a bull.

Lorelei wiped her tears discreetly and got onto her feet. Her face was stone cold, showing no weakness.

The moonlight whitened the man's teeth as he grinned at her. "Imma hunter. Time to go home, girlie." He spoke in a combination of thick East Texas and Norwegian accents.

"Lynbrook isn't my home. Meccanicville isn't either."

"I ain't talkin' those places. Kan is gonna be yer home. It's mine 'n yers." His eyes widened and glistened.

"I'm not going to Kan."

"This can be easy or hard. Yer choice."

"I do things the hard way."

"So I've been warned," he said, wiping away sweat. "Ah, c'mon, don't look at me like that. Yer've been out here Fri-daay night…Satur-daay mornin'…Satur-daay night…Sun-daay mornin'." He bent his fingers down and stretched out the syllables and vowels. "Issa been rain-in'…hot…rain-in'…wet…mosquitahs—"

"It's not hot. It's around forty degrees."

"It feels like eighty degrees! C'mon with me. I wanna get this over with."

"I'll stay out here until I'm done." Lorelei cracked her knuckles and prepared to reach for her shovel. It was hidden right where she needed it.

"You gonna stay out here with all these trees everywhere?" He reached into his holster and pulled out a switchblade.

Lorelei narrowed her eyes. "Yes, with all the trees."

"You gotta excuse me. I ain't seen a tree in a while. All I see is snow, icebergs, and polar bears when they let me go outside."

Mouth agape, Lorelei was lost for words.

"You gotta be gettin' tired…huuungry…boooooored…looooooonely…"

"I like being alone, and you should stop talking like that. You sound stupid."

"We wanna have you at Kan," he said, slicing his hand with the blade. "All we evah talk 'bout is havin' a girl around."

She gritted her teeth. "I'm not going to Kan!"

"Ah! That's right. Nobody told ya. Yer brother and you ain't goin' to Meccanicville no more. You're property of VOK now. They sent me to come get ya." He showed her his bleeding hand. "Wanna come with me to Lynbrook or tough this out like how we settle things in the arena?"

The hunter's blood leaked onto the ground beside his boots. The pony licked it, ingesting its way into becoming submissive to the hunter's leash. Lorelei partially understood what she would be dealing with. The hunter was Blood Leash Capable like Mr. Sparrowhawk, possessing abilities that were engineered through experimentation. She suspected his power replicated the capabilities of the Equestrian, or else he wouldn't have that abomination of a pony with him; he would've had a canine or raptor instead. How and why his pony looked like a mixture of three or more species baffled her. Uncle Eric had never mentioned something like that before.

She stepped back to gain distance. "Which surgery did you have?"

"My heart. Got it last year. That's a stupid question, by the way. I ain't got a uterus, and brain surgery is a death wish," he said. "There are a lot of *us* men at Kan who got the heart surgery."

"I'd rather die than go to Kan where they make Capable freaks like you." She sliced her thumb with a jagged edge of her shovel.

The hunter cackled. "If I'm a freak, then what does that make you, girlie?" He held his bloody hand out for his pony creature to lick directly.

Lorelei held up her bleeding hand and blew her whistle, summoning her hawks. One arrived. The other seven were too far away to reestablish their Link with her.

"Only one. Ain't that a shame. Me and my pony are three-time champions in the arena. We done beat Capable Falconers bigger and stronger than you."

Lorelei knew nothing about the arena. She took a deep breath, determined not to appear rattled and frustrated.

"Ya scared, Lorelei. I see it. Ever fought one of us before?"

"I'm not scared of you," she said, refusing to answer his question.

"Be scared. That moon up there is goin' full tonight. Means it's the Canine Moon—the Handler dominates."

"So what? You have a pony. That means you operate under the restrictions of the Capable Equestrian. You can't dominate me until third quarter. You're about a week too early. We're equally disadvantaged."

"Ah, you know more than I thought." He closed in on her.

Lorelei lunged backward, dodging his punch. "I can teach you a thing or two!"

Her hawk flew away and then circled back around. She pointed at the man and commanded the hawk to fly towards him. The hawk immediately tightened its body like an arrow and went beak-first for his eyes. The pony intercepted the hawk with a powerful hindleg kick. The hawk smacked flat into a tree and slid down into a pile of its own feathers.

The hunter laughed. "Seen that comin'. They say falconers are one trick ponies. Then I get offended 'cause I am too." He threw his hand out again. "If it ain't broke, don't go fixin' it!"

"*Mateo, vas!*" Lorelei called out.

The sound of a whistle tooted and was followed by a bell jingling. Mateo swooped at the pony. He struck and sunk his talons into the pony's back.

Meanwhile, Lorelei and the hunter engaged in hand-to-hand combat. He punched her a few times, but Lorelei managed to strike him in the nose hard enough to break it. Behind them, the pony stood on its hindlegs, twisting its neck, gnawing at Mateo's wings. Mateo dipped, left wingtip leaned downward. He managed to hover, but slowly.

The pony recovered and galloped at Lorelei. Feet aching, she stumbled away and looked up to ensure Mateo flew safely above her head. An easy tree to climb caught her eye. She scaled it halfway up to a stopping point where she could catch her breath. The pony stopped at the trunk, contemplating.

Then it rammed into the tree with its horns like a bull.

"Git up there, dammit!" the hunter shouted, grabbing his bleeding nose.

The pony whinnied and scaled the tree trunk, inverted like a mountain goat. Lorelei, without time to comprehend the absurdity, climbed higher. Mateo perched on her left shoulder and huddled close to her. She started moving more carefully to avoid injuring him. She looked down. The pony was gaining on her.

The hunter projected his voice. "You hit like a man, girlie. I ain't gonna kill ya for it. VOK wouldn't like it if ya got mutilated or killed."

Below, the hunter looked much smaller. She was almost to the top, but the pony had more than halfway caught up to her. The nearest branch thick enough to carry her weight was about six feet away. She readied herself and pounced moments before the pony impaled her with its horns.

She caught the other branch but wasn't strong enough to pull herself up onto it. Below her was a more accessible branch, but she wasn't sure if it could support her. She swung slightly to position it directly underneath her and then dropped onto it. When her weight struck the branch, it trembled and then snapped.

Lorelei clung onto the trunk and slid down about ten feet. The bark scratched deeply into the side of her face. Mateo launched off her shoulder.

"Mateo! Don't leave me!" she cried.

The trunk began vibrating. Lorelei looked down. The pony was scaling upward with its horns pointed at her. She hugged the tree tightly and closed her eyes, activating Bird's Eye View. When she opened her eyes again, she was inside the hawk, controlling its movements.

The hawk leapt off the ground, still in pain from the pony's kick. She commanded the hawk to ignore its injuries, shutting off its senses. It flew upward towards the pony's blind spot. It swerved to the left and struck the pony off the tree before its horns could jab into Lorelei. While the pony fell to the ground, Lorelei spearheaded the hawk towards the hunter's chest and maximized its flight speed. Cancelling Bird's Eye View, she relinquished control of the hawk a split second before it pierced through his shoulder blade, ripping through his flesh like a bullet. The pony crash landed. The lifeless hawk landed on the other side of the man, covered in blood. Everything happened in three seconds.

Lorelei regained control of her body. Through her own eyes, she looked down and saw the pony splayed on the ground and the hunter grasping at the gaping hole in his torso.

"You!" he shook his fist at her.

He rummaged through his holster for emergency gauze, ripped the pack open with his teeth, and began packing his wound. Lorelei watched him, panting. Afterward, he stumbled over to his pony, hoisted it over his shoulder, and limped towards Lynbrook with his hand covering his packed wound. After losing sight of him in the thick forest, Lorelei loosened her grip on the tree trunk and slid down until she safely touched the bloody ground.

She collapsed and caught her breath. Adrenaline coursing through her body muted pain she would feel later. Every time she had pushed a hawk to its limit, she felt its agony hours afterward. That was why she'd canceled the Bird's Eye View before killing the hawk. She didn't want to experience the full feeling of death alongside it. Whenever each hawk was on the brink of death, she had sensed their doom and bailed out. Being inside of them as they flew the skies and swayed in the wind was fine. The dying part wasn't.

Uncle Eric had warned her that Kan was a place where men danced around the boundaries of ethics and morality, but she had no idea this was what he meant. Even though she felt like she and the hunter both were immoral and unethical for relying on animals to do their fighting, she was determined to believe his evil was stronger. She had been born a Pure Blood Leasher. She had no choice, but the hunter consented to experimenting on his heart to become Blood Leash Capable. He'd chosen his path.

Her dead hawk was an arm's length away. She clasped it between her fingertips, wiping off as much of the man's blood as she could. Mateo returned to perch on her shoulder as she sat up and cradled the hawk in her arms.

"I'm sorry I turned you into a missile," she said to it. "Next time, if I use one of you like that, we'll face death together."

Mikayla Birdwing

6:51 AM

The Washington Monument loomed far away in the distance. Fresh, powdery snow covered the ground, absorbing Mikayla's giggles. She hid behind a fir tree on the Christmas tree farm, on the lookout for Isaiah. She almost slipped on a patch of ice and fell into the snow but grasped a branch to catch herself. Her laughter grew louder.

She covered her mouth and leaned out of hiding to see if Isaiah was coming after her. A golden labrador pounced behind her and stuck its nose up her dress. She yelped, running to a pine tree across the way. Another lab, a black one, barked at her and wagged its tail. Laughing, she ran away, letting it chase her. Hundreds of dogs of various breeds decorated festively in lights and tinsel appeared, rushing after her.

She hurried down the center aisle, calling Isaiah's name. Wearing Santa's hat, Isaiah jumped from behind a spruce and grabbed her waist. He spun her around. The dogs vanished one by one as he stared into her eyes. She leaned into him for a kiss, barely touching his lips before waking up.

Coughing, Mikayla felt more congested. She sat on the edge of her mattress, feeling weak from head to toe. It seemed like every dream she had was vivid and lucid.

Her favorite showed her dad slurping noodles from a bowl of beef pho at their favorite Vietnamese restaurant. He'd introduced her to pho when she was eight. Once a week, they would eat a bowl and share dumplings or spring rolls for appetizers.

Her second favorite dream came in the early morning hours. It was just Isaiah and her, no one else. She was too bashful to fully immerse herself in her memories of what they did together. A few scenes flashed before her eyes, and it made her blush.

What's wrong with me, thinking about him at a time like this?

Naomi suddenly dropped a long-sleeved white blouse, a black sweater, a gray skirt, and a pair of black stockings into her lap. "Leslie had an extra uniform. She noticed yours had gotten too loose, so she said you can have hers."

Snapping out of it, Mikayla turned her head towards Leslie's area of the dorm. Brushing her hair, Leslie caught Mikayla's eyes and waved, smiling. Mikayla thanked her.

"Leslie said don't worry about doing anything in return," Naomi added.

Feeling a bit better, Mikayla changed. The stockings were the perfect cross between thick and comfortable. The fleece sweater secured her body's warmth. The blouse and skirt fit tighter than usual since Leslie was extra petite, but she blushed at herself in the mirror, amazed at the outcome. Never had her uniform fit her in such a flattering way.

She took her pawn out of the pocket of yesterday's pants. The abalone trim still shimmered beautifully, even underneath the dorm's dim lighting. She felt a gentle pair of hands parting her hair to make room for a black scarf that suddenly stretched across her shoulders. She quickly hid the pawn behind her back.

Naomi fluffed Mikayla's hair. "You look like a doll! So pretty."

"Thanks, but I don't feel like one. I feel like I've been hit by a truck."

One of the girls walked up to Mikayla. Her name was Shianne. "You look nice today. A lot of us felt bad about what happened to your dad yesterday. It's the least we could do, since your clothes weren't fitting right anymore."

"Thanks, Shianne," Mikayla said.

"We know you were trying to help us, and we're sorry," another girl said.

Others gathered around and collectively spoke over each other, apologizing to Mikayla.

"Can you tell us more about your dad? Do you think he'll be able to get out from the Kites holding him hostage?"

Mikayla sat on the edge of her bed. She showed them the pawn. "My dad carved this out of onyx. He's a talented guy." They marveled at it. "But he's got bad knees, and he's getting old. I don't think he'll get away."

"Do you think he'll be alright?"

"Yeah," Mikayla said confidently, not only for herself but for the others. "I think if the Kites wanted him gone, they would've done it already. They see value in him." She rolled the pawn around in her palm. "I remember being with him at his job. It was a small office, but not like those offices where phones in cubicles are constantly ringing and people are walking fast. It was him and one other guy drawing maps on computers."

"Maps, like what's on a globe?"

"Nah, I don't know what they're called exactly, but he said I should think of him as the man who can map the skies." She expected confusion on their faces. "In the sky, planes fly on invisible highways. He drew those maps for pilots."

"Mine worked on an oil boat, gone most of the time—you know, out in the ocean. Wow, your dad sounded like he had a cool job."

Smiling, Mikayla briefly reflected on last night's dreams about him. He was a well-respected man, smiling, and had a large office with a panoramic view of a flatland. She wanted to believe in those dreams. They were bright, vivid, and beautiful.

"Tell us more about him," a girl said.

Mikayla glanced at Naomi, who nodded and gestured her to go ahead. They saw the glint in everyone's eyes. They needed a moment of relief too.

Mikayla relaxed her shoulders. She chuckled under her breath, thinking about that day. "He's lactose intolerant but goes crazy around ice cream. One time, he ate an entire gallon of vanilla. All by himself. Nobody even knew it was in the house. Then he got diarrhea."

"Sounds like my dad. Man, I miss him," a girl said.

"My dad's a goofball like that, but my mom's worse," another admitted. "She'd get like three or four scoops on a cone. It falls over every time."

"My dad and I like going fishing. There was this pesky trout, a big one with a heart spot. We were about to leave the dock, then it came onto the hook like a magnet to a refrigerator. He said that my spirit was there, his lucky charm."

As the girls continued sharing silly stories about their parents, Mikayla sat quietly, listening to bits and pieces with a smile on her face.

Naomi tapped her shoulder. "Can we talk about last night?" she asked.

Mikayla sighed. She didn't know whether to bring up her dream of Naomi's and Jericho's horses and children. She wondered if Naomi's feelings for Jericho went beyond a fling. What if that dream wasn't a dream? What if it was a vision that'd come true, like the one of Miss Kestrel taking her notebook? Was Mr. Sparrowhawk in her head again, trying to upset her?

Naomi pulled Mikayla to the side and lowered her voice. "When I said that I want to join them, I didn't mean that I want to turn evil. I mean that I want to be with people who can make a difference—the people who get what they want."

Mikayla made sure no one was listening. "Jericho lied to everyone yesterday when he said the CSB were criminals."

"He admitted that he lied."

"Only to you, right?"

"Yeah."

"He won't tell everyone else the truth, will he?"

"He can't. His father threatens him."

"And yet he's supposed to save us."

"I think he will, Mika. He's reaching his breaking point. Don't go talk to Headmaster Kite. I'll ask Jericho to help us."

Mikayla stared long and hard at Naomi. "What's really going on between you and him?"

Naomi gasped and crossed her arms over her chest, head tilted away. She closed her eyes and exhaled. "Mika, I love him."

In her chest, Mikayla felt the load Naomi's conscience carried. It was a thousand pounds and counting. She wanted to scream.

"How? We just got to this school."

"We talk all the time about making our own world—one without guns and murder. He has a good heart."

"Isaiah does too, but you don't see me walking around saying I l-word him." Mikayla couldn't help but grin at her next question. "Ready to say the quiet part out loud?"

"What do you mean?"

"You want him for his money."

Naomi looked at Mikayla. Mikayla looked back at her.

"Okay," Naomi said. "I want his money."

"I knew it."

"Mika, imagine all the stuff I could get. A mansion. My own private beach off the coast of Asia. First pick of the highest fashion on the planet, tailored to my body." She twirled, letting her skirt lift a little. She had a slim hourglass figure everyone envied. "I could get my mouse comics turned into a TV show—no, a movie. Mika, stop laughing. I could get a supersonic plane that flies me from New York to Paris, where I can shop all day in boutiques where the associates will take me in the back room to show me the good stuff. A castle of my own. Mika, I'll buy you a castle too. Just tell me what country you wanna live in."

"I think you're about to start foaming at the mouth." Mikayla pulled it together. "Gawd, Naomi, his father kills people and said our mothers want nothing to do with us. Before you marry the guy, make him answer why his father said that stuff to me."

"That can't be true. Headmaster Kite said that to make you sad. He says mean stuff to Jericho too. Jericho's nothing like his father."

The dorm's door opened. Mrs. Secretarybird stepped inside. A gust of air lifted some loose papers and blew through girls' hair. Mrs. Secretarybird wore braided Bantu knots and orange stilettos with her black and white pantsuit. She was an elegant lady, more polite and poised than Miss Kestrel. Out of all the Raptor Admins, she was seen the least but the most respected. Scared stiff, every girl stopped what she was doing. Mrs. Secretarybird kindly told everyone to go back to their activities as she sauntered towards Mikayla and Naomi. The other girls resumed preparing for the day but subtly watched over their shoulders or out of the corner of their eyes.

"Naomi Maus, are you ready for the day?"

"Yes, ma'am."

"Come with me."

Naomi pointed to herself. "Am I in trouble?"

"That is not my question to answer. Hug your friend goodbye."

"I'm not coming back?" Naomi asked.

Mrs. Secretarybird gave her a vague, not so reassuring look.

Shocked, Naomi hesitated, then embraced Mikayla tightly. They held each other for a while. Mikayla wanted to yank her back as their hug ended, but she let go because she had to.

"This isn't goodbye," Naomi whispered.

"Of course not," Mikayla said, wiping the corners of her eyes. "Don't let the Kites change you."

"I'll be changing them before they ever get to me. You know how I am." She sniffled and smiled a little.

Naomi followed Mrs. Secretarybird out of the dorm without looking back. The door closed, and Mikayla felt everyone's eyes on her. She slowly turned around, facing the confused and worried girls.

"Naomi will be okay," she said to them. It came out as a whisper.

Ten minutes later, she left the dorm alone. Her stomach growled, anticipating Sunday's breakfast: eggs, sausage links, and grits. Enjoying a warm breakfast before confronting Headmaster Kite with her request was a good idea. She had two services in mind for him: pulling weeds and cleaning the campus. If he told her no and wanted her to cook meals every day, she would request the recipe book and an apron. She was willing to do anything to save her dad.

The cloudless sky was a crisp shade of blue she hadn't seen since last week, before the bad weather. A cold front had pushed yesterday's thunderstorms further east. Birds flew high in V-shaped formations above the forest. Forty-one degrees, the air pierced her cheeks like icy needles. Thick fog covered the area. She could barely see her way to the cafeteria without looking directly down at the cobblestones. The morning dew attached grass blades and clots of dirt onto her flats.

"Git in there, boy!"

"I didn't do it!"

"Git in there now!"

The voices were familiar. Mikayla froze in place. The yelling came from the supply office near the boys' dorm. It sounded like Isaiah. Girls took off running towards the cafeteria. One of them bumped into Mikayla.

"Mikayla, don't go back there. Mr. Falco's chewing someone out."

"Who?" Mikayla asked.

"That quiet boy who likes bologna and peanut butter," she said before leaving.

Allowing Lynbrookians to pass, Mikayla stepped off the cobblestones and ran in the opposite direction. The harsh white light inside of the supply office showed Mr. Falco strong-arming Isaiah inside the portable building. Without thinking, she darted up the short ramp, slipping through the door before it closed.

"Hey, git out, girl!" Mr. Falco yelled. He had clamped Isaiah in a chokehold with his arm.

"What are you doing to him?" Mikayla demanded.

"Mika, leave!" Isaiah struggled. "Don't stay in here! Go!"

"Listen to yer friend, Birdwing. Us men are talkin'."

Mikayla clasped her hands together. "Please don't hurt him!"

"Imma make you git out!"

Mr. Falco dropped Isaiah and lunged for Mikayla, pushing her into a shelf of packaged uniforms and shoes.

Isaiah slipped his hand in his back pocket. He ambushed Mr. Falco and swung his hand back out. Blood splatter dotted the floor. Mr. Falco stumbled backward, covering his bleeding cheeks and nose. He'd been slashed deep by the serrated metal object Isaiah had placed between his fingers. The wound started underneath his right eye, extending down to the left side of his chin.

"Mika, run!" Isaiah shouted before he heaved at the sight of the blood.

Mikayla got on her feet and spun for the door. Mr. Sparrowhawk, standing in the open doorway, clutched her shoulders. She searched for another exit. There wasn't one.

Mr. Falco snatched Isaiah's right wrist and dug his fingers into the pressure point. Isaiah involuntarily opened his hand. The metal fell onto the floor and rolled into a shelf. It was a bullet's spent casing.

Mr. Falco bent Isaiah's wrist backward. Isaiah tried fighting back, but Mr. Falco's size and weight was much greater. Wincing, Isaiah dropped to his knees. Mikayla screamed at Mr. Falco, begging him to stop. The man pressed harder. Isaiah couldn't hold back any longer. He screamed as his wrist twisted. A bone snapped.

The sudden howling of coyotes outside hushed everyone except Isaiah.

A syringe drove into Mikayla's neck above her scarf. Mr. Sparrowhawk pressed the plunger, injecting the needle deep inside her. She saw the last of his blood emptying out of the barrel.

He lifted her chin saying, "Now you're on my leash."

In seconds, the room began spinning, blurring, and splitting into two halves. The howling and voices became distorted. Mr. Sparrowhawk let her go. She tried running, but the room turned upside down. Her feet were on the floor but looked like they should've been on the ceiling. The blood rushed to her head, making her congestion worse.

She couldn't stay balanced, even though she knew she was upright. Everything felt backward. Left was right. Up was down. She collapsed beside Isaiah, panting. He reached out. She went for his left hand but wasn't sure which hand was his. He grasped her fingers, squeezing. The distortion faded.

"She looks like a retarded deer that got hit by a pickup truck."

"My vertigo attack works well. She'll never counter me again."

"Keep it up. You'll be runnin' the Trinity in no time. You'll kick Kite Boy aside, huh?"

"Don't humor me. I'm more capable than you all think. The Kite boy will eventually be his own demise. He's weak."

"Yeah, yeah. Speaking of weak, these dumb kids think they're smarter than us with their plans."

Mr. Falco kicked Isaiah's rib cage. Winded, Isaiah dropped Mikayla's hand and grabbed his chest. Mr. Falco picked up the ammo casing. Mikayla lost focus again.

"Half of the gunpowder in hundreds of these 22 long rifle casings, gone. This boy here had been very busy tamperin' with our respirators, HAZMAT suits, and ammo. Who knows what else? Imma punish him real good!"

He kicked Isaiah again. The boy whimpered.

"Careful, Birdwing has deep feelings for him. Don't set off her fight or flight."

Mr. Falco grabbed Isaiah's hair and pushed his face into Mikayla's. "Now, what's yer daddy gonna say about you bein' in love with this skinny little white boy? You think he's cute? Imma make him ugly. Imma mess him up."

Mikayla garnered the strength to seize Mr. Falco's arm. "Let him go!"

He swatted her off him. "Ain't she 'posed to be unable to do that?"

"Impossible," Mr. Sparrowhawk gasped. "Don't let her touch your blood!"

"Then put her to sleep and git her out of here!"

Isaiah screamed again. The drawn-out howling outside intensified. It sounded distorted again. Everyone's voices slowed down, echoing.

Mikayla fought to rise. She fell onto her back. "Make it stop!"

Mr. Sparrowhawk kneeled, then lifted her until she sat up straight. Her eyes darted left and right, unable to focus. He snapped his fingers. The vertigo stopped, and she took in the horrid sound of Isaiah's screaming and the coyotes howling.

Mr. Sparrowhawk restrained her and brought her in close so that only she could hear him. She shuddered, feeling his breath on the nape of her neck.

"Your mind is sweet, so innocent. I'll tell your father about that sweet, innocent side of you." He wiped her tears. "He'll miss you so much. The sweet, innocent stories of his daughter will keep him working for us at Meccanicville until he drops dead. Don't worry that pretty head of yours. I'll make sure you *forget* this, but I will punish you for humiliating me."

Grinning, he let her drop out his arms. Darkness surrounded her before she hit the floor, and she felt like she was being pulled into a black hole.

Jericho Kite IV

Jericho left his pack of cigarettes on his nightstand unopened. Starting from that moment on, he was quitting smoking for good. He opened his balcony and took a deep breath, letting the chill hit his bare chest. It made him feel something.

In a small black box on the top shelf of his walk-in closet awaited Naomi's next surprise. He opened it. A 20.89 carat diamond, flawless clarity, princess cut, glinted on a gold band. The ring had once belonged to his mother.

After washing up and shaving, he got dressed in his usual attire, minus a cigarette pack and a lighter. Then he stepped into the bal-chatri for the 8:00 AM meeting. Soon, Secretarybird would arrive with Naomi, and his father would make a big fuss about it. He couldn't wait to rub that he had power to get his way in his father's face.

Osprey and Condor left their respective rooms around the same time. Osprey wore his usual button-down shirt in a muted color and khakis pulled over his protruding gut. He probably sat on his recliner all night, feet up, watching football with a beer, or maybe he sat at his desk, gluing airplane models together for painting. Most of his collection consisted of military tanker refuelers and large commercial jets, plus a few prop planes. No matter what, he slept peacefully.

Condor, on the other hand, didn't. His eyes were red, his face swollen like he had been crying. He wore a brown hoodie, red sweatpants, and ragged sneakers. Jericho couldn't see Condor's room from where he was standing but had had been in there many times before. Multiple computers logged onto different networks, a landfill of empty coffee cups and energy drinks stacked to the ceiling. The man was an unappreciated genius on the computer. Jericho imagined his father forced Condor to stay up all night, launching cyberattacks on Ravensbourne's company. Last night wouldn't have been the first time Condor had pulled an all-night hacking session.

"Good morning, Honorable Kite," Condor said over a yawn before he went to his stained-glass window, gulping an energy drink.

Osprey waved. "Good morn, young Kite."

Jericho acknowledged Osprey with a firm nod. "Condor, are you okay?"

Condor smiled weakly. "Yeah."

Kestrel stormed out of her quarters, slamming her door against the wall. In her sparkling blue heels, she sauntered past Jericho without acknowledging him and stood at her stained glass window with her hands on her hips. Vulture came down the hallway dressed in his brown three-piece suit and red tie. He stood across from Kestrel at his window.

"Kestrel, your posture is unflattering," Vulture said with a smile.

She took her cell phone out of her pocket and showed him her middle finger. The glitter on her nails matched her heels.

"What's her problem?" Osprey asked.

"If you want to know what my problem is, ask me instead of talking like I'm not here!" Kestrel growled, clenching her phone.

Jericho stepped up to her. "Kestrel, your attitude isn't welcomed."

"Shut up, Kite Boy. Your cousin injured our bounty hunter from Kan early this morning. He's in the infirmary because she flew one of her hawks into his body and put a hole in him!"

Jericho gasped, unable to process what she'd said. It made no sense.

"And you're upset because...?" Vulture asked with a grin.

"Shove it, Vulture!" she screeched, showing him her middle finger again.

Vulture turned to everyone. "Boss told Kestrel she has to take care of the bounty hunter and his pony. Bandage their wounds, bring them food, make sure they get healing..."

"And he's making me fly out to Kan with them!" she added before cursing excessively. "Who would want to go on a seventeen-hour flight across two effing oceans with Falcon, a pony, and a man who hasn't been around a woman in years?"

"Obey Boss's orders, and then one day you'll gain some seniority and can push back on such request," Vulture said. "You're the new one, so—"

"No! Sparrowhawk was the newest hire after me."

"And yet…" Vulture smirked. He was smug, even jovial. "He's more useful than you."

Kestrel stamped her feet. "I've proven I'm as useful as any of you men!"

Coyotes outside began howling.

"You hear that, Kestrel?" Osprey said. "The mongrels are crying you a river."

The men laughed. Jericho normally would've joined in, but he was confused.

"Can somebody explain to me how Lorelei flew a hawk into a man's body and why he brought a pony with him?" Jericho asked. No one spoke up. They ignored him. "Where are the other Raptor Admins? Falcon, Sparrowhawk, and Secretarybird are missing."

He knew Secretarybird was going to get Naomi, and he'd included to avoid suspicion. What the others were doing was a mystery.

"I saw Falcon and Sparrowhawk going downstairs together twenty minutes ago. They didn't say where they were going. Secretarybird was gone hours ago. She had breakfast duty," Osprey replied.

"I'll go find them. Father's meeting will start soon," Jericho said, heading towards the staircase.

Outside, Jericho searched left and right for Naomi and Secretarybird. Fog covered everything more than ten feet in front of him. His nerves started going bad. He wanted a cigarette. *Pathetic*, he thought. Not an hour had gone by, and he was already considering backsliding into old habits. He stuffed his hands into his pockets and went back into the main building.

Downstairs, the Lynbrookians were in the cafeteria, eating whatever Secretarybird had prepped that morning. At a quick glance, Naomi and

Secretarybird weren't there. He checked upstairs in the library. Empty. He zipped back downstairs. The private dining hall doors were shut tight. He shoved open both doors, forcing his way in.

Sparrowhawk sat in front of a fancy chessboard across from Mikayla. He seemed focused on planning his next move in a game against himself. He sat on the side of the white gold pieces but was staring at the onyx and abalone pieces. Mikayla was slumped forward, her eyes wide open, unblinking.

"What the hell?" Jericho ran up to her. He waved his hand in front of her face. No response. Shook her arm. A soft whimper and head tilt. Her coiled hair fell over, curtaining her dulled, lifeless eyes. "Sparrowhawk, what did you do to her?"

Sparrowhawk suddenly spoke without turning around. "This chessboard was made for no one poorer than a billionaire. Fine craftsmanship, high carat gemstones." His voice shifted menacingly. "I'd kill for one of these."

For a split second, Jericho marveled at the pieces. Kites loved shiny gemstones and precious metals. Refocused, he shifted his body towards Sparrowhawk. "I asked you a question."

"Robert Birdwing brought this board." Sparrowhawk moved a white gold bishop to take an onyx rook. "How does a retired aeronautical analyst have access to materials of this quality? I tried to pick her brain, but the answer isn't in there. There's a black pawn missing. She's hiding it from me."

Jericho's nostrils flared. The fact Sparrowhawk was too occupied to have the decency to turn around and greet him properly pissed him off too. He slapped the onyx rook out of Sparrowhawk's hand. "Is she dead? Did you kill her?"

"She's overwhelmed." He smiled. "I'm inside of her head. She'll recover."

"Sparrowhawk, stand up and look at me when you're talking to me."

Sparrowhawk continued moving pieces around the board. He paused for a moment, not contemplating Jericho's request, but as if he were thinking deeply about his next move. Jericho felt invisible.

"Answer this, Sparrowhawk." Jericho waited until he reached for another piece, and the timing was perfect. "How could Lorelei command a hawk to fly *through* a man?" He pointed to Mikayla. "How did you activate her yesterday? What is it that you're doing to her now?"

Sparrowhawk took a couple of seconds longer than usual to pick a piece. He eventually spoke, but with his back facing Jericho. "You've wasted your one."

"Huh? My one what?"

"Demand out of me. You are a traitor to your father and the Trinity. It won't be long before you're banished out of your legacy, out of the Kite Clan. I see clearly that will happen."

Jericho pulled his fist back to punch Sparrowhawk, but the Raptor Amin swiftly caught his arm. Now, he had Sparrowhawk's undivided attention. His pupils were fully dilated. They scowled at each other for a few moments, sizing each other up. Jericho tried to hide his fear. Sparrowhawk's eyes made him appear possessed.

"Help me. Make him stop," Mikayla whispered. A stream of tears poured down her face.

"*Silence!*" Sparrowhawk snapped at her. She seized back up into her lifeless state. "I can't fight you right now. I'm busy inside of her."

Jericho snatched his arm back. "You're a fucking predator."

"The pot calls the kettle black." Sparrowhawk turned his back to Jericho again. He leaned over and tenderly caressed Mikayla's stiff, wet face.

"*Ugh,*" Jericho muttered.

"She's putting up a fight. I know she knows where that pawn went. Oh, her mind is too innocent for her power. She wastes it dreaming about her parents getting back together, talking to friends, and silly dates with Isaiah Marksman. I should have her power. She represses the darkness within her, unable to truly activate her zenith. I'm going to pry deeper and deeper to see what else I find, deep in her id. No, I'll go deeper than that. I want to see what's below that."

"She's not your little doll to play with!"

Jericho stormed out of the dining hall. His hands were shaking. He needed a cigarette now. Where were Naomi and Secretarybird?

Along the same hallway, he continued searching for them until he stumbled upon the lounge where the teachers once gathered. The two women were there talking on the couch, facing each other. It looked like a mother and her daughter. Jericho stormed inside and closed the door.

"Jericho!" Naomi hopped onto her feet. "She told me you're trying to save me from going to some place called Kan. I don't get it."

"I didn't have a chance to explain more than that, Honorable Kite," Secretarybird said.

Panicking, he looked away from Naomi, unwilling to see her reaction. "Secretarybird, Sparrowhawk has Mikayla Birdwing. He's in the dining hall, torturing her."

Naomi began firing questions and stumbling over her words.

Secretarybird got to her feet. "What did you see him doing to her?"

"It's hard to describe. She looks like a zombie, or more like a puppet. She's sitting in the chair, not talking or blinking. There was a moment she asked for my help, and then he put a spell on her, telling her to be quiet. She went back to looking dead, not moving or saying anything."

Secretarybird immediately left the room.

Naomi balled her fist and pounded Jerico repeatedly. It felt like a series of nudges, but he knew she would've hit him a lot harder if she could've.

"Why didn't you help Mika? Why? Why? Why?"

If Mikayla hadn't been present and vulnerable in the room, he would have taken on Sparrowhawk. No doubt. He hated the man more than his father. He hated his smug face. He hated his nonchalant demeanor. He hated his serial killer energy. He wanted to break him in half.

Naomi wailed, tears streaming down her cheeks and down to her neck. "Mika's never done anything to deserve all this abuse and pain. Your people keep hurting her."

"Hey! Sparrowhawk is *not* my people! Not Falcon and Kestrel either! If I had a choice, people like them would never, ever be here. I asked Secretarybird to take Mikayla because Sparrowhawk won't put his hands on her."

"Why not?"

"Because she's one of my father's senior Raptor Admins. If he hurts her, it'll piss Father off. It's not in Sparrowhawk's best interest."

"Mika will be okay?" Naomi sniffled.

"Yeah," Jericho said, holding Naomi's hand and motioning that she should sit back down. "She will."

"You promise?"

"I promise. Secretarybird is like a mom to me. Well, she took my mom's place in a w-w-way," he stuttered. He wasn't used to describing his buried feelings about Secretarybird. "She has a momma's heart is what I meant. She's gonna get Mikayla out of there, take good care of her."

"Mika told me Sparrowhawk hurt her yesterday. She said it felt like he got into her head, and he was able to control her dad's body. I didn't understand."

Jericho didn't either. He bit his lip. "Naomi, I've been as confused as you."

She crossed her arms over her chest, made herself small, and pressed her back into the corner of the sectional. "How could you not know what he's doing to her?"

He sat closer and palmed her cheek gently. "My father and his Raptors are keeping secrets from me. I'm now seeing that."

He pressed his lips together and listened to every word she cried. She shared thoughts that made sense and others that came out jumbled. And then there were the thoughts that made him look at her and himself.

She turned her head and nudged him away. "Nobody was supposed to know we're together, and now they're sending me away. They're hurting Mika..."

"You and I being together has nothing to do with any of that."

Naomi pouted and turned away from him, exhaling through her nostrils. "You've been hiding something from me. There's no way you knew nothing the entire time, Jericho." She looked into his eyes. "You're hiding something else, aren't you?"

Without thinking, he left the lounge and bolted upstairs to the bal-chatri. Nobody was there. He hurried into his room and grabbed for an unopened pack of cigarettes. As the packaging crinkled, he realized what he was doing. He threw it against the wall. The cigarettes scattered.

"What is wrong with me?" His fingers clawed at his forehead.

He snatched off his blazer, ripped off the cravat, and picked off the pearl cufflinks. Now he was down to a white Oxford and pants. He scuffed his hair and undid a few of his top buttons. After going into the closet for his mother's ring, he went back downstairs.

Naomi crossed her arms and turned her back on him. "You left me."

"Naomi. I'm sorry."

She didn't turn around, but she did cock her neck enough to see him through her peripheral.

"You don't realize how vulnerable you've always been, you and Mikayla both."

Naomi's eyes moved, contemplating. There was silence until she shook her head. Whatever she said came out softer than a whisper, and Jericho couldn't hear it. She cleared her throat and spoke louder. "What are you trying to say?"

He paused and thought carefully about his next words. "You two were in grave danger from the day your—" He cut himself off and cursed under his breath. "Naomi, there's no easy way to say this. Those Friday nights you came to me sad about another week going by without your mom mailing you were hard on me because I knew all along exactly why. I—I knew why she hasn't mailed you." He sighed. "Lynbrookians are Kite Express property. Your mom sold you."

"You've gotta be kidding me." Naomi's eyes watered.

"Lynbrook is a part of something we call the Trinity. My father targets families in astronomical amounts of debt and advertises Lynbrook as a way they can save themselves. I'm assuming your mom was in law school debt."

Naomi nodded and whispered, "So much, it kept her up at night."

"My family uses Kite Express to trick families into thinking this place is a reputable boarding school that'll teach their kids about aviation. In reality, it's a trap to get them sucked into airfield labor at Meccanicville."

"And what happens at Kan?"

"I have no idea."

Naomi got quiet, and then she asked, "How much did my mom get?"

"Something in the six-figures, up front, I think. Maybe more. Every year after you're eighteen, my father will pay her much more. There are ex-

Lynbrookians who've died at Meccanicville in the Texas heat while moving cargo or fixing a jet. Their parents are still being compensated, unaware their kids are gone. Secretarybird told me about that last month."

Naomi buried her face in her hands.

"Unfortunately, that's not the worst part. Your mom and Mikayla's put you both through surgeries when you were twelve. I don't know what was done to you, but it put you both on a list to go to Kan."

"Why?"

"That's the other half nobody's explaining to me. I'm sorry, Naomi. I wanted to tell you sooner, but my father would have killed me."

She punched Jericho's bicep and began sobbing.

Ashamed, he sat quietly. Every passing minute felt like an hour, but he didn't stop her from crying. He felt like he deserved to wallow in discomfort and humiliation.

The intercom buzzed.

"ALL RAPTOR ADMINS AND MY SON: REPORT TO THE BAL-CHATRI IMMEDIATELY!"

Jericho heeded the rage in his father's voice.

He felt like his time was up with Naomi. He reached into his pocket for the diamond ring, showed it to her. She balled her fist, hiding her fingers in refusal to submit. He waited for his heart rate to slow down.

He held the ring up again, sure to make his voice sound confident and unwavering. "This was my mom's engagement ring. Wear it. Don't wear it. Whatever you choose, take it as a promise ring—not for marriage but as a symbol of my apology and my vow to never lie to you again." Naomi swiftly turned around. He pounded his heart with his right hand. "I have a feeling in my gut this is my last chance to be here with you. I want you to trust that I'm doing everything I can."

She swiftly turned towards him, eyes wide open, eager for more. He had already taken her left hand. "Help Mika *and* everyone else."

"Yes, my mouse, I'll try. There's nothing I can say or do to make my father stop because a Kite wants what they want and gets what they want."

"You're a Kite too, Jericho." She looked him in the eyes, shuddering. "Get what you want. You keep talking about saving me. But that's not all you want. Save everyone. You can do it."

He slipped the ring on her finger and sat beside her. He lifted her chin and made her look him in the eye. "I'll do it. I'll break the Trinity if that's what it takes."

"What's going to happen to me?"

"You're not going to Kan." He pulled her in for a kiss, then stood up and brushed the wrinkles from his clothes. "Stay here."

"Will you come back?"

"No, it's best that I'm not seen with you again." He headed for the door and turned back around. "Can you trust me?"

"I can relearn," she replied.

He nodded. "That's more than I deserve. I love you, Naomi."

"For all it's worth, I love you too, Jericho."

Lorelei Avian

Lorelei, somewhat rested after her battle with the hunter and his pony, began gathering all the dead hawks along her way to the mass grave. There were four hawks in her bag and one in her hand. Cause of death was unknown, though she suspected they died of exhaustion. She put those hawks through hell and back yesterday, successfully launching them to thwart Headmaster Kite's spy planes. Their deaths weren't the only costs; her morality had been taxed.

Time was up too. The lunar phase had shifted from the Raptor Moon to the Canine Moon, in favor of the Handler. Her Blood Leash power would wane and remain weakened until first quarter returned in December.

The mass grave where all the teachers and staff were dumped after Mr. Falco and Miss Kestrel executed them was sort of a sleepy place where the only movement was lizards scurrying onto trees. A few rodents moved about here and there. Badly injured, Lorelei crouched awkwardly on a patch of grass between the grave and a tree. Mateo perched on a branch above, falling asleep instantly.

She wanted the man who was burned alive in his vehicle not to be a CSB investigator. She wanted him to be a figment of her imagination. Scrunched into the fetal position, Lorelei began sobbing. In her mind, his death was her fault. She'd called them to come.

An hour later, she pulled herself together and crafted five crosses. Each consisted of two branches bonded together with pine needles. Next, she gathered whatever pebbles were nearby. She began digging five shallow graves with the hand shovel until the hard handle made her hand ache. She snatched up a yard's length of crabgrass to make way for her hands to scoop through the earth. Though her hangnails and cuticles ached, she continued digging.

Two feet below, the soil was cool, moist, and easy to break through. She went at it for so long, she didn't realize her body had gone stiff until she rose up to straighten her hunched spine. Her bones crackled, and she sighed in relief.

The graves were complete. She kissed each hawk before burying them and placing pebbles on their graves.

Landon crossed her mind as she listened to the distant howling—the Canine's Howl.

"Is Landon in trouble?" she whispered.

Canines in the vicinity of the Handler tended to bark and howl for their master's affection and command. The Canine's Howl was a cry for mercy. Lorelei wished she could return instantly, but she didn't want to get caught and sent to Kan. She wondered why she and her brother were being diverted to Kan instead of Meccanicville. The Kites already knew about their Blood Leash. What had made them change their minds?

"Something happened. Is Landon activating?"

She patted the sides of the graves to make them look pristine and rectangular before placing the last pebbles. When her task was complete, a realization hit her. They were going to send Landon to Kan whether she came back or not.

"I'm going to put an additional restriction on my Blood Leash power in the name of you five." She got onto her hands and knees, a prayer position. "You all were like Mateo: a gift from God, really. If it weren't for you guys, I would've gotten caught yesterday. You were good to me. From now on, any time a bird or raptor I use faints of exhaustion, I faint of exhaustion too. You have a heart attack; I have a heart attack. You die; I die."

She arranged the five crosses and made the sign of the cross herself.

After her prayer, she gathered her belongings and made her way towards Lynbrook. With a sprained ankle and low energy, she surmised it would take hours. She wished she had one friend, one human soul, to accompany her. Then again, she felt like a terrible person for killing those hawks. Who did she deserve to have in her life? Not one single person came to mind. Not even Landon. She'd abandoned him.

"Mateo, am I going to hell?"

Hoot.

Jericho Kite IV

9:26 AM

Upstairs in the bal-chatri, all the Raptor Admins stood before their respective stained glass windows with their hands behind their backs at parade rest. Secretarybird, Osprey, and Condor were among the first, standing on the right side in the order in which his father hired them. Vulture was on the center of the left side in front of Falcon, Kestrel, and Sparrowhawk.

Jericho held his head high, feeling the eyes of all the Raptor Admins on him as he passed between them. In the back center, he took his place at the stained glass window depicting a baby swallowtail kite in a nest.

His blazer, cravat, and cufflinks were strewn on the floor in his bedroom. The cool air touched his chest through the opening where his buttons were undone. Though there were eight people in the hall, enough bodies to keep each other warm, the cold crept underneath his sleeves. Hairs stood on his goosebumps, and yet his hands began to feel clammy. A mixture of emotions brewed inside his mind.

Falcon broke the silence. "Sure 'bout presentin' yerself like that, Kite Boy?"

Jericho glared straight ahead, waiting for the doors to open and reveal his father, the only opponent he was focused on right now.

"Falcon, you have a cut and dried blood on your face. Are you sure you want to present *yourself* that way?" Osprey asked.

"It's called a battle scar. Yer fat ass wouldn't know. At least I ain't dressed like a disgrace."

Secretarybird broke in, "It isn't our place to judge and convict Honorable Kite."

"You coddle him, Secretarybird. Whenever he needs to man up, he goes to you. He's soft because of you. He's in love with that Afro-German mixed breed because of you," Falcon said.

"I am the first Raptor Admin! Honorable Kite is his name, and he's your next master and the next leader of the Trinity! If you don't like it, leave! Sparrowhawk was reminded earlier, and I remind you too, Falcon, Kestrel. Know your place!"

"You couldn't be more wrong, Secretarybird!" Falcon bellowed.

Jericho stomped his foot. The click of the titanium plate bolted to his heel echoed. The room fell into silence again.

Fifteen more minutes passed. The double doors at the end of the hall opened, revealing Headmaster Kite. Everyone snapped to attention. His father stopped mid-step, glaring at Jericho's attire—or lack thereof. He continued walking forward, and his admins bowed as he passed them. At the end of the hall, he looked Jericho in the eyes, almost as if he were daring him to strike.

"You think you hate me now? Wait until the end of this meeting, boy."

His father took his place before his stained glass, the central window that dominated the entire bal-chatri.

"This will be our final meeting together. Now that Lorelei has stopped attacking our airspace, four helicopters are already well on their way here. Arrival time will be around 8:00 PM, maybe earlier. Half of us are flying directly to Meccanicville. The other two helicopters are going to an uncontrolled airport where a plane awaits. Those people will be going to Kan."

"Sir?" Falcon raised his hand. "We're leavin' the campus? Why?"

"After what Edmund Rabbit revealed, I decided we should evacuate the campus."

"Thank goodness!" Secretarybird cheered.

"Does Alexander know about this evacuation plan?" Vulture asked.

"No, and I want it to stay that way. The last thing I want is to make that brat aware of what we're doing. There will be contractors coming at the end of the month to fix the gas leak. We'll return afterwards."

Jericho couldn't believe what he was hearing. For once, his father had a reasonable idea. Finally.

His father listed everyone going to Meccanicville first. "Myself, Edmund Rabbit, Robert Birdwing, Secretarybird, Osprey, Condor, and Vulture. Any objections?"

Condor and Osprey looked at each other and shook their heads. Secretarybird bowed her head, showing her concurrence. Vulture did the same.

"Kestrel and Falcon, you two will be staying back with Eric Fowl, the bounty hunter, and the pony to dispose of the Lynbrookians and shut the campus down. A helicopter will then take you to the airport for a flight to Kan much later this evening. Any objections?"

Kestrel grinned.

Falcon shook his head and raised his hand slightly. "Sir, why are we executin' the Lynbrookians?"

"They are damaged goods. They know too much and have seen too much. They're not educated enough to send to Meccanicville, and they're beyond useless for Kan. Keeping them will cost too much money. It's cheaper to get rid of them and keep paying off their families annually."

"Fair enough for me!" Falcon replied.

And just like that, Jericho lost hope in his father again.

The headmaster continued, "On the list to go to Kan: Sparrowhawk, Landon Avian, Lorelei Avian, Naomi Maus, Mikayla Birdwing, and my son. Shortly, Mikayla Birdwing will be sent to find Lorelei, using the contract Vulture and I have written up. Any objections?"

Jericho maintained his composure. His father glared at him, but Jericho refused to show fear.

Sparrowhawk stepped forward. He didn't tack on his usual smirk. Something was off about him. "I have multiple objections, sir."

"Explain," the elder Kite said, obviously annoyed.

"Sir, Isaiah Marksman should be going to Kan."

"Why so? I don't have a clue who that is."

"You should!" Sparrowhawk insisted. "My apologies, sir. I'll explain. Now activated, Mikayla Birdwing's visions show the future. She is capable of lucid dreaming. Some of her dreams are literal. Others, a series of convoluted symbolism. I have a working theory that if she masters Blood Leash, she will be able to view the past, present, and futures of her targets." He paused and recovered. "There's a chance that the visions I was able to uncover this morning are related to future targets, *including me.*" He shuddered. "I saw my fate through her eyes, I think. I don't know. All I get are snippets, never the big picture." Sparrowhawk's eye twitched. He whispered, "I don't want to be a kitten."

It was a sight to see. The man was falling apart. Kestrel and Falcon started laughing.

"Sparrowhawk, pull yourself together," said Kestrel.

"Yeah, stop bein' a pussy," Falcon snickered and opened a small bag of pork rinds.

"Sparrowhawk, Mikayla Birdwing is a tiny girl, need I remind you. I think you'll be okay," Vulture said, laughing along with the others.

Condor chuckled lightly. "Sparrowhawk, I'm afraid what you said doesn't make any sense."

"I told you Sparrowhawk doesn't know what he's doing!" Kestrel held her belly. "The only Blood Leasher with a clue about her abilities is out there raising hell in the forest with thousands of birds."

"Let's get back on topic. Sparrowhawk," Jericho's father began. "You didn't explain why Isaiah Marksman should be sent to Kan. You went off on a psychotic tangent."

"It's not a tangent, sir. Some of those dream snippets show Isaiah Marksman is the Handler! He's the one who can control canines. They howl for him! The coyotes! The Canine's Howl!"

Jericho saw everyone in the bal-chatri either shift or make a subtle facial expression of discomfort and confusion. He was glad they were as confused as he was.

"You're creepin' us out, man. Them coyotes are always hangin' out by the fence because Eric Fowl's autistic nephew hangs out with him in that cabin nearby," Falcon said.

"I never thought I'd say this, but I agree with Falco. You're not making sense, Sparrowhawk," Condor said. "Eric Fowl told us that Landon is the Handler. That makes more sense because he's Lorelei's twin."

"Yeah, and Isaiah Marksman's eyes are brown, not silver like Jericho and the Avian twins," Osprey added.

Sparrowhawk raised his voice. "Honorable Kite's hair is jet black, but the twins are blonde. Genetic outcomes shift generation to generation as some recessive genes trump more dominant alleles!"

He had studied genetics and eugenics closely. With everyone aware of this, nobody refuted his statement.

"I know what I saw! Isaiah Marksman is the Handler!" Sparrowhawk declared.

"Who is Isaiah Marksman? Nobody's answered my question!" Jericho's father shouted.

Kestrel spoke up. "Sir, he's just a regular kid. Brown curly hair, freckles—"

"He's bird-chested, quiet. Little. Breakable," Falcon added.

"He worked in the supply office," Condor said.

Vulture chuckled. "Your fall from grace is mighty right now, Sparrowhawk. It's impossible for Isaiah Marksman to be the Handler. That would mean he's of the Trembley bloodline, related to the Kite Clan and the Avians through the same grandmother. Unless Carolyn Trembley had an additional child with another man before her death nobody knows about."

"Perhaps he could be from a Trembley completely unrelated to Carolyn," Condor suggested.

"No, I am one-hundred percent positive Marksman is a descendant of Carolyn Trembley. I need to go back inside of Mikayla to review that relationship from the past." Sparrowhawk pointed at Jericho. "Then I'll have proof that Isaiah Marksman is your cousin!"

"Headmaster, I believe Sparrowhawk is calling your mother a whore, sir, and he should tread carefully," Secretarybird said, glaring at Sparrowhawk.

"Sparrowhawk's claim is ridiculous. Do we all agree on that?" Jericho's father asked.

"Yes, sir!" all the other Raptor Admins responded adamantly.

The headmaster was now visibly angry. "Sparrowhawk, why were you inside Birdwing's head again? I was fine with it weeks ago, when you discovered her secret plan, but lately, you've been proving you shouldn't be doing this."

"Sir, I wanted to understand how Robert Birdwing could afford that chess set he brought in, and then I saw them—the visions..."

"Headmaster, I can confirm this. Sparrowhawk was clamped onto the table in a state of shock when I found him. Some might say he was petrified," Secretarybird explained. "I had to pry him away from the table, one finger at a time, and drag him out of the dining hall. I went back later for Mikayla Birdwing. She had a fever and symptoms of an anxiety attack. She's asleep and recovering in the dorm, alone."

Jericho covered his mouth, hiding his smile. He knew Secretarybird would come through, but it also sounded like Mikayla had managed to unintentionally one-up Sparrowhawk again.

"Alright, that's enough of this," the headmaster said. "Sparrowhawk, not another word from you."

"But, sir! If I am correct, the Trinity will have all three. Lorelei Avian, the Falconer. Isaiah Marksman, the Handler. Your son, the Equestrian. The eugenics at Kan will take off! The Victor of Kan will be pleased."

"What did he call me?" Jericho asked.

Everyone ignored him.

"Sir, your original plan was to dispose of Isaiah Marksman, along with the other Lynbrookians," Sparrowhawk said. "Landon Avian would have gotten to Kan, and it would've eventually come out he's not the Handler. You would look incompetent before the Victor of Kan, thus looking incompetent in front of the rest of your family."

"*Hmm,*" Headmaster Kite muttered, thinking. "Where is this Isaiah kid? I want to speak with him. I'll talk to him about his family tree. If he has Canadian origins, I'll look deeper into him. Vulture has his guardians' contacts and will speak with them."

"Sir, don't entertain Sparrowhawk," Falcon said nervously.

"I have no choice. If either you or Kestrel kill Isaiah Marksman tonight and it comes out that he is the Handler, the Victor of Kan will make me pay."

"And his *price* is high," all the other Raptor Admins grimly chanted in unison.

"My brothers would also banish me from the Kite Clan."

Falcon gulped. "I understand, sir, but there's a thing about Marksman you need to know. See these cuts on my face? He did this." He pulled a jagged bullet casing from his pocket. "He confessed he was up all last night, turnin' this little thing here into a tiny knife with a nail file."

"Why? Hurry up and make this make sense."

"Boss, Marksman admitted to tamperin' with our respirators and weapons. He's the one who took half of the gunpowder out of hundreds of rounds of ammo. He took all the projectiles out too. That's why we couldn't shoot any of those hawks yesterday."

"When did he have time to do all that?" Secretarybird asked.

"Freedom Hours, I bet. Seems like he took advantage of us being distracted with the gas leak fallout last month," Condor said.

"He took only half the gunpowder out of the bullets? Why only half?" Osprey asked.

"Takin' half makes the bullet more likely to injure the person usin' the weapon. At best, the weapon would malfunction. He turned all our ammo in the supply office into half-filled blanks. That's why I beat the livin' crap out of him. He was tryin' to kill us."

Vulture was stunned. "I did not have enough coffee this morning."

"Falcon, elaborate on what you meant when you said you 'beat the livin' crap out of him,'" the elder Kite ordered.

"Well, y'know, Boss." Falcon lowered his voice and shrugged. "I had to get him to talk."

"Answer the question." His father stepped to him, fist balled.

"He told me he understood weapons because he loves huntin' and shootin' at the range." Falcon paused, then spoke quietly. "I gouged his eye, his dominant one. His good eye—the eye that makes him a sharpshooter."

Secretarybird gasped. "Oh, my goodness! That poor boy. You took his eye?"

"I got carried away. I know. But I felt like that was what he deserved."

The headmaster looked upon Falcon with conviction. "The Victor of Kan will make you pay, if Sparrowhawk's claim is correct."

"And his *price* is high," all the other Raptor Admins chanted in unison again.

"We will spare Marksman's life, for now. Sparrowhawk, Falcon, you better hope you both were wrong for the sake of your egos. Pray to God that Marksman is another nobody. Osprey, after this meeting, go relieve Eric Fowl from library watch and have him report to my office downstairs."

"Yes, sir," Osprey said.

Jericho had heard words that were new to him. Blood Leash. Canine's Howl. The Falconer. The Equestrian. The Handler. Trembley bloodline. It all sounded insane, yet more undeniably relevant. He had a million questions, but he stayed focused. An opportunity would arrive soon.

"This meeting is over," the headmaster declared. "I will see how much I can find out about this Marksman kid. Everyone else, prepare for tonight. Pack only the essentials and leave nothing pertinent behind. The helicopters will depart fifteen minutes after they arrive."

"Sir, I volunteer to stay back." Sparrowhawk ran into the center and bowed in complete submission, forehead touching the floor. "I will singlehandedly ensure Mikayla Birdwing brings back Lorelei Avian, and I will dispose of the Lynbrookians, save for Isaiah Marksman."

"You want to redeem yourself? That's why you're doing this?"

"Yes, master," he said, tucking his body in, making himself small.

"Get Lorelei, Mikayla, and Isaiah—if it turns out he's the Handler—on that helicopter with you to Kan by midnight."

"Yes, master."

Jericho's opportunity arose. He stepped forward. "Father, I will stay behind and assist Sparrowhawk, then join them in Kan."

His father looked him in the eye. "Can you pull the trigger when those Lynbrookians beg for mercy?"

"Yes, Father."

"Leave no witnesses."

"Yes, Father. I'll even make them dig their own graves beforehand."

"Finally, you've taken initiative. Perhaps the Trinity will be in good hands after all."

Jericho had bought himself more time to save as many lives as he possibly could, but the clock was ticking. Sparrowhawk would be looming over his shoulder, but he didn't care. He had made Naomi a promise he intended to keep.

"This meeting is over. Dismissed."

Everyone bowed their heads as Headmaster Kite left the bal-chatri. Osprey and Condor exchanged worried looks with Jericho before they departed. Sparrowhawk stood up and glared at him. They were the last two remaining.

Sparrowhawk's arrogant grin came back. "I will ensure you keep your word, *Honorable Kite.*"

The man turned and went to his quarters. Jericho waited until his door's lock clicked before he walked diagonally towards Secretarybird's quarters and knocked once. She opened promptly, looking disheveled. Her Bantu knots, taken down, hung loose on the sides of her shoulders. She had a glass of wine in one hand and a cigarette in the other.

"Can I come in?" he asked.

"Sure. Hurry up before the others see," she said. Jericho stepped inside. She closed the door. "I usually smoke on my balcony, but what's the point in it now?"

Her room—colored white, beige, and gray—was a standalone representation of her personal chic, clean style. She'd helped design the Lynbrookians' uniforms and other elements of the campus. Aside from her current cigarette, the room had an underlying scent of fresh cotton and linen.

"Don't mind me. Want one? It's a menthol." She showed him her cigarette, stained with burgundy lipstick.

Jericho desperately wanted to say yes. He wanted three or more, in fact. "I quit this morning."

Her eyes lit up. "Good job, Jericho. I'll put mine out to keep from tempting you. I'm so proud. I'll be right back!"

He rested on her beige chaise lounge and kicked his shoes off. *Ugh!* He thought to himself, wishing he had said yes.

"Help me understand," she said, taking the armchair across from him. "Early this morning when we spoke, you were concerned about the Lynbrookians. Now you're going to help Sparrowhawk? Hon, taking someone's life isn't—"

"I lied to my father," he said. He turned to her with a smirk.

"You've got something up your sleeve?"

"Working on it."

She sighed with relief. "I hate that your father is sending you to Kan. I really do, hon. Vulture went right over to his office first thing this morning and told him you planned on marrying Naomi Maus. He decided on the spot that he'd send you over to Kan."

"He thinks I don't care about the Trinity." He crossed his arms behind his head. "I do care about the Trinity, but not in the way he wants. I want to change it, make it better."

"I know, hon. Falcon took that boy's eye. I've always wanted to believe he wouldn't hurt the kids…" Her voice trembled.

They got quiet.

She took a sip of her wine. "Well, what brings you here?"

"Secretarybird, you meant it when you said I'll be your next master and leader, right?"

"Yes, hon. Every word."

"This is a direct order." Jericho sat up and looked her in the eye. "Explain Blood Leash to me right now. I want to know every single detail of everything everyone's been hiding from me."

She put her glass down. "I suppose if you're going to Kan, you won't get far without understanding. Kan's economy is based on battles between Blood Leash fighters in an arena."

She began with reexplaining that his grandmother, Carolyn Trembley, was from Quebec, Canada and immigrated to the United States. She married a Kite before the Kite Clan created the huge conglomerate, Kite Express.

After the divorce, she moved back to Canada but went to Ontario instead and started a new family, which led to the Avian twins. She revealed the three Pure Blood Leash powers descendants of Trembley blood may inherit genetically. Lastly, she explained the three eugenic surgeries, mentioning the bounty hunter from Kan, Naomi, Mikayla, and Sparrowhawk as examples. Her explanation finally helped him understand what activation and Blood Leash Capable meant. By the end of the hour, Jericho was completely taken aback.

"All I have to do is cut myself, make a horse lick it, and then I can make that horse do whatever I want it to do?"

"It's much more complicated than that, if you want to use Blood Leash efficiently. But yes, to function on a novice level, that's what you'll do as the Equestrian."

"That's weird. Kinda unethical too. Like, who was the first guy to slice himself and say, 'Here doggy, come lick my blood so I can make you sit and roll over and play fetch?!'"

"I know, hon. It's a lot to take in."

"I'm scared of needles and sharp stuff."

He was so afraid that he had never received any vaccinations. Since he never left the campus and Lynbrookians arrived fully vaccinated, it was a nonissue.

"You can't be a Blood Leasher without some level of comfort with sharp objects. The blood must come out, one way or another." She pondered for a moment. "Then again, female Blood Leashers have their periods, and I guess if you induce a nosebleed, that could work too. Blood is blood."

Jericho palmed his face and groaned. "Why did I have to be born this way?"

She patted his back. "I know it's hard."

"Is that how Lorelei was able to make a hawk go through a man's body? She cut herself, fed a hawk her blood?"

"I think so. I know it sounds *out there*, Jericho, but that's who she is. That's who you are too."

"And Landon can control dogs? Make the dog lick his blood? Make it sit?

Do dog tricks like shake paws, dance, and bark? All it needs is his blood?" His face distorted with disgust.

"Allegedly. I've never seen it. Eric Fowl claimed that was his power. That's why nobody believes Sparrowhawk. It makes zero sense for Isaiah Marksman to be the Handler. Sparrowhawk is fairly new at being Blood Leash Capable. I think he got his brain surgery eight years ago, when it wasn't as safe. He doesn't know what he's doing, and maybe he's experiencing complications."

"I think he's wrong too," Jericho said. "I get it now. My father is sending us freaks to Kan because we'll make him and the Victor of Kan a lot of money there."

"Bingo. He's making Kestrel and Falcon go to keep you all in check. The rest of us are going to Meccanicville to ensure it stays business-as-usual there until we all return. That's my assumption."

"Secretarybird, I have another order for you."

"Don't push it, Jericho."

"Take Naomi to Meccanicville with you."

"I knew you were going to say that."

"Secretarybird, please take her. Kan sounds dangerous and evil. Lorelei will hold her own. She'll protect her brother. Mikayla can put up a fight too. Naomi won't do well. Please take her with you."

Secretarybird poured the rest of the wine into her glass and gently swirled it. "I suppose I've lived a good life. I helped raise you. You turned out okay."

"What do you mean?"

"Hon, your father will execute me for taking Naomi Maus."

"No!" Jericho cried, grasping her leg. "He values you."

She shook her head. "Not like he used to. I'm afraid Condor, Osprey, and I don't neatly align with who he has become. Vulture toes the line. Those other three are perfect. They are who he wants."

"Sick psychopaths," Jericho grumbled.

"Indeed, my dear. I'll do it."

Jericho wiped off a runaway tear. "You'll take Naomi to Meccanicville?"

"The helicopter seats five, including the pilot. She'll ride next to me.

Condor and Osprey will be there. The other helicopter will have Edmund Rabbit, Birdwing's father, Vulture, and your father. It works out perfectly."

"Secretarybird, hire one more helicopter for me. Have that pilot show up after you all leave." He took note of her eyes widening. "I'm not going to Kan. I'm going to Meccanicville."

She palmed her forehead. "Please, don't do this. It's going to be chaotic enough tonight. Don't get yourself killed."

"Apparently, my blood is worth more than a cave full of gold. You said so. They're not going to kill me or anyone I care about! I'll be right there at Meccanicville in the morning, by your side!"

In tears and at a loss for words, Secretarybird bowed her head and promised him she would do everything she could to help Naomi.

"One more thing: wrap up that fancy chess set in the dining hall," he instructed. "Gift it to Naomi in a couple of weeks from now. It'll be her birthday. We'll give her a birthday party—me, you, Condor, and Osprey, kind of like a real family." He hugged her and buried his head in her bosom.

"I'll see you again in the morning, Jericho. What else is up your sleeve?"

"Other than time, I don't know," he replied.

Mikayla Birdwing

1:48 PM

Something moist and cool soothed Mikayla's forehead as she awakened in Lorelei's bed. She rolled over, and a small washcloth fell off her and smacked the floor. As she reached to pick it up, the soreness in the muscles in her arm traveled up into her shoulder.

She scratched her head, reading the clock on the wall. "How long have I been here? Let's see…it's ten minutes till two. What? So much of the day passed by."

The last thing she remembered was Mrs. Secretarybird taking Naomi from the dorm. She also remembered heading to the cafeteria for breakfast. Whatever happened afterward, those memories were gone. She scrunched into a ball, fighting to remember. It felt like she had been in a coma for the last six hours. Her dreams were all black, like she had been knocked out with anesthesia. She thought for a while, massaging her forehead. She remembered hearing voices but not what they said. She began talking to herself, hoping it would stimulate a memory or two.

"Naomi went with Mrs. Secretarybird. I waited. She didn't come back. I went to get eggs and sausage, but I didn't get any. Did I? I'm so hungry now. I guess I didn't eat. I was going to tell Headmaster Kite that I would do anything to save Dad, but I didn't. Did I? Maybe I did. That's why I'm hungry. I must've done that instead. And then the fog this morning was really bad. I couldn't see in front of me. What made me skip breakfast? Why

179

am I in Lorelei's bed? I remember feeling sick yesterday. I feel much better now."

She took another moment of silence to piece things together, but then she continued talking in circles, only to reach no conclusion. Those memories were gone. Her dad's onyx pawn was still in her pocket. She squeezed it tight, releasing hunger pains.

"I wanted one thing to go my way," she mumbled.

Had yesterday gone as planned, she would be in her dad's backyard, reading a book, or taking a walk in the park to get herself used to Oklahoma's cooler weather. She would've already spent Saturday night drafting the letters to the other Lynbrookians' parents and had them stamped, ready to mail on Monday.

The dormitory's door opened. Mikayla quickly sat on the pawn and her hands. Mr. Vulture entered, carrying a briefcase in one hand and a platter in the other. He pulled up a chair next to Mikayla's bedside. She scooted to the other side of the bed and balled up in a fetal position.

He placed the platter down and revealed what was underneath the lid. A pulpy glass of orange juice next to a plate of sunny side up eggs and a well-seasoned, medium rare tenderloin steak. The yolk oozed over the meat like glaze. A smaller plate had a blueberry muffin toasted to a golden crisp.

"Enjoy the food."

Mikayla shook her head at him.

"Mikayla Birdwing, I know you and I have never spoken to one another before. I am an attorney. I do not intend to hurt you in any way. I know Sparrowhawk did some suspicious things to your food yesterday. I have not done any such thing today. That would be unbecoming of me and most definitely disbarment worthy. Besides, I'm not the one who prepared this. Secretarybird did." He opened the briefcase. "We need you to bring Lorelei here, so eat and let's talk about that."

Clenching the comforter, she inhaled, taking in what felt like her last breath. "Why not send Landon? Lorelei is more than twice my weight and muscular. How am I supposed to get her? I've never been out in the woods before. There're bears, bobcats, snakes. I don't know how to navigate or survive."

He took out a laptop. He wouldn't look her in the eye. "That's a direct order from the headmaster. You want your father?"

"Yes, sir."

"You want your father alive?"

"Please."

"Then you have to give us Lorelei—tonight."

He began typing, then turned the laptop around for her to view. She paused, her grip on the comforter slipping between her fingers. It took every ounce of self-control she possessed to stop herself from pressing her face against the screen. Her dad was handcuffed to a bar embedded in a brick wall, chained next to Mr. Rabbit. Their heads drooped sideways, somewhat lethargic. They seemed deprived of rest.

Where's the other CSB man? Mikayla wondered.

"This is a livestream, not a recording. As soon as I press this button, they will hear us." Mr. Vulture's finger hovered over a button with a microphone emblem. "Want to speak to your father?"

Nodding, she leaned into the screen. Mr. Vulture activated the microphone.

"Dad! Dad! Can you hear me?! Dad!"

Her dad sluggishly lifted his head, turned it left then right in search of the voice.

"Dad! Look up. The camera is up! Dad, look up!"

He weakly threw his head back against the wall and stared directly into the camera. A small smile came—a silent goodbye type of smile.

Mr. Vulture swiveled the laptop around to face himself and turned the screen off. "He's alive, correct?"

"Yes, sir, but—"

"Then you've seen what you needed to see."

He pushed a ballpoint pen her way. She caught the pen before it tumbled off the edge of the bed. Then he set down a paper labeled "NONDISCLOSURE AGREEMENT" in capital letters.

"*In summary,*" he explained sternly, "Headmaster Kite will award you three million dollars, your freedom, and your dad's freedom. All you have to do is sign this and bring Lorelei to us by midnight."

He slapped an identical document beside the other. It had her dad's signature and the date at the bottom.

She gulped. Her mouth became drier every time she swallowed. Her voice came out as a raspy whisper. "I bring back Lorelei...and I get three m-million dollars. Cash?"

"And freedom. Sign the document. Your father already has," he spoke loud enough for her to hear him over her beating heart.

She nodded and read it slowly. It was an agreement stating she was not allowed to disclose anything about Lynbrook to anyone for the rest of her life. Headmaster Kite's signature and the day's date were already scribed below. There was one empty slot for her signature.

She gripped the pen, then put it back down. "I don't see anything about three million dollars or my freedom. This is only about me never speaking about Lynbrook. I don't even think I'm allowed to speak to another Lynbrookian again if I sign this."

"It's in your best interest not to talk. Headmaster Kite's monetary deal is unwritten, a verbal agreement he added after his signature."

She looked him in the eye. "My mom taught me never sign unless everything I want is in writing."

He laughed. "Did Samara teach you the best deals happen under the table or in the judge's chambers? This is one of those deals."

"How do you know my mom's name?"

"Take the deal."

She gritted her teeth, glaring at the NDA, unsure if her dad's signature was authentic. It looked like his chicken scratch writing, but was it truly his? Did he sign under duress? Was he aware of what this meant for him? He'd get no justice for what they'd done to him. He and Mikayla could never talk about it; however, they would have freedom if Headmaster Kite honored his word.

She twirled the pen around her fingers. "All I have to do is bring Lorelei back tonight?"

"Other agreements haven't changed. You're ordered to leave the campus by 8:00 PM this evening."

She bit her bottom lip. "I'd like to speak to all my friends one last time."

"Birdwing, most people do what they have to do." He put his leathery hand on her shoulder. "Take the money and live with regret, darling. Flawless victories don't exist. No one wins with zero regrets."

"What if I want the freedom instead of the money, and I want the CSB guy and all the other Lynbrookians released? Freedom for all, no money."

"I'm sure that could be arranged," Vulture said with a toothy grin.

Hopeful, she stared at her dad's signature again, then quickly scribbled her full name on the line and dated it with crooked numbers. As she glanced at what she had done, she realized her signature was as frantic as her dad's.

Mr. Vulture notarized the documents with the golden wax seal of a swallowtail kite and snatched it from her. He set the stamps aside to let it cool off.

"Rest and take it easy over the next few hours, Birdwing." Mr. Vulture broke the silence. "We will allow you to speak with friends during Freedom Hours. Then, you'll be prohibited from speaking to them again. Do not discuss anything about this agreement."

She lowered her head and mumbled, "Yes, sir."

Mr. Vulture turned his back on her, then left. She traced her finger along the lace trimming on the cuff on her sleeve. She inhaled and slowly breathed out, wondering what she had done.

Hungry, she couldn't take her eyes off the food. She checked underneath the sunny side up eggs and the steak. No sign of human blood. She bit into the steak. As she chewed, a tear rolled down her face. It was delicious. She ate both eggs and the muffin in inconsolable tears. Her own mother had never made breakfast this good. The woman hardly slowed down to do anything nonobligatory for Mikayla. She never went to her chess club matches, helped her pick a homecoming dress, or asked about her day. There was always a big case, bigger than the last, and it needed Atlanta's best environmental prosecutor on the stand.

Did her mother know the Kite Clan took her dad? Would she even care?

Mikayla cried herself to sleep, avoiding spiraling into those thoughts. She didn't dream.

Two and a half hours later, Freedom Hours carried on as usual. The Lynbrookians were released from the library. They dispersed across the campus in their cliques. Mikayla walked amongst them in search of Naomi or Isaiah. She eavesdropped on conversations. Some groups gossiped about the thousands of birds that flew over the campus and the coyotes howling. Others talked about Mr. Falco attacking someone. A few discussed Naomi's disappearance.

Sado sat with a large group of guys gathered around him. He spotted Mikayla, left them, and joined her.

Light posts activated automatically one by one as she and Sado trudged along the cobblestone walkway into the courtyard. Stars shimmered brightly above the milky orange and purplish clouds. One star looked more like a white dot of light shooting in an arc. Now daylight savings time, the sky darkened much sooner. Gnats buzzed around the lightbulbs. Moths swarmed over the surviving milkweed. Cicadas hidden in the grass sounded like tambourines. Still feeling sick, Mikayla was thankful she could breathe out both nostrils again and experience nature's essence.

"They say Isaiah has one eye and a messed-up hand now, like this." Sato bent his wrist ninety-degrees, close to his torso, and closed one eye. He grunted obnoxiously.

"I don't get it." Mikayla shook her head, grimacing. She didn't think Sado's joke was funny. "Have you seen Naomi?"

"Nope. You, Naomi, and Isaiah were missin' all day."

She sighed. "I was sick."

Landon walked by and bumped her shoulder. She felt him slipping something into her hand before he made a sharp turn to go elsewhere.

Mikayla opened the note and read: *Ened Ot Ltak Ot Uyo. eeMt em yb eth apmle rete. On'wt akte pu Oto ucmh fo oyur imte.* The message, translated from Lynbrookian to English, read: *Need to talk to you. Meet me by the maple tree. Won't take up too much of your time.*

"Creepy." Sado shuddered. "He walks 'round with that hood on like a grim reaper."

"Saw him putting bugs in a jar the other day. Never found out why. I don't think he's creepy. I think he's really shy."

"Whatever, he's a mute. He ain't said a word since his sister left Friday night. C'mon, ignore him and let's sit."

"Don't you want to find Naomi? I do."

"For what? She picked the Kites over us. She's a *traitor*."

She glanced at the scarf Naomi had wrapped around her earlier. "I don't want to feel that way, Sado. There's a lot Naomi didn't get to say to me, and I want to talk to her."

"Well, nobody knows where she is. Let's sit."

They sat underneath a Southern magnolia—a spot where it smelled sweet, like honey on citrus—where she and Naomi loved to sit together. Sado scooted closer to her, which caught her off guard. He held her hand. She traced her finger along the dirt with her other hand, avoiding his gaze. At least she wasn't alone, but where was Isaiah? She wanted him instead.

They sat quietly, listening to the crickets and the rustle of the trees. Iridescent clouds surrounded the full moon like the mother-of-pearl coating on an oyster shell. Beau Heights caught her eye. She couldn't help but stop and take in how immense and mysterious she was. She imagined a beautifully crafted matrix of brick, gears, and a wooden spiral staircase ascending upward to a loft surrounding four crystal clock faces.

"Mika-Chou, why won't you look at me?" Sado asked.

A small, forced smile raised her cheeks. "I have a lot on my mind, and I'm trying to think of everything but that stuff."

"You think if we had met in either of our hometowns, you'd date me?" he asked.

Here he goes again. Mikayla pulled her hand away. "I think we'd be friends."

"That's it? Nothin' more?"

"I don't think so."

He sighed and mocked Mikayla's "I don't get it" from earlier.

"You don't get what?"

"You and Marksman."

Mikayla felt like what she and Isaiah had was nobody's business.

"He's a goofball *and* clumsy. You and I are popular. In a normal school, people like us would be together. Ya wouldn't look twice at him. Tell me I'm wrong." Sado put his palm on her knee, easing his fingertips up to her thigh. He gave her a seductive look with a daring undertone that said *I bet you won't stop me.*

Mikayla slapped him in the mouth and pushed him down. She staggered onto her feet and kicked dirt in his face. Lynbrookians pointed and began whispering. The girls laughed, cheering her on. Sado stared forlornly at the ground.

Mikayla stormed off towards the maple tree, feeling spiteful towards Landon but mostly still upset with Sado. She felt like Landon should trade places with her, go out there, and find his own sister.

At the tree, Landon leaned against the trunk, folding creases into a sheet of red construction paper. He had that same caterpillar from days ago perched on his shoulder. Without saying anything, he tossed the folded red paper to her.

"My uncle told me to tell you this, but I don't feel like talking to you, so here."

She cupped the origami butterfly in her palms. Her fingers flipped a panel above the wing where the letter "S" written in black ink bled through the paper. She carefully unfolded the creases until the words "when you learn our other family secret" written in the center struck her fingers motionless. In cursive, under another flap, she read: *Rfogive Su Sa Ew Vhae Rfogiven Rouselves.* It translated to *Forgive us as we have forgiven ourselves.* Mikayla stood for a while, not sure what Mr. Fowl was trying to tell her.

"I gotta go," Landon said. "My uncle said we're leaving soon."

"Leaving to where?"

"Kan."

"Where's that?" Mikayla waited for him to elaborate, but he didn't. "Do you know where Naomi is?"

"She's in the bal-*chatri*. She's coming with us to Kan."

"She's in what? What is Kan?"

"Bye, Mikayla. I'll see you on the plane when you get back with Lorelei."
He squeezed his hoodie's drawstrings to hide his face.

Mikayla watched him walk off. Grimacing, she threw the origami inside
the first trashcan she found. She felt no need to put effort into mulling
over that interaction. Landon hadn't taken it seriously, so she didn't feel she
should either.

#

Twenty minutes till six, the infirmary doors remained open downstairs
in the main building. Bars covered the window on Isaiah's door. The sign
taped on it read: SEND ON LAST FLIGHT OF THE NIGHT. DO NOT
DISTURB.

It was unlocked, but she knocked first. Nothing happened. She looked
through the window. The lights were off, and the glass was chilly. With the
hall clear on her left and right, she twisted the doorknob and stepped inside.

Across the room, Isaiah rested in his bed, not moving. His left eye was
covered with an eyepatch, and he wore a cast on his right arm. She somehow
felt his pain from looking at all his injuries. Her hands trembled, and she
felt flustered, leaning her back against the door.

His uninjured arm dangled over the side of the mattress. She tip-toed
closer, knelt, and firmly grasped that hand. It was icy all the way from his
wrist to his fingertips. There was a pulse, strong.

A lump or some sort of tightness clogged Mikayla's throat to the point
she was forced to cry to relieve the pain. She positioned herself to rest her
head on his chest. His heartbeat was steady. She patted his bruised forehead.
Some of his curls draped the back of her hand.

"Isaiah, what happened?" She wiped her tears from her face and his with
her sleeve.

His face was still. She waited for him to react, but nothing came. She
leaned closer, caressing his bruised jawline and cupping his hand gently
with her other hand. All the blood in her body rushed up to her cheeks.
Something about his expression turned more relaxed, less tense.

"Hey." He opened his one eye. His smile reached it, intense as if he still
had both.

"You're up!" She scrambled off him. "What happened? Are you in pain?"

"A lot. I got initiated into the US Pirate Association."

"I'm glad you're okay for jokes."

"I'm a pirate now, Mika, so I guess I gotta be funny." He gave her a serious look. "You were there? Forgot what happened?"

Mikayla shrugged. "I'm sorry…I can't remember."

"Lucky." Isaiah sighed.

He explained what had led up to Mr. Falco's attack.

"Why did you tamper with their inventory?"

"I figured you needed the extra help, so I did what I could to disadvantage them. I also didn't want them to be able to use weapons so easily." He paused, clenching the sheet. "I've been worried sick about you all day. Don't tell me Mr. Sparrowhawk hurt you?"

"I don't know," she shuddered. "I woke up with a headache in the dorm. That's all I know."

"I'm so sorry, Mika."

"It's not your fault."

"No, I mean about everything. Your plan. Your dad. Me being an idiot."

She was at a loss for words. They got quiet.

"There's a sign on your door that says 'send on last flight of the night.'"

He bit his lip. "I guess they're sending me to Meccanicville with Lorelei and Landon for what I've done with the ammo."

"Is that what they've told you?"

"They told me nothing, Mika. But we both knew this day would come. I turn eighteen on the twelfth of next month."

"This is it? I won't see you again?"

"We'll meet again in February?"

Mikayla shook her head, reluctant to share the details of the non-disclosure agreement she signed earlier that morning.

"This sucks," he said.

"Yeah."

He opened his palm. "Wanna stay?"

Nodding, she took his hand and leaned into him. He managed to sit up on his elbow. He winced from the pain, then drew her closer by the small of her back. She made it easy for him to pull her in, recognizing that without his dominant arm, all his movements were awkward. Her legs bumped into the metal bed frame. They laughed softly.

She turned around and sat on the edge of the bed, on his left side. He sat up all the way beside her before plopping onto his back, yanking her down with him awkwardly. They laughed again, then got quiet as they realized what was happening. The bed was soft. They were alone. The infirmary outside was silent, lacking Raptor supervision. It felt like the entire world had forgotten about them and they had nobody but each other.

He combed his bangs over his eyepatch. She scooted closer. He pulled away.

"Sorry. I haven't kissed a girl in a while…a while meaning never."

"Wait, you and Naomi didn't kiss, not even a peck on the cheek?"

"Never came up." His hair moved off the eyepatch. "*Ugh.* Falco ruined me."

"No," she said, touching his face. "After my brain surgery, I had a shaved head. Got lots of nasty looks. Got bullied. That was a hard year, but I got through it somehow. You're the most positive person I've met in a while. You'll bounce back fast. It's a new face to love."

Isaiah chuckled nervously, turning red all over. She moved his hair away. A howling coyote broke the tension, and they laughed. Mikayla got up and opened the blinds, revealing the full moon. Grunting in pain, Isaiah slowly readjusted and sat up against the headboard. He tilted his head towards the right side of the bed. She climbed in beside him, twiddling her thumbs. His eye softened.

"It's easier on me if you're on my right. I can see you better." He got quiet, then said, "Before I asked Naomi out, I thought you and Sado were together because he was constantly around you, doing stuff for you."

She sighed. She didn't want to make him feel guilty, but at the same time, she needed him to know how frustrated she had been. "I know. He was hard to make go away, and then it didn't help that in the back of my mind, I felt like you asked Naomi out to get back at me."

He shook his head, looking regretful. "I didn't mean it to. I did it because she's your best friend, and I wanted to get close to you without *him* looking over our shoulders," he said, referring to Sado's persistent nature. "It was the best my peanut brain could come up with. It worked."

Mikayla chuckled. "It did, but I was…jealous."

"There was nothing to be jealous about." Isaiah grinned. "Between you and me, I think Naomi was using me too. That's why she didn't care about *us*."

"You think so?"

"Oh, yeah." He paused. "I think her and Jericho Kite are into each other, deep. I gotta admit that if they had a secret fling for months, they did an excellent job hiding it. These last couple of days…sloppy."

Mikayla reflected. There were people getting what they wanted at her expense. Naomi was closing in on marrying one of the richest men in the world. Sparrowhawk had punished her for humiliating him, although she had no idea how she'd managed to do that. Headmaster Kite had trapped her into being used for gains beyond her understanding. There was no way an evil man like him was going to benefit nothing from that NDA.

With little time left and someone special by her side, Mikayla finally had her chance to enjoy a shrivel of agency in her life.

"Isaiah, don't you think there's something we can do, together?"

"Like what, Mika?"

"You know."

"I don't get what you're asking."

"Are you going to make me say it?"

"Say what?"

They stared at the moon for a while, not saying anything else. Their nervous smiles faded into rapt gazes at one another, silently telling each other yes but neither budging.

Jericho Kite IV

While Jericho was standing in the bal-chatri, an insane idea popped into his head. He thought about calling Alexander Ravensbourne. He had no idea how it would go, but he needed a level of help he couldn't find elsewhere. Condor was the last Raptor Admin to have been in contact with Ravensbourne's personnel, but he was reluctant to share how their conversation went. And now Condor was gone with the rest, preparing for departure.

Jericho made his way towards Condor's quarters to see if he had taken notes on the call somewhere. Inside, Jericho stumbled into a mountain of energy drinks, coffee cups, and scrunched balls of damp facial tissue. A hundred computer monitors lit the room in the shade of the blue screen of death. Every single display had an animated cartoon image of a cowboy beating a dead horse and an error message informing him that the machine had been irreparably damaged by malware.

There was an additional message: THIS IS ALEXANDER HERE TO TELL YOU THAT YOU SUCK AT DEFENDING NETWORKS. YOU'RE A FLIPPING 34 YO LOSER, MATTHEW JACOBS! IT MUST SUCK TO BE 34 AND STILL A LOSER. NOBODY LOVES YOU, NOT BECAUSE YOU'RE 34 BUT BECAUSE YOU'RE A LOSER AND 34. THAT PRETTY RUSSIAN GIRL YOU WERE CONNECTING ONLINE WITH WAS ONE OF OURS. SHE'S A HONEYPOT AND A MAN! YOU'RE A DISGRACE.

YOU CAN'T CALL YOURSELF A REAL NETWORK ANALYST.

Matthew Jacobs was Condor's real name. Feeling bad for Condor, Jericho left the room and went back into the bal-chatri to ruminate.

"No wonder Condor looked like crap this morning. I guess I'm playing with fire."

He had no idea how to deal with Alexander. The man seemed unpredictable, more like lightning than fire. Condor had managed the Trinity's network for years. Alexander's people had struck it down like nothing.

He paced back and forth within the circle of moonlight that shone down from the skylight above. A ray of light washed over him like a streaming shower. Everyone except for Sparrowhawk had left their quarters and were downstairs on the lawn below on the east side of campus.

Jericho thought about smoking and how he would gently inhale, letting it fill his lungs. He missed leaning against a post and closing his eyes, listening to the sounds of the night with a cigarette between his fingers.

"Get it together, man. Think straight, you addict." He knocked on his forehead with his knuckles.

Four searchlights on the horizon whitened the stained glass on his right side. The rotor wash of four helicopters deafened his hearing. At a low altitude, they flew together in a tight formation, directly over the skylight. The walls and glass vibrated all around him. He ran into his room and went out onto his balcony where he could watch the helicopters land.

"They came early," he whispered. "That means I'm stuck with Sparrowhawk already."

Below, everyone lined up for departure. In the first helicopter were Edmund Rabbit and Robert Birdwing, both handcuffed. Vulture followed closely behind them. The men looked defeated and tired as they stepped into their seats. Last to board was Jericho's father. Their pilot loaded their luggage and closed the door.

At the same time, Falcon boarded the second helicopter while the pilot loaded luggage. Kestrel, in high heels, stepped on the pilot's hand, and then she kicked him in the face with the point of her heel because she felt like he was in her way. The bounty hunter, bandaged and sluggish, struggled with the climb up the steps. Falcon snagged him by his collar and threw him to the other side of the helicopter before slamming their helicopter's door shut.

At the third helicopter, Eric Fowl had his back pressed against the obstinate pony, shoving it to force it up the stairs. Landon joined him. Naomi stood behind them, biting her fingers.

Jericho leaned forward. "C'mon. C'mon. Now's the time. Everyone who'd care won't see it."

Secretarybird, in line for the last helicopter, waited until Condor and Osprey boarded. She quickly ran over to Naomi and grabbed her hand. Naomi snagged her duffle bag and stumbled behind her to board on the opposite side. The two men were visibly upset but let the pilot load the remaining luggage and close the door.

Yes! Jericho pumped his fist. "I owe you, Secretarybird. When I get to Meccanicville, I'll make sure my father doesn't lay a hand on you."

Two pilots helped Landon and Eric Fowl load the pony onto their helicopter. They tossed the luggage in behind them and closed the door. Five minutes later, all four helicopters departed.

Jericho reentered the bal-chatri. *And then there were two.*

He wondered what Sparrowhawk was up to. The man had gone missing after his humiliating moment at the meeting this morning. Jericho rubbed his hands together, ridding his fingers of the outside chill. He passed the stained glass of Sparrowhawk's mighty imagery and pressed his ear up against his door. The man was in there, talking to himself. Jericho could barely hear it, so he quietly cracked open the door.

All four walls were covered with drawings, diagrams, scholarly journals, and documents, all interlaced with yarn like a detective's evidence board. The floor was covered with broken vases, cotton from ripped pillows, torn bedsheets, and clothes. Jericho peered closer, horrified. One corner of the room had been dedicated to pictures of Mikayla Birdwing's movements. A picture showed her lying her head on Isaiah Marksman's lap near a patch of dandelions as he blew on a dandelion with his eyes crossed goofily. Many of the pictures showed Mikayla and Isaiah cuddling in various positions with each other in inconspicuous areas on the campus. A knife had been lodged into the center of Isaiah's forehead on a picture of him nearly kissing Mikayla in the courtyard.

"I'll kill you, gatekeeper!" Sparrowhawk drew an X on a picture of Eric Fowl with a red marker and cursed at the top of his lungs again. "You lied to us. You knew all along who the Handler really was, didn't you, you sonofa—oh, when I get to Kan, Eric Fowl, I'll kill you. You won't stand a chance in those mines. I'll hide your body where the sun doesn't shine!"

Jericho tried to ease the door closed.

"I know you're out there, Kite Boy. Get in here."

"You don't order me around, Sparrowhawk."

Sparrowhawk crooked his neck. *"Get in here."* His voice carried a demonic undertone.

Against his free will, Jericho opened the door and entered. He beheld the immense destruction Sparrowhawk had inflicted on his quarters.

Sparrowhawk closed the door. "You thought Mikayla Birdwing was the only one I can control? I can control whoever I want. Don't forget about what I did to her father. *Kneel!*"

Jericho collapsed to his knees. "I can't move. How are you doing this to me?"

"I put my blood in that tomato soup you ate an hour ago," he said. "I told you I will ensure you keep your word, *Honorable Kite.*"

Sparrowhawk snatched a diagram off the wall and shoved it in Jericho's face. It showed the eight lunar phases. First quarter, full moon, and third quarter were all circled. The paper was titled THE CYCLE OF THE HUNT.

"Tonight is the full moon. You know what this means?" Sparrowhawk asked.

"Get inside my head and work for the answer."

"Your mind isn't worth searching. It'd be like walking by tumbleweeds on an open field. I know Secretarybird explained Blood Leash to you earlier."

"She didn't talk about that moon crap."

"This isn't 'moon crap.' It's what you depend upon, Equestrian. One week from now, yours will be the dominant element, and I know you plan on going to Meccanicville."

"Not true."

"It is true, you moron. Weren't you listening to me earlier? When I was inside of Mikayla, I saw the future. You plan on launching a coup, and you'll win. Why wouldn't you? Texas is full of horses on ranches. Wide open land. It'll be your playground."

"I don't know what you're talking about."

"I told you. I saw a snippet of the future," he said through his teeth. "Mikayla saw—or whoever's blood she'll possess saw it. You'll marry Naomi Maus. Three children. Lots of guards. Oh, it's grand. A sight to see." Sparrowhawk turned his back on him. "You'll get your way. A Kite wants what he wants—"

"And I'll get what I want," Jericho completed the saying with a smile.

Sparrowhawk bent to Jericho's eye level and pinched his cheek. "Now that was a fun moment there, Kite Boy. I bet you pictured it too. You'd be all grown up. Living on your own with a pretty, faithful woman. Power. Control. I can take that away. All I have to do is send you to Kan instead."

"Did you figure out if Isaiah Marksman's the Handler or not?" Jericho asked. He wanted to get under the smug, prideful man's skin.

"Your father didn't bother looking into it. He sent Vulture to speak to Mikayla to put her out there chasing down Lorelei. He didn't even talk to Eric Fowl."

"Sounds like nobody believes you. You're driving yourself insane."

"Isaiah Marksman is the Handler, and tonight is the night he dominates. But I will already know what's next, so I'll be ready for him."

"Okay, God," Jericho muttered sarcastically. He chuckled. "Doesn't Isaiah only have one eye and a broken wrist now? Oh, what a mighty god you'll be when you take him out."

"Wait until we get to Kan. You'll be stripped of your title, banished!"

"I saw the way Falcon and Kestrel treated the hunter. Looks like Blood Leash Capable people are underclassmen and Pure Bloods like me outclass you."

Sparrowhawk's eye twitched. He stood up, sauntered to the back wall of photos, and took hold of the knife that he had stabbed through Isaiah's forehead. He pulled out three more daggers from his pocket, then lodged the knife over his shoulder back into Isaiah's forehead. He threw one dagger across the room at a picture of Lorelei sulking alone with a pigeon in the courtyard. Another at Mikayla laughing with Naomi and a large group of girls. The last dagger went into the floor between Jericho's legs.

"You four won't get the best of me tonight! I already know what you're going to do! I will make every single one of you bend to my will!" Sparrowhawk caught his breath and fixed his disheveled hair. "We will begin the Lynbrookians' executions at 8:30 PM. Now, *get out!*"

Suddenly, Jericho felt his muscles relax. He flexed his fingers and toes to make sure he had free will again. Careful not to slice himself on the dagger, he rose and fled Sparrowhawk's quarters. The door closed, and Sparrowhawk went back to yelling and breaking things.

Jericho's hands were shaking. He really wanted a cigarette. "I dodged a bullet because he thinks I'm stupid. And I kinda am, but at least he doesn't know what I'll do next. And I don't either."

He sprinted downstairs to his father's office. The entire room had been ransacked. Books had been thrown everywhere, and all the drawers were left open, emptied. He sat in the massive desk chair. It was like a throne.

He spread his hands apart on the desk, feeling for the loose slot. His father hid passwords and numbers underneath puzzle pieces embedded in his desk. A part of a thin wood slat shifted. Jericho dug his fingernail through and lifted it up. He unfolded the paper and saw the labeled numbers. It was one of the few things his father bothered sharing with him.

Jericho picked up the jade and turquoise phone and put it to his ear, upside down. The dial tone sounded far away. He flipped it around and heard it loud and clear.

He pressed the numbers. His heart started racing.

"Confirmation number." The voice sounded sweet.

"Code zero-one-three-seventeen-five," Jericho read from the paper.

"Say request, Jericho Kite third in his name."

"This is his son. I'd like to speak to Alexander Ravensbourne." He gulped.

He had never made an important phone call, let alone spoken on the phone before.

"Standby, Jericho Kite fourth in his name. Alexander will be with you right away. A brief hold."

"A hold? What's that mean?" Jericho asked.

A prerecorded message took over. Soft music played in the background. *"Thanks for calling Alexander's Electric Company, where we value your static satisfaction! Standby. Processing request. You are on hold. Standby. Processing request. You are on—"*

"Surrender yet?"

Jericho clenched the phone. Alexander's voice was feminine, pleasant, eerily soothing.

"Not calling to surrender, Alexander."

He chuckled lightly. "Oh, it's just you, Jericho. Please call me Alex. We're the same age, same echelon. No need to be formal with me, my friend."

"We're not friends."

"Not yet." A pause. The sound of sipping. "I've been waiting on this call, though I expected I'd be speaking to your father."

"My father isn't available."

"That's terrible, Jericho. I've heard that you're sheltered—a horse who's never left the stable."

Alexander had a prominent Northern accent, strong and tight, no twang and drawl like the Southern voices he was used to. Jericho felt like he was speaking with a foreigner.

"I'll cut to the chase, asshole. You beat my father."

"Well, Jericho, I know I said drop the formalities, but it'll please me if you don't cuss. My kitten is nearby in bed with me." He whispered. "He can't take words like that. By the way, I already know that I beat your father. Where is he?"

"He sent me to call on his behalf."

The light chuckle again. "Oh, darling, you are funnier than they say you are. Now, where is he?" Alexander growled. The aggressive side Jericho had heard about had emerged.

Jericho took a deep breath. He didn't want Alexander to launch an attack on Meccanicville.

"My father is headed to Birmingham to negotiate a deal with the Chemical Safety Board."

Alexander's gentle voice returned. "Oh, goodie! Good for him! I suppose I'll lie low and wait for the icky, nasty gas pipelines to be gotten rid of, and then I'll move in later. I've purchased tons of copper. Definitely going to install some fiber optics down below the clocktower, then I'll update the electric grid. Lynbrook has an antique, gothic feel to it. I'll keep the gothic part but make it more modern, more innovative. It'll be *amazing*," he tittered.

"F—screw you."

"You haven't heard? I already have a partner. You and I should speak more often so that you're not out of the loop, darling." He took another sip. "Okay, let's see. Your father is in Birmingham? Good, good. Well, that's all I wanted to know upfront. Now you can tell me why you're calling."

"I was calling to tell you that you can have Lynbrook now."

Dead air. A sip. "*Mhmm*, that's a good mojito. Jericho, have you ever had a mojito before?"

"I don't know what that is."

Light chuckle. "Oh, Jericho. You poor, sheltered soul. I suppose you don't know what sex is either."

Jericho couldn't believe this was *the* Alexander Ravensbourne who had been coming after Kite Express.

"Jericho, it seems as though I've stunned you. I'll explain. It's when the mommy horse and the daddy horse fall in love and go *boink, boink*."

"I know what sex is!" He wanted to slam the phone down.

"Just checking. Just checking. The Kite Clan has a history of being so, so prudish, which contradicts your barbarian nature. Explain that. Anyway, I had to make sure you're okay. You have had sex before, haven't you? Because you can know what it is without ever doing it, get what I'm asking?"

Jericho breathed fast out of his nose. "Did you hear me, Alex? I said you can have Lynbrook."

"Oh, yes! I definitely, definitely heard that. My Electric Company and I so happen to already be in Talladega, servicing your area. They can swoop by as their last stop of the night." A sip.

"But there's a catch," Jericho muttered.

"Baby, there's always a catch. You know what? I like you. You're much more fun to talk to than your father. Call me Al."

"No."

"Now, Jericho. If you want me to come, you have to call me Al."

"No."

"Fine. I won't come tonight. Thanks for calling."

"Wait!" Jericho clenched the phone. "I know what you want. You want to destroy the Trinity."

"It's not even a want anymore, baby! The Trinity is actively collapsing right before your eyes. You see, the pieces were laid into place for me years ago." A sip, then another. The sound of ice clanking against glass. "Your father made his bed when he didn't fix the pipeline under Beau ten years ago. I knew Lynbrook had another natural gas leakage as far back as August because my infrared satellites pointed at your school detected the fumes. Our tech is very high-end and sensitive to even small leaks. Ever seen what methane looks like through an infrared lens?"

Jericho's eyebrows furrowed. "No."

"Of course, you haven't! You poor, sheltered horse! Now, where was I? Wait a minute." A sip. "Oh, yeah, and then your father invited those Pure Blood Leash cousins of yours into Lynbrook and treated them like human trash. Oh, Lorelei hates your father's guts. I thought about having her call the EPA, but they carry guns and have power. They would've have gotten to have all the fun putting him in prison." He laughed and quickly composed himself. "But then you would've inherited the Trinity, and I'd run circles around you. Boring!"

"Why do you want the Trinity so bad? Why come after it?"

"Well, my family is already dominating in energy production, and that's getting dull. The truth is my gripe is with your father, not you. Back in July, at an energy convention in Denver, your father's pork rind-munching bodyguard bumped into me and called me a faggot. Nobody nearby laughed out loud, but I saw them smirking, looking away. Snickering."

"Oh, Falcon," Jericho said under his breath, slapping his palm to his brow.

"No, a falcon didn't call me a faggot. Raymond Johnson called me a faggot. I call those *Raptor Admins* by their government names." He said Raptor Admin facetiously. "Your father didn't even apologize because he's a bigot too. His brothers are bigots."

"Is this why you're coming after us?"

"I'm not coming after you. I'm coming after the Trinity. What happens to you is collateral."

"What if I apologize? I'm truly sorry he called you that and even more sorry my father didn't display professionalism standing up for you."

"Too late! I'm petty, Jericho. I'm a very petty person. I asked my father, can I play with Kite Express? My father said no. Kite Express is his. I said pretty, pretty please can I play with Kite Express? My father said fine, you can play with the Trinity!" His aggressive side emerged again. He laughed maniacally. "You Kites kill people who get in your way. That's how you operate. Impulsive decisions. But, baby, I'm a Ravensbourne. We like a long game—a long, long game." He suddenly giggled. "What, honey? Huh, I'm flirting with him a little. C'mon, you know tonight you're my one and only, kitten. Get me another drink, will you?"

Jericho heard a smack and another laughing man in the background. He sighed, staring at a dot on his father's desk. "Al, the catch? You ready for it?"

"Yes, I am!"

"I want you to leave Meccanicville and Kan alone in exchange for Lynbrook."

"Huh? Those are the fun places. How am I supposed to brag about shafting the Trinity if I only get a third of the way through? Okay, it's a deal. I'll leave Meccanicville and Kan alone."

"Really?"

"Sure thing. I'll give you three years, baby. I wanna watch you grow up. Nice 'n strong."

"Three years?"

"Uh-huh. Is that not long enough? I can throw in another day or two."

Jericho balled his fist. "Three is plenty."

"Oh, you're wonderful. Now tell me all the gossip. Why are you giving Lynbrook away? *Hmm?* It's your home. The only home you've ever known. The only place you've ever been in your entire, pathetic life." He laughed sadistically.

Jericho waited patiently for the laughter to end. He answered, "The government won't have to find out about the leak. The rest of the Trinity will operate."

And Alexander Ravensbourne could be held liable for the dead bodies in the forest beyond the gate. Jericho left that out.

"Okay, okay. I sympathize with you there. The government can get bent! Yeah, I'll take good care of New Lynbrook. No government will show up." He chuckled. "Did you hear me call it New Lynbrook? That's what it's going to be called from here on out. I suggest you drop the term the Trinity. *Awkward…* Makes no sense after tonight, heh! Get what I mean? Maybe you can call it the Duet. Or, whatever, don't mind me. You know what? Don't even stress it. I'm taking them all anyway, year three and one day."

Jericho gritted his teeth. He had one more reason to sacrifice Lynbrook. "There are over fifty Lynbrookians here whose lives need saving. I need your company here by 10:00 PM because my father ordered for them to be executed. The executions are supposed to start at 8:30 PM, but I can stall them."

"This night keeps getting better and better. You know when I take over that those Lynbrookians will be mine."

Jericho dropped his head. He supposed leaving the Lynbrookians under Alexander's control was better than death or the Trinity pipeline. "I know, but there are some you can't take."

"Now, Jericho. I'm greedy. I want them *all.*"

"You're not getting them all, bastard!"

"Who am I not getting?"

"Lorelei, one that's Blood Leash Capable, and an alleged Pure Blood Leasher. They're going to Kan. They're already property of the Victor of Kan."

"I don't give a f-flip! Oh, kitten, I had to catch myself there. I almost swore." Alexander broke out into uncontrollable laughter, then he took a sip. The other man in the background giggled. "You want me to forgo two Pure Blood Leashers and a Capable? Do you think I'm as obtuse as you are? You didn't think this call through, did you?"

"You won't know who they are."

"Baby, I'll be able to tell. My Electric Company doesn't operate like barbarians in the dark age. Nice talking to you. See you tonight. We'll be there around 10:30. Wear something that shows off your chest. They say you're a big, muscular guy!"

The phone clicked.

"Thanks for calling Alexander's Electric Company, where we value your static satisfaction! Standby for a brief survey. Your satisfaction is our upmost priority. Rating us five stars confirms we've pleasured you."

Jericho snatched the phone out of the wall and hurled it through the bay window. "Fuck."

Mikayla Birdwing

7:40 PM

Mikayla's shoes, scarf, and sweater were strewn across the foot of the bed. All the rest of her clothes were on the floor. She had her arms wrapped around Isaiah while he lightly petted her, occasionally kissing her cheek. She giggled, leaning in for another long kiss on his lips.

The clock on the wall showed her their time was almost up.

"No," she whispered, breaking away.

His smile faded. He sat up and read the clock. "Ah, darn."

"I have to leave now." Panting, she jumped out of the bed so quickly her head began spinning. Her hands scrambled for her undergarments. "It went by so fast. I got caught up in it." She put her skirt back on crooked, buttoned her blouse's buttons, and wrapped the scarf around her neck. It covered the hickeys on her nape. Her stockings felt bunched up from putting them back on in a hurry, and she had to fix them too.

"Wait." Isaiah held her shoulder. "Slow down for a sec."

Mikayla paused. His hand slid down her arm, taking her fingertips into his. They sat quietly for another two minutes.

"What now?" Isaiah squeezed. His palm was sweaty.

"I don't know," she mumbled.

She had no idea she had it in her, but she liked it.

"Okay, well, I guess this is the part where we say bye."

"I'm not a goodbye person."

He looked directly into her eyes. "If or when I get out of this place or Meccanicville, I'll find you."

She looked away. "You'll never see me again."

"Why?"

"Because," she began before letting out a long sigh, "I signed an NDA, okay? Don't tell anyone. I'm not supposed to mention this. Vulture came to me this morning. He said I have until midnight to find Lorelei and bring her back here. Then, I can have my dad back, and I'm not allowed to see or speak to anyone from this place ever again."

"Oh, Mika," Isaiah said. He fell back against the headboard, not saying anything else for a while.

Mikayla finished adjusting her clothes and hair.

Eventually, Isaiah began unclasping a chain from his neck. It took a minute because he was using his nondominant hand. "Here, I want you to have this." He handed her his necklace.

"I can't take that."

"Take it."

Mikayla hesitated before she slowly put it around her neck. She leaned in, eyes twinkling. "What's the TY engraved on it mean?"

"Ty. That was my old hound's name. He was shot by another hunter by accident in the forest. Sorry, it's not romantic."

"I'm honored you gave this to me."

His smile lightly puckered. She kissed him again.

The door slammed against the wall, putting a dent in the drywall. Mr. Sparrowhawk lowered his leg and stormed inside with a pair of handcuffs.

"Hey there, doggy boy! Thought I forgot about you?"

"Who's doggy boy?" Isaiah asked.

Wide-eyed, Mikayla tore away from Isaiah. She wiped her lips, crossed her arms behind her back, and pressed her thighs together. Isaiah covered his bare chest with the sheets. Mr. Sparrowhawk paused and glared skeptically, as if his instinct knew what they had been doing for the last two hours. He ripped the sheets back, horrified.

"What gives!" Isaiah growled, taking the sheet and covering himself again.

"Having sex? With a broken arm and one eye? You determined bastard," Mr. Sparrowhawk muttered before handcuffing Isaiah's unbroken arm to the bed post. "There's blood on the sheets. Why didn't I see this coming? Damn it! I should've prevented this from happening!"

He took a syringe out of his pocket and stuck it into Isaiah's neck. Mikayla glared at it, then narrowed her eyes at Mr. Sparrowhawk.

"You might've forgotten what this is, but your nervous system remembers," he mocked Mikayla.

"I don't understand what you're saying," she said.

"You and doggy boy have a Link. He's on your Leash."

"What?" she asked.

"Mika, ignore him! He's crazy! Leave!" Isaiah shouted.

Mr. Sparrowhawk snapped his attention to her. He looked deranged. "You heard him. You have a contract to uphold!"

"No." Mikayla shook her head, backing away slowly.

"Don't worry about me, Mika. I'll be..." Isaiah began fading as if Mr. Sparrowhawk had put a sleeping spell on him. He struggled to get the words out before drifting off.

In her rush out of the infirmary, she immediately bumped into Jericho Kite as he left his father's office. He stumbled forward, brushing the wrinkles off his blazer.

"I'm sorry, Honorable Kite," she muttered, running away.

"Hey, Mikayla!"

Trembling, she jerked to a halt and turned her entire body. "Yes, Honorable Kite?"

"Naomi is going to be safe. Tell Lorelei to save some fight in her for tonight. We've got work to do. If you can get her back here before ten, that'd be nice."

"Mr. Vulture said I have until midnight."

"Shoot for ten."

Mr. Sparrowhawk reentered the hallway, walking towards them. Mikayla ran away. Outside, the Lynbrookians began migrating towards the south side of the campus, headed for the dorms. She continued north towards the fence.

"Mikayla, you're going the wrong way! Mikayla!" one of them shouted.

She ignored them.

Mr. Fowl had left the gate partially open and all four of its padlocks unlocked. She took one last look over her shoulder at Lynbrook's steep, hipped roof, wondering what Jericho meant when he had said Naomi was safe. Was she hidden somewhere?

Preparing for the cold, dry air, she tightened her scarf. It still smelled like Naomi's perfume on some threads and like Isaiah on others. She trudged forward.

After about twenty minutes, every small branch or twig that snapped felt like splinters pricking the arches of her feet. She felt every uneven surface, every rock. She began chafing. Her lungs and the muscles in her legs felt like they were about to burst. Thinking about the worst happening to her dad and friends propelled her forward.

Croaking crickets and cicadas hushed suddenly. Appearing from dark pockets amongst trees and bushes, packs of coyotes trotted towards her. She froze, stiffening like a board. The biggest coyote, possibly the leader, approached her. As it sniffed, she realized how fast she had been rushing since she left the infirmary and how slow the coyote moved as it inspected her. Licking its snout, it breathed out, shook off, then went along its way. The rest followed. Dozens of golden, focused eyes surrounded her and soon revealed themselves as more coyotes. A few pups tagged along. They all disregarded her on their migration towards Lynbrook. She counted at least eighty.

Trembling, Mikayla collapsed. Leaves fell around her. Above, Lorelei dropped from a tree branch with her knees slightly tucked. As she neared the ground, she untucked, landed on her feet, and went into a controlled roll that propelled her until she stood directly in front of Mikayla. She immediately fell, grasping her ankle. Feathers, animal entrails, and dirt were stuck onto her torn clothes. Her hair, disheveled and littered with twigs, was tangled around her whistle's chain. Her barn owl swooped from the tree and landed beside her.

"Ugh! I thought I could handle that." Lorelei grimaced.

"Why were you up in the trees?" Mikayla asked.

"I don't know, maybe it's because there were like a hundred coyotes." She grabbed Mikayla's arms. "Look, if you're here to kill me, get it over with."

"What? I don't want to kill you!"

"Why are you here?"

"To bring you back."

"I'd rather die. I felt death over and over and over, three times. I felt it every time one of them died."

"What are you talking about? Who died?"

"My hawks, Mikayla!" Lorelei made a fist. There were dozens of half-healed cuts along her wrist.

Mikayla calmed her voice. "Call me Mika, okay? I'm not here to hurt you."

"You want me to call you Mika, like your friends?"

Mikayla nodded. Lorelei fell onto her side, got quiet, and began sobbing. The owl hooted softly. Mikayla sat with them, patting Lorelei's back, incredibly confused.

Hopefully Lorelei will explain, she thought. Their time was running out.

Jericho Kite IV

8:50 PM

Jericho checked his wristwatch. Alexander would arrive in one hour and forty minutes—if he was a man of his word. He looked up from his watch, facing the Lynbrookians standing in a horizontal line before him. Boys were separated from the girls, each grasping a shovel. They were on the east side of the campus.

"Honorable Kite, please explain what's happening," someone down the line cried.

"Are we gonna get killed like the teachers?"

"Where's Naomi?"

"And Mikayla?"

"We've been good, loyal…"

"I thought you were the good Kite."

"The Avian twins are gone. Y'all killed them! They ain't do nothing!"

"Can we go to Meccanicville instead?"

"Send us home!"

Many of them began chanting "Send us home!"

Jericho stood with his hands behind his back, keeping a straight, unemotional expression. He took shallow breaths, fighting back tears.

He whispered, "I'm sorry my home hasn't been good to you."

Sparrowhawk drove up in a red flatbed pick-up. The Lynbrookians silenced as soon as the engine turned off. He stepped out of the vehicle,

208

armed with a rifle geared with an extended magazine. Wrapped around his torso was a bandolier full of ammo and syringes full of blood. He stood on Jericho's right side, holding the rifle at port arms.

"Any objections?" Sparrowhawk asked the Lynbrookians.

They stared straight ahead. Some shook their heads.

"Dig six feet deep. That's your final order," Jericho ordered, staring through them. His eyes were fixed westward on Beau Heights.

Coyotes howled in the distance as the Lynbrookians began digging.

"You hear that, *Honorable Kite?*" Sparrowhawk addressed Jericho spitefully in the presence of the Lynbrookians. "That's the Canine's Howl."

Jericho glared at Beau's hands. 3:17. He wanted no conversation.

"Landon Avian is long gone. They howl for Isaiah Marksman."

"Okay, God," Jericho muttered.

"You haven't seen God yet," Sparrowhawk said with a grin. "I've written hundreds of research papers about the Canine's Howl. Every Pure Blood Leasher has their own niche that makes them unique. The Falconer can make use of Bird's Eye View. The Equestrian has Emperor's Charge. There're more, but they're harder to research, less known. I've spent all day trying to understand how Isaiah Marksman was the Handler this entire time underneath our noses. He's been at this school through two full moons—no indication. The coyotes following him around at the fence is anecdotal evidence. Those coyotes have followed others before, begging for food. You've grown up seeing that. At first, I thought it was Mikayla Birdwing who activated him. No, I was wrong. She's too shy to use our methods. She knows nothing about being Capable. It was Falcon."

Jericho gave Sparrowhawk a quick glance. "Falcon activated Marksman?"

"It happened in the supply office. I walked in right when it happened. Falcon pushed Birdwing. It upset Marksman, and he sliced Falcon's face. That's another reason why Falcon broke his wrist and gouged his eye out. Isaiah's blood spilling, his screaming, and the full moon activated his power."

Yesterday, Jericho would've asked Sparrowhawk if he had been using drugs. Today, he believed the man because of his conversation with Secretarybird.

Sparrowhawk pointed to the fence line. "Behold, the tangible proof Isaiah

Marksman is the Handler. They're trying to come in and find him."

"You just said that coyotes at the fence aren't proof."

"When it's that many, yes, it is."

Distant golden eyes stared from the bushes. The nearer coyotes pawed at the fence, barking and growling.

Jericho checked his watch. "This doesn't prove he's my cousin."

"I know what I saw when I was inside of Mikayla. Her visions are crystal clear, like watching in real life. Proving he is your kin will be trickier. That will come in due time."

Jericho remained nonchalant so as not to alarm the busy Lynbrookians. "You're going to mow us all down? Is that what the weapon is for?"

"Honorable Kite, you are the Equestrian, property of the Victor of Kan. Pointing the barrel and firing upon you and the other three would be counterproductive." His grin was wide and toothy.

"You put up a good front, Sparrowhawk. The man I saw earlier in your quarters is the real you—a eugenics cuckoo head who doesn't know what he's doing. You only know theory, not practicality." His watch showed fifteen minutes had gone by.

"I think you need a brief reminder of who you're talking to."

Jericho's muscles began stiffening, feeling like a charley horse coursing throughout his entire body. In excruciating pain, he was stuck in his clock-watching position. His tears blurred the faceplate of his watch.

"Mr. Sparrowhawk! My shovel broke in half!" a Lynbrookian shouted.

Sparrowhawk had taken his eyes off Jericho to tend to the Lynbrookian and his broken shovel. Jericho relaxed and recognized what was happening. Whenever Sparrowhawk got distracted, he didn't use his Blood Leash well. Earlier, when Sparrowhawk had Mikayla on his Blood Leash, he lost complete control of her when Jericho had distracted him. That was how Mikayla was able to beg for help before Sparrowhawk established his control over her again.

"All I have to do is keep him distracted until Alexander comes," Jericho muttered under his breath. "I think I know who'll help, hopefully."

Behind him, Sparrowhawk was busy searching for another shovel in the truck's flatbed. Jericho darted away with another crazy idea. He ran along the fence, headed northbound towards the gate. Some coyotes began tracking him aggressively. Most of them pawed at the fence near the center of the main building where the infirmary was. Sparrowhawk's theory was coming to fruition. Nobody else but Isaiah Marksman rested in the infirmary.

"You want your Handler?" Jericho said to the coyotes that followed. "I can take you to him. C'mon."

He ran to the gate and pulled it open, letting the coyotes run rampant onto the campus. First a few or so scurried through, headed towards the infirmary. They were the bigger ones, brisk and burly. Moments later, dozens of the mid-sized coyotes stampeded. The smaller, slower ones filtered in last.

"Oh, what have I done? There's no turning back," Jericho said breathlessly. "Isaiah, you better be *the one*."

He ran inside the main building's center entrance and took the shortest path to the infirmary. Panting, he toggled each of the six doorknobs until Isaiah's unlocked door flung open. He stormed into the room. Coyotes were already pawing at the window or gnawing at the bars. The mid-sized ones whined and barked. Isaiah was dead asleep. Jericho grabbed Isaiah's left arm and shimmied the handcuffs off his small wrist.

Sparrowhawk wasn't thinking about how leaving Isaiah like this was a bad idea. He didn't bother locking him up or making it hard to get him out.

"Isaiah, get up!" Jericho bellowed. "I need you to wake up! What happened to you, man? Wake up!"

He spotted an empty, unlabeled syringe near Isaiah's bedside. Thinking on his feet, he picked up a small chair and threw it through the window, shattering most of the glass. He picked up a large shard, wielding it like a dagger, and rushed back to Isaiah. Lifting the other boy's unbroken arm, he remembered Secretarybird's explanation of how a Blood Leasher should never cut near or along a vital artery.

"I feel like I'm going crazy right now. Is this the rush serial killers like Falcon and Kestrel experience? I feel dirty." He pressed the glass against Isaiah's arm. "I was jealous of you and Naomi's fake relationship, but not enough to do stuff like this, man. I'm so sorry, but I don't know what else to do. I hate this feeling!"

Jericho sliced. As blood poured out, snaking around Isaiah's arm, the coyotes went insane. The bigger ones leaped at the bars on the window. Others pawed through the grill, trying to claw their way in.

Isaiah jolted awake. "What!"

Jericho dropped Isaiah's arm. He bolted to the window and began unfastening and punching at the bars' frame. The coyotes nipped at him.

"Honorable Kite, what are you doing? You're not going to let them in here, are you?"

"Tell them to stop biting me!"

"What?"

"Tell the coyotes to stop biting me!"

"Stop biting him?" Isaiah said unconfidently.

The coyotes fell back and started howling. Jericho continued beating away at the bars.

"What the hell is going on? I'm so confused."

"You're the Handler. You might be my cousin! I don't know! *Ugh!*" Jericho managed to rip the window frame away with his brute strength alone.

"What? Why's my arm bleeding like crazy? Blood makes me nauseous! I can't do this."

"I cut you. I'm sorry."

"What? Why? Imma throw up."

"It's the full moon, and the coyotes want you. They want your blood! I had to do it."

"The puke is coming!"

"You have a power to control them. They *want* you to control them, I think. I don't know. I learned about this stuff today."

Isaiah leaned over and vomited. Being afraid of needles and other sharp things, Jericho couldn't judge him.

"I think Mr. Sparrowhawk overdosed me on painkillers when he gave me that shot. He's losing his mind or maybe it's me losing my—"

"He was trying to incapacitate you. This is actually happening, Isaiah!"

Jericho kicked out the last few bars and used the chair again to hack away more glass, making way for the coyotes' entrance.

"Oh my God!" Isaiah scrunched into a ball, trembling.

Aimed at Isaiah, the ones at the front darted inside first and jumped onto the bed. They licked Isaiah's arm and his other wounds. Disgusted, Jericho backed himself into a corner as the others climbed into the room. Within seconds, fifty more coyotes assembled, all attempting to connect with Isaiah. The coyotes outside barked and whined. The smell was wretched, and the room became covered in muddy paw prints.

"Leave me alone!" Isaiah shouted, pushing the coyotes away with one arm.

They silenced and jumped off the bed. All the others gradually hushed.

"Tell them to sit, Isaiah," Jericho said.

"Like a regular pet dog? They're wild."

"It doesn't matter. You're the Handler. They'll do it!"

"I don't know what the Handler is!"

"Tell them to sit!"

"Sit?" Isaiah asked timidly and quietly.

They sat.

"No way," Jericho trembled. "He's the Handler. It's really him."

Huffing, Isaiah sat up and pressed himself against the headboard. He and Jericho locked eyes. Jericho feared what his awakening would be like next week with whatever horses he would find in Texas. The thought of cutting himself made him tremble.

"Isaiah—"

"The next words out of your mouth better explain what the hell this is!" Isaiah growled. His chest puffed out, and he turned red all over. The coyotes growled, pointing their fangs at Jericho.

Jericho pressed into the corner. "Make them calm down. I think they're mirroring your emotions."

"You started this, and you don't know?"

One of the coyotes chomped at Jericho's blazer and wouldn't let go.

"Calm down before they take me out!"

Isaiah shouted, "Settle!"

The coyotes laid down and kicked their legs out like common pet dogs following commands. Isaiah looked at Jericho, gesturing for an explanation.

"It's Blood Leash. You and I have this power, except I can control horses. You're the dog Handler, and I'm the Equestrian."

"You're full of crap."

"Isaiah, I know this is messed up. I'm sorry."

"No, no, no. I'm high on drugs. Earlier, a girl I like came in here and we had—" His mouth hung agape, and he got quiet. The way he clutched the bedsheets made Jericho certain the guy was completely naked. "She let me kiss and touch her all over. She was making cute sounds and saying sweet things to me. Me, with one eye, wearing a cast. There's no way that happened either. All this is fake. I'm on hallucinogens."

Jericho paused for a moment until he remembered seeing Mikayla leave the infirmary earlier. Putting together his run-in with her and what Naomi told him last night, it was safe to assume Isaiah was not hallucinating. Unreal. Average, goofball Isaiah Marksman had gotten more action in one night than Jericho had in his entire life. He had never gotten that close with Naomi. The jealousy crept back.

"You're not high. This is really happening."

"No! I've hunted deer and boar using dogs with my stepdad. Grew up with dogs everywhere. I never had this type of control over them."

"Your power was dormant until Falcon beat you earlier today. The full moon is strengthening it. You're part of the Trembley bloodline, or else this couldn't be happening."

"I'm adopted. What are you talking about?" Isaiah pulled his hair over his eyepatch and palmed his face. "This makes no sense. This is the worst day of my life. I should've minded my own business and left everything in the supply office alone."

The coyotes all began howling and whimpering.

"No, Isaiah! Don't shut down on me. I need you to help me. Sparrowhawk is out there. He's going to kill everybody on this campus except me and you. I need you to help me keep him distracted until help comes."

"I'm sure that's working right now! Coyotes all gathered in one place. He sure can't miss that!"

"Help is coming. I called someone to help us."

"I'm dead! I'm dead! I'm so high."

The whimpering grew louder.

"No, calm down, Isaiah. You're not going to die. Sparrowhawk's not going to kill us. You and I are worth a lot of money. Sparrowhawk is loyal to the headmaster. He won't kill us, I swear. Lorelei can control raptors. She's the one who made thousands of birds cover the sky yesterday. She's like me and you, but she's the Falconer. She'll be here to help us."

I hope, Jericho thought, blinking hard.

Isaiah cursed under his breath and mumbled about being high. "What about Naomi? I know you know where she is. And Mika's dad? Where is he? Is he okay?"

"Isaiah, I need you to focus. You're right. Sparrowhawk is going to show up. I need you to help me keep him distracted for another forty-five minutes until help comes."

"Keep him distracted? Doing what?" Isaiah clenched the comforter.

"The leader coyotes are on your leash. You can make them do whatever it takes because your blood runs in them."

A pup whimpered. Another yipped loudly. Jericho stepped away from the corner and peeked outside, searching amongst the packs of coyotes for the crying pups. Isaiah climbed out of the bed and stood beside Jericho. Another coyote yelped. Three seconds later, another followed suit.

Wielding shovels, Lynbrookians shuffled towards the packs of coyotes with hunched shoulders. They were slow and uncoordinated with the same dull, lifeless eyes Mikayla had earlier. One bludgeoned a pup with the back of the shovel and continued shuffling forward, unfazed by the blood splatter on his face. Isaiah and Jericho looked at each other in horror.

"Riley just beat that coyote to death with a shovel!" Isaiah screamed Riley's name, but the boy continued mindlessly bludgeoning more pups. "Did the zombie apocalypse start too?"

"That's Sparrowhawk's Blood Leash power. He's like a puppeteer."

"He's the Marionette Master, if you give it one of those names you're coming up with," Isaiah said.

"Yeah, I guess so. That's what he did to Mikayla this morning. He turned her into one of those," Jericho said, watching a different Lynbrookian beat another coyote mercilessly with a shovel. "You ready to take Sparrowhawk on with me? We gotta last forty minutes."

"I can last however long it takes." Isaiah's nostrils flared.

As Isaiah clumsily got dressed in his clothes that were spread out on the floor, Jericho tried his hardest to tune out the chaos going on outside. Dressed, Isaiah turned around and looked at the coyotes. He was overwhelmed.

"All you have to do is control the leaders. The rest will follow," Jericho explained.

Isaiah nodded. "What are the other rules?"

"I don't know. I just learned about this stuff today. I have no idea what my power can do exactly."

Isaiah looked at him. Jericho looked at him back.

"We're gonna get hosed." Though he wasn't confident, Isaiah went along with it. "Stand!"

The coyotes on the floor rose as one.

Jericho went to open the door. "Follow me. We're going to the north side to gain some distance from Sparrowhawk's army."

Isaiah caught up to Jericho and ran along his left side. "I'm trusting you to watch out for me, Honorable Kite. I can only see out of the right side."

"C'mon." Jericho started running. "You can run, right?"

"Yup. My feet work." He was barefoot.

"Where are your shoes?"

"I don't know."

"Okay…I'll watch your back, Isaiah."

"I'm gonna crap my pants."

Jericho felt the same but wouldn't dare say it out loud.

"What will happen to us after this is over, Honorable Kite?"

"I have no idea."

It got quiet, save for the crying pups outside and the clicking of fifty coyotes' sharp claws tapping the tiles. Jericho's titanium plates also clicked against the tile.

Outside the center door, Sparrowhawk greeted Isaiah and Jericho with fully dilated pupils. He held a young girl's braids as a means of restraining her, and injected his blood into her neck with a syringe pulled from his bandolier. She immediately stopped fighting and became compliant like the others.

"The Handler and his coyotes. Picture-perfect, like the vision," Sparrowhawk said with a grin. "Isaiah Marksman, welcome to the Blood Leash family. I won't even pull you two into my submission. I'll thrash you fair and square."

Lorelei Avian

9:25 PM

The moonlight gleamed, casting a bluish tint along Lorelei's pale skin. She stabbed the tip of her shovel along the rim of an aluminum can of peas. Mateo perched on her shoulder and hooted. She snuggled the owl against her cheek and kissed his belly. He warbled, stretching both wings up and back simultaneously.

"What are you looking at, Mika? Mateo is my best friend."

Mikayla stood with her arms crossed, foot tapping. "Lorelei, you have to hurry up."

Lorelei pried open the can. "I'm not in the biggest hurry to get back. My ankle is killing me." She rolled a lidded jar of applesauce over to the other girl. She felt like Mikayla missed too many meals. "Eat."

Mikayla planted her foot on it ready, to kick it back. "Got anything else besides apples?"

"Being picky at a time like this? Bad idea."

"Is this all you have?" She picked it up.

"That's my last bit of food."

Mikayla reluctantly unscrewed the jar, pressed her lips against the rim, and let applesauce slide down her throat. She spat it out immediately. "How were you able to survive this whole time out here alone? I've barely done this for an hour, and I'm miserable."

"Camped in Ontario." She left out the part of how she was used to being alone.

"Wow."

They were quiet for a few minutes as they ate. Mikayla choked down the applesauce. Lorelei finished her last bite, smiling at Mikayla's twisted expression.

"You don't give up at anything, do you?" Lorelei asked.

Mikayla shook her head and shrugged at the same time. "Not really."

"You're the most selfless person I've met. There's a highway not that far away. Most people would've left the forest and hitchhiked to Georgia or something."

"I'm not leaving anyone behind, and you wouldn't either. That's why you're still out here, right?"

Lorelei looked her in the eye and said, "I'm out here because I don't want to leave my brother. Look at me, I'm maimed. Where am I going anytime soon? I know you're not out here on your own. It's safe for me to assume Headmaster Kite sent you, but why you?"

"I bring you back, and I'll get my dad back," she said, putting the jar aside.

Humbly, Mikayla briefly explained that her plan had failed. Her dad and one CSB investigator were hostages. The other CSB investigator had gone missing. She described what Mr. Sparrowhawk had done to her and her dad during their chess match, and then what Headmaster Kite had said to her in his office regarding her mother knowing about the natural gas leak before Miss Kestrel put her outside. Then she recounted Mrs. Secretarybird taking Naomi away from the dorm and Mr. Falco punishing Isaiah because he tampered with inventory in the supply office. She finished off with Mr. Vulture's non-disclosure agreement.

Lorelei's head spun. She'd thought *her* last two days were wild.

"I don't have a plan," Mikayla said at the end. "I want Dad back. I wasn't supposed to talk about the NDA, but I feel like I have to because I don't know how else to convince you why coming back with me is important."

"Good news for you. I was on my way back to the campus anyway, just not very fast."

They got quiet.

Lorelei remembered the dead man behind the wheel of the scorched SUV. "Oh, no," she whispered.

"What?" Mikayla asked.

Lorelei's appetite disappeared. She put the can down. "I saw the CSB man who was missing. I wish I hadn't called them."

"Headmaster Kite told me my mother didn't call them. I wanted it to be a lie. So, it was you. How'd you do that? Can you call more CSB? Better yet, call the FBI. Call the police!"

Lorelei shook her head, grinding her teeth at the thought of the consequences. Sure, the Raptor Admins and the headmaster would go to prison, but Uncle Eric would return to prison as well. With his criminal record, he would never see the light of day again. Jericho would also be locked up, deprived of any chance to live like a normal human being. Otherwise, Lorelei loved the thought of the rest of them getting what they deserved.

Lorelei replied, leaving her other concerns out, "The phone I used is dead. Even if I had a way to bring the battery life back, I wouldn't. Alexander used me."

"Who's Alexander?"

"Alexander Ravensbourne," Lorelei clarified.

Mikayla gasped. "Ravensbourne? *That* Alexander! Like, heir of Raven Dynamic?"

"Yeah, that guy. He has his own faction called *Alexander's Electric Company*. He somehow found out about the leak and had one of his men come up to me at the gate last month during Freedom Hours." Lorelei remembered him clearly. He had a gaunt appearance and a raven tattoo behind his ear. It was a secret meeting nobody saw because everyone was scrambling with the gas leak problem. "He gave me coordinates to a cellphone and told me to make my move when I was ready. I waited too long. That's why the phone's battery was no good by the time I got to it. He promised me that they'd save me, Landon, and Mateo. That was a lie."

"Oh, Lorelei, I'm sorry." Mikayla stopped fidgeting. "Your cousin told me he had a way to help us, as long as we get back to Lynbrook by ten o'clock."

Lorelei motioned for Mateo to fly off her. She began packing her bag.

"Like I said, I was already headed that way. I think Landon is in trouble."

"Why?"

"The coyotes are howling." She hoisted her backpack onto her shoulders, ignoring Mikayla's confused expression. "Let's go."

They began the short hike to Lynbrook. Lorelei felt a pain shooting up her leg. She feared her Achilles tendon was damaged as her limp became more pronounced.

"Lorelei, Landon told me he was leaving tonight to go to a place called Kan."

"When did he say that?" Lorelei winced.

"Around five. He said he and Naomi were going with others." Mikayla paused. "Hey, are you okay?"

"Yeah, I'm fine. When did he say when he was leaving?"

"He didn't say, but he seemed in a hurry."

"We gotta move faster. We're following the coyotes' path."

"Why?"

"Because of the Canine's Howl."

"What's that?"

Lorelei's eyes widened. She had forgotten Mikayla knew absolutely nothing about Blood Leash lore despite being subjected to a eugenics experiment.

Another pain shot through her leg. "*Ugh,*" she grunted.

"You're limping."

"I'll be fine."

They got quiet again. Lynbrook was about a mile and a half away. At their pace, they would arrive after ten o'clock.

"Sparrowhawk scares me, Lorelei," Mikayla said. "He stuck a syringe in Isaiah before I left. It put him to sleep."

Mikayla explained what Mr. Sparrowhawk made her see and do against her will. Lorelei listened, but the pain in her leg started drowning out Mikayla's voice.

"Hold on," Lorelei said, stopping to lean against a tree.

"Lorelei, my contract with Vulture says I have until midnight. We're not making it by Jericho's timing. Let's stop here for a while."

"No," Lorelei said, blowing through her lips as if it would lessen the pain. "That stuff Sparrowhawk is doing—it's Blood Leash."

"Blood Leash?"

"Yeah, Sparrowhawk is somebody who's called Blood Leash Capable—or just Capable, for short. That's why he was able to control you and your dad."

"I don't get it."

"Most people don't. It's not exactly one of those things everybody knows about. You have to know people who know people who know people to get on a list to become Capable. It's the fastest way to become a millionaire too because you get paid for it. Sparrowhawk found a network and got on a list for eugenic experimentation. He's the only Raptor Admin like that."

"How did he control us?"

Lorelei looked away. "He put his blood in you. That's how he entered your body and took control of it. His power is like a cross between telepathy and telekinesis. Well, all Blood Leash Power is like that," she clarified. "I can do it too. That's why Mateo's been following me all day and night. He's under my control."

"Why are you telling me this? It was a secret, wasn't it?"

Lorelei groaned and shifted her weight to the other side of her body. "I don't know. I don't care anymore. I'm so sick and tired of keeping all this bottled up." The pain radiated. She grabbed her leg. "It's decades of eugenic experiments making freaks of nature."

"Lorelei, it's okay if we don't make it on time. Let's sit."

"No, give me a minute!" Lorelei snapped. She winced and apologized softly.

"It's okay, Lorelei. I understand." Mikayla stood beside her at the tree. "I've read stuff about rich people experimenting with eugenics. I thought it was a crackpot conspiracy theory."

"That's what *they* want regular people to think. The Kite Clan and the Ravensbourne family are two of many trillionaire families in the world investing in eugenics. A few take special interest in Blood Leash experimentation."

"But I thought the Kites were in oil and gas."

"Barely. Electricity dominates everything now, Mika. You know that. It's like how coal phased out. The Kite Clan is pivoting to stay relevant *and* wealthy. Eugenics is the next gold rush." Lorelei paused for a moment. She couldn't believe after years of silence all this information was flowing out of her. Her gut felt right about it. "That place—Kan—that Landon was talking about is where Lynbrookians go after their time at Meccanicville. It's where the Kite Clan do their eugenics experiments and arena fighting, I think. A man they call the Victor of Kan runs the place. Early this morning, Headmaster Kite sent a hunter from Kan to capture me using a mountain goat-pony chimera thingy."

"He used a what?"

"Some animal that was experimented on. I don't know what to make of it. Anyway, we got into a fight, and that's why I'm hurt."

"You said a lot there. I don't even know…" Mikayla's voice trailed off.

Lorelei felt embarrassed about going on a tangent. "All you need to know is the Trinity is like a school-to-prison pipeline. Ever heard of that saying before? Got it from Uncle Eric."

"My mom said it every once in a while."

"Here's how the Trinity works. First, you come to Lynbrook to get indoctrinated on how to support an airfield, then you go to Meccanicville Airport. There, you help the Kites' oil and gas business on a flightline that supports refineries for Kite Express gas stations. Then, you go to Kan, where they do the Blood Leash Experimentation and arena fighting."

Mikayla grumbled. "You sound insane."

"I'm not. Jericho knows this goes on. That's why he always smokes and why he's stressed out. Landon knew. That's why he doesn't talk much. Uncle Eric too. We were threatened not to say anything, so we didn't because…" Lorelei shuddered. "Talking gets you handcuffed to a steering wheel and set on fire or your eye gouged out or whatever punishment they feel like inflicting."

Mikayla shook her head. "No."

"Mika, listen." Lorelei grasped her shoulder. Balancing herself began to hurt. "I'm telling you this because if they send me off to Kan, then they can't prove it was me who told you. I've been keeping this from you."

"Keeping what?"

Lorelei gulped at the panic in Mikayla's big eyes. She made sure not to look away this time. "Your mom sold you to Headmaster Kite."

Mikayla crossed her arms. "No. She wouldn't do that. She wouldn't send me to a place like Lynbrook if she knew what it was. It makes no sense. She spent so much money on my brain surgery; she wouldn't throw me away like that."

She's Blood Leash Capable, same as Sparrowhawk, Lorelei remembered. She had no idea how to break the news to Mikayla. The information she was sharing was already overwhelming enough.

"You're almost eighteen, right?"

"In February." She was agitated.

"Every year, after you're eighteen, Headmaster Kite will pay your mother to keep you in the Trinity pipeline. He makes so much off the labor he gets from former Lynbrookians at Meccanicville and Kan that it's nothing to him. He tells the parents to never contact you again. That's why I was suspicious when he let your dad write *and* come to Lynbrook. They want your dad, Mika. If they told you bringing me back would get you your dad back, they're lying! They're using you!"

"No!" Mikayla cried. "I thought I was going to actually be able to do something to help myself and the others. I'm useless."

Lorelei winced again at her own bluntness. She had grown used to bearing the gravity of the truth, and she had forgotten how she felt heartbroken, depressed, and useless when she first learned about it.

"Mika, I should've said it differently. I didn't mean to say it like that."

"It doesn't matter," she sniffled and sighed. "You can't sugarcoat evil and make it sweet."

Lorelei pushed off the tree. "Let's keep moving."

Crying softly, Mikayla dragged herself forward. Lorelei limped behind her quietly. It took them over twenty-seven minutes to cover a mile. With half a mile left, Mikayla suddenly stopped walking and burst into inconsolable tears. Lorelei found herself at a loss for words but knew exactly how numb she felt inside.

"Mika, don't hate your mom," Lorelei soothed. "I lost my mom when I was thirteen. She was a devoted church goer. I hated going, but there are days I wish I were in a pew next to her."

Lorelei looked at her hand. She couldn't believe all the oversharing on her part so far. Her loneliness was worse than she'd expected. Mikayla could've been a skunk or another bird, and the same word vomit would've spilled right out.

"Mika, ignore me. I'm dehydrated."

She sniffled. "Hate is too strong for how I feel. Whatever word comes between love and hate…that's how I feel about my mom. I've always felt like she didn't care. And yesterday, for the first time, I had faith she was the one who answered my letters and called the CSB. I kept holding onto that for nothing. Out of all those businesses who violated environmental regulations, she brought many to justice. Why not Kite Express? I guess it's because she's another person who traded her beliefs for money. Perhaps her job was just that: a job. What she fought for in the courtroom was never a part of her identity and values. It was a job."

Lorelei was amazed. *She's working through it better than I did. This girl is strong-willed.*

Intermittent howling echoed in the distance.

"Mika, you're about to see me do something weird, but know I'm okay no matter what you see."

Mikayla glared but didn't react.

Collapsing, Lorelei transferred her conscious to Mateo, activating Bird's Eye View. The owl flapped upward and soared above the trees. He banked left and flew above the dirt road. Below, a succession of royal purple vans with lightning bolts painted on the top headed towards Lynbrook. The horizon showed two searchlights of helicopters, also approaching Lynbrook at a low altitude.

After two minutes of drifting with the full moon in the background, Mateo glided down along Lynbrook's fence line. A coyote pounced at him. The owl dodged, flapping his wings furiously, encountering more coyotes and Lynbrookians in his path. He darted and weaved every which way, avoiding fangs and shovels ascending above the unrest in search of Landon.

Below, Jericho tackled Mr. Sparrowhawk from the side. They hit the ground, rolling. Jericho threw multiple punches. Mr. Sparrowhawk thrust his pelvis up, bucking Jericho off him, and managed to strike him in the chin with the pointiest part of his shoe.

In a flash, Mr. Sparrowhawk and Mateo made eye contact. Disoriented, Jericho staggered onto his feet. He reached for a shovel and swung it like a bat against Mr. Sparrowhawk's spine. They both collapsed.

Isaiah angrily pointed at Mr. Sparrowhawk, commanding the coyotes to charge. Mr. Sparrowhawk recovered, but he was obviously exhausted. He pointed, commanding the Lynbrookians to swarm Jericho and Isaiah. The students fell into a zombie-like state and started forward.

Dodging Lynbrookians, Jericho went after Mr. Sparrowhawk. His punches were either dodged or blocked. And yet, the strength in both their fists and stamina was something supernatural—inhuman almost.

Mateo dived into the army of Lynbrookians. Landon wasn't amongst them. Twisting and turning, he avoided the shovels, rising sixty feet above everyone again. He desperately soared, looking for Landon's whereabouts along the fence line. A green laser dot flickered against the tree leaves.

Mateo flew a tight one-eighty. Yards away, Jericho had been subdued. He laid on the ground, unconscious. Mr. Sparrowhawk stood beside him, armed with a rifle, tracking the owl's haphazard movements. He pulled the trigger, rapidly firing multiple bullets twenty yards into the air. The gunshots pierced the night, rattling Mateo's eardrums. He lost control and began diving, confused about the direction and believing it to be an ascent. Suddenly, Mateo jolted to a halt and fell out of the sky.

He had been shot in the chest.

Lorelei's consciousness returned. She fought to get back into Mateo, and when she did, a numbness stretched across her chest, and it radiated. It became hot, then burned. The pain was excruciating, like a thousand-degree branding iron. She started crying.

Mikayla knelt beside Lorelei and held her in her arms.

"Lorelei, you're back. What happened? Your eyes rolled into the back of your head. It looked like you were having a seizure. Are you okay?"

"I'm okay. Mateo's not."

"Did you hear that? There was shooting. I lost count of how many shots were fired…"

Mikayla's voice was drowned out amongst the cacophony ringing out across the campus in earshot of Mateo. There were gunshots, screaming, howling, and the rotor wash of helicopters flying over them.

Lorelei grimaced and grabbed her chest. "It hurts. I feel it, Mateo. I'm here. I'm here. I feel with you. I won't leave you to die alone. Shhh…"

The other half of Lorelei's consciousness felt Mikayla's hand wrapping around her limp hand.

"Lorelei…Lorelei, you okay? Lorelei? Lorelei…don't die. Please, don't die."

"I'm not dying. Mateo is," Lorelei replied, breathing sharply.

"I don't understand."

"It's what I was trying to explain earlier. I'm like Mr. Sparrowhawk, except I can control raptors." Lorelei took a deep breath, wishing taking in more oxygen could rid her of the pain. "I went inside of Mateo and flew to Lynbrook. There's a battle. Sparrowhawk shot Mateo. I can feel him dying. I couldn't find Landon."

"Lorelei, I'm so sorry. Let's stay here until you're ready."

They sat quietly, holding hands. In minutes, Lorelei felt one hundred percent of her consciousness returning as Mateo passed away.

She stood up one leg at a time, preparing herself for whatever came next. "Now. Jericho and Isaiah need us."

"They're in trouble?"

"Yeah, Sparrowhawk is using his Blood Leash power to control the Lynbrookians. He's using them to fight off Isaiah and the coyotes. Jericho is unconscious."

Mikayla held onto Lorelei. "Use me to help you walk. I know I'm little, but so is a cane."

Lorelei embraced Mikayla, finding her balance. She sighed and looked up at the moon. "Mika, there's one more thing that's going to be hard for you to take in. We need you to fight Sparrowhawk."

"Me? I can't."

"Yeah, you can. You're the only one who can reach him on a level we can't because your blood already runs through him and you're Capable. You and he have a Link."

"A Link?" she asked.

"Yeah, a Link is established when a Blood Leasher intoxicates you with their blood. There's a distance and time limitation on it. I haven't figured out to what extent, but I know it exists. Normally, you want to avoid injecting your blood into another Blood Leasher because it makes you vulnerable to them. Long story short, you can stop him, Mika. All you have to do is subdue him. Get into his head. Attack him."

"But I'm way smaller than him, and he knows what he's doing, and I don't—"

"Don't sell yourself short. Think about what he did to you and your dad. He's hurting everyone you tried to save. He's ruthless and selfish. Focus on that, Mika, and you'll find the power within to take him out. Listen to your instinct."

With Mikayla supporting half of Lorelei's weight, they both slowly made their way towards Lynbrook's north gate. It took them roughly fifteen minutes to cover the distance, and Lorelei elaborated more on Mikayla's abilities as they traveled.

Near the fence line, Lorelei shakily scooped up Mateo. He was light and unresponsive to the touch, but he had a peaceful look on his face. She wrapped her friend's corpse in a cloth and packed it in her bag.

"I'm glad you didn't die alone, Mateo. I would be there all over again if I had to."

Mikayla stood by, watching with her fist clenched as her friends struggled in a battle none of them could believe was happening.

The Triad and The Dreamer

10:16 PM

Watching the ongoing battle, Lorelei and Mikayla silently hid behind bushes near Lynbrook's north gate. Sparrowhawk, eyes fully dilated, stood in a defensive fighting stance with zombie-like Lynbrookians looming behind him. Isaiah and the hundreds of coyotes behind him faced Sparrowhawk. The scene was a snippet directly from Mikayla's short nightmare from Saturday night. She had nearly forgotten it.

"*Déjà vu*. I saw this in a nightmare," Mikayla whispered. "How is Isaiah able to control all those coyotes?"

Lorelei was in awe. She had a hunch on the answer but had no time to think about it or explain it to Mikayla. She clasped the other girl's shoulder. "Go help Isaiah."

"But those coyotes will come after me."

"No, they won't."

"What makes you so sure?"

"I don't have time to explain. Go out there. I'll find a way to distract Sparrowhawk. He can't control all those people and take on a big distraction at the same time. That's every Blood Leasher's weakness."

"What do I do?"

"Literally anything."

"But you're hurt."

"I can still use my power without being able to walk. I did it earlier, remember?"

Mikayla nodded. "You'll be okay?"

"Yes. Go."

Mikayla ran through the gate and waved her hands. She shouted, "Hey!"

Isaiah turned around and smiled lightly. The coyotes mirrored his movements, barking softly and whining excitedly at Mikayla.

Meanwhile, Lorelei rummaged through her bag for the shovel. She sliced along her wrist, creating her Gauntlet of Fury. Blowing her whistle, she raised her bloody hand to the sky, releasing her scent.

"C'mon, c'mon, c'mon," she repeated under her breath in hopes for a parliament of owls to come her way.

Jericho opened his eyes and sat up, groggily coming to. He had double vision, and the ground felt like it was bobbing up and down like ocean waves. His fingertips inched for the nearest shovel as his eyes zeroed in on Sparrowhawk's backside. He waited until the feeling of motion sickness subsided.

Isaiah spread his arms. Half the coyotes shifted left. The rest moved right, making an aisle for Mikayla to run directly to him.

"Isaiah, what are you doing?" she asked.

"I don't know. I have no idea what I'm doing, but they do whatever I want. Sparrowhawk's getting tired." Isaiah pointed at Sparrowhawk. "Sic 'em again! Don't bite anyone but him!"

The coyotes charged at Sparrowhawk, but the Lynbrookian front lines formed a barrier around him, absorbing the brunt force. They began swinging shovels at the coyotes to fend them off. The coyotes dodged and darted in different directions, trying to get to Sparrowhawk. Some crawled underneath Lynbrookians' legs. Others had enough energy to jump right over the students. Sparrowhawk broke away from the barrier.

Jericho ambushed Sparrowhawk and swung the shovel at the back of his head. Every Lynbrookian's shovel dropped, and their bodies fell like ragdolls.

Mikayla spotted a few of her friends. She ran up to them and touched their wrists for pulses. They were normal but faint.

A parliament of five great horned owls rushed in a straight line towards Sparrowhawk's head. He ran, haphazardly swatting at the birds.

"Get him now! Bite his booty!" Isaiah shouted with a grin.

The leader coyotes lunged for Sparrowhawk's backside. The smaller ones howled, scurrying behind them.

Mikayla lifted Leslie by her shoulders and began dragging her towards the fence. Jericho joined her. He hunched over and stacked three Lynbrookians on his back for the fireman's carry. Together, the two of them rescued nine more.

Sparrowhawk grabbed onto an owl's legs and swung it to smack the other four out of the air. He kicked some of the coyotes in their snouts and shoved away others.

"Enough of this child's play!" he shouted. *"Bond!"*

Jericho dropped a husky young man. Both of his arms contorted behind his back. Mikayla looked around. Isaiah had fallen to his knees. He was paralyzed. Every coyote on the campus fell sideways and howled.

Sparrowhawk swiftly spun around and made a clawing motion at Mikayla. *"Vision!"*

A migraine took over. She grabbed her head and fought to keep her mind focused on positive images. Naomi and her children in the grand hall. Jericho and his horses on the ranch in Texas. Isaiah shooting a bullseye at the range. Lorelei hugging her brother. Herself sharing a bowl of beef pho with her dad. She blocked Sparrowhawk's dark energy from creeping into her brain.

"You're not making me do what you want this time! You're not getting inside!" she shouted.

He was taken aback, but his smug smile returned. "Mikayla, look around. I can make whatever I want happen."

She closed her eyes. "No. Not true! We came together to beat you. That's what will happen."

"Beat me for what?"

"To save everyone!"

"The one you care most about is gone."

Mikayla opened her eyes. "My dad is gone?"

Sparrowhawk grinned. "Yes, he left hours ago in a helicopter to Meccanicville."

Mikayla balled her fists and gritted her teeth. "You're going to hell!"

"I expect to." He made a pulling motion, forcing her to draw nearer to his clutches. His pupils grew wider.

"Fight him, Mika! Don't let him turn you into one of these zombies!" Isaiah shouted.

"Mikayla, you can do this! You fought him off twice before! I saw you do it!" Jericho yelled.

Lorelei called out from a distance. "I'm summoning more owls, Mika! Hold out a little longer!" Her whistle tweeted.

Sparrowhawk snatched Mikayla's chin and pulled her in. "You and I are the same, Mikayla. We are the only two people in the world alive after having the Blood Leash brain surgery. I checked this morning. People who've gotten it recently died. There's something special about me and you. They call us Dreamers. If you accept an alliance with me right here, right now, I can give you what you want. I'll give you your dad. I'll make your mother answer for what she's done."

"I want nothing to do with you."

"Mikayla, I've already been inside of you once. I know all your deepest insecurities and secrets. I know doing this will drive some of that darkness to the surface."

Sparrowhawk twirled his finger. Isaiah started screaming and writhing on the ground. The Canine's Howl echoed.

"Leave him alone!"

He stopped and grabbed Mikayla's neck with both hands. "What do you say, little Mikayla?"

She tried to shake her head. It became hard to breathe.

"Mikayla, your power is incredible—godly—and you have no idea how to tap into it. I know how. We can be an amazing duo—the Dreamers. Look around at what I did alone. Imagine the power we'd have together."

"No...I wouldn't...do anything...like...this," she gasped.

"Mikayla, we can save your dad."

"Say no, Mikayla! He's lying to you!" Jericho shouted.

"Mika, keep fighting!" Isaiah added.

"Almost there, Mika! The owls are coming."

Sparrowhawk clenched harder. "Do you honestly want to make an adversary out of me?"

Lightheaded, Mikayla fought to keep her eyes open. Spots and blackness closed in around Sparrowhawk's smirk. She stared straight into his eyes through her slitted lids.

Her instinct spoke to her. It whispered *"Oblivion."* Mikayla repeated it.

Eyes widening with shock, Sparrowhawk dropped her. He seized up and froze in a petrified state. Mikayla hit the ground, coughing. She stared at the fear frozen on Sparrowhawk's face, confused about how she could do such a thing to another human being.

It was possible because of their teamwork, she realized. The four of them had failed to rebel alone, but together, they made a change.

She locked eyes with Isaiah for a moment, hoping he wouldn't think she was a monster. He, a few coyotes, and Jericho ran up to her. Lorelei hobbled over, two owls soaring above. The Lynbrookians gradually regained consciousness and began wandering the campus, asking each other if they were okay and figuring out what happened. Many of them had been bitten by coyotes or hit by shovels.

Isaiah hugged Mikayla. "You okay?"

"I should be asking you."

"I'll be okay. Just waiting to wake up from this nightmare."

She managed to break a small smile. "I've been waiting for days."

Sparrowhawk had called her a Dreamer. Perhaps she wasn't meant to wake up. She shuddered and refused to let his words sink into her heart and soul.

Lorelei limped up to Sparrowhawk and flicked his nose. He didn't budge.

She chuckled. "This happens to Blood Leashers who wield more leashes than they can handle. It was too much, wasn't it, Sparrowhawk? You tried leashing over fifty people simultaneously. It makes you weaker, not stronger."

"Is he going to stay stiff like a stone?" Isaiah asked.

"Not forever," Lorelei replied, smirking at Isaiah. "I've only been gone two days. What's with the coyotes?"

Jericho stepped between Lorelei and Isaiah, huddling them against either side of him. "He's one of us. Isaiah here is the Handler."

"You know about Blood Leash now?" Lorelei asked. "Who told you that you're the Equestrian?"

"Secretarybird."

Lorelei paused, sighing. "Then if he's the Handler, what does that make Landon? Where is he?"

"Everyone else thought Landon was the Handler too. Because of that, they sent him to Kan a few hours ago," Jericho said.

"What?" Lorelei gripped Jericho's shoulders. "Please tell me he's not alone."

"He's not. Eric went with him, and a couple of the Raptor Admins—"

"Please don't say—"

"Kestrel and Falcon."

Lorelei dropped her head. "No."

"I'm sorry, Lorelei," Jericho said. "Wait…it's not too late for you to go see him. There's a helicopter coming."

"Really?" Mikayla asked. "Where is it going, Jericho?"

"To Kan. Sparrowhawk was tasked with murdering all the Lynbrookians and delivering the four of us and himself to Kan. Well, there's two helicopters coming. I requested Secretarybird order the other. That one is going to Meccanicville."

Lorelei and Mikayla bombarded Jericho with praying hands. Lorelei begged for the helicopter for Kan. Mikayla pleaded for the one going to Meccanicville.

"Where's Naomi?" Mikayla asked. "You said she was going to be safe. Is she out here?"

"No, she's headed to Meccanicville. Your dad and Edmund Rabbit too. I'm going there after this to make sure they stay safe."

"But why is Naomi headed to Meccanicville?"

"Because my father was going to send her to Kan. I asked Secretarybird to take her. She's riding with Condor and Osprey."

"Why did he want to send her to Kan? Is she going to be okay with those three?"

Mikayla glanced at Lorelei for her unbiased opinion. She nodded, making Mikayla feel slightly better.

"Please let me go with you, Jericho. I need to see my dad."

Tears filled Lorelei's eyes. "Jericho, let me take the helicopter to Kan. I have to be there for Landon. If he's not the Handler, then he'll struggle at Kan."

"Jericho—I mean, Honorable Kite—say something," Mikayla pleaded. "Let me go with you to Meccanicville."

"Jericho, did you hear me?" Lorelei asked.

Jericho stepped backward. His heart began racing. He had no idea what to say.

Isaiah tapped Jericho's shoulder. "Uh, what's supposed to happen to the rest of us and Lynbrook?" The campus was in disarray—lots of wandering Lynbrookians and coyotes. "How do I make the coyotes go away? Do I say shoo? Or…"

Headlights whitened the grass and blinded everyone. Multiple purple vans drove through the north gates. Freezing in place, the coyotes' ears perked up seconds before they scattered in every direction. Screaming Lynbrookians broke out into hysteria, dodging the coyotes.

"Calm down!" Jericho shouted.

Lorelei's two owls departed. They spun upward and soared into the forest.

Uniformed men and women wearing black leather jackets and black pants exited the vans with urgency. Many of them snagged nearby Lynbrookians. Above, two small helicopters banked left towards them, searchlights brightening the campus even more. They descended slowly to an isolated area further east. The rotor wash rustled the grass, throwing around debris. The wind and noise were incredible.

At the gate, a man wearing dark clothes—a modern stylistic cross of steampunk and goth—walked directly up to Jericho. Two bodyguards flanked him, a step behind. Fingertips pointed downward, the man held his hand out for an elegant handshake. All his studded rings and black diamonds reflected the moonlight.

"Alexander Ravensbourne. Charmed to finally meet you in person, Jericho Kite."

The Triad and The Dreamer

10:30 PM

More purple moving trucks labeled *Alexander's Electric Company* reversed onto the campus. Workers began unloading furniture, boxes, and wheeled wardrobes. Other workers created an assembly line, passing down Alexander's extensive collection of electric guitars from a separate truck.

Every Lynbrookian had been captured and stood still in the grasp of a uniformed worker. Scores of extra workers stood by, awaiting Alexander's next order. Alexander, however, was preoccupied caressing Sparrowhawk's chin with the tip of his black fingernails.

"Who is that guy?" Isaiah whispered to Mikayla.

"A Ravensbourne," Mikayla replied.

"Fair enough. I'll shut up forever," Isaiah said before sucking his lips into his mouth.

The man holding Isaiah had a tapered undercut revealing a fine-lined tattoo of a raven behind his black earrings. Mikayla's captor also had a raven tattoo on his neck that matched his black and purple eyeliner. Lorelei's was a woman wearing a studded leather jacket. Half her hair was shaved.

"Alexander, what are you doing here?" Lorelei squirmed to get away from the woman.

Alexander ignored her and continued adoring Sparrowhawk's frozen face. He ran the back of his fingers down Sparrowhawk's cheek.

"I asked Alexander to come," Jericho muttered. He had no captor, but he felt far from free.

"Are you serious? After all he's done?" Lorelei said.

"My father wanted Sparrowhawk to kill every Lynbrookian. I traded Lynbrook for everyone's lives."

"Why are we being captured if we're spared, Jericho?" Lorelei asked.

Alexander finally spoke. "Liam Galton, it's actually you."

"Is that Sparrowhawk's real name?" Mikayla asked.

Jericho nodded.

"Liam here is one of the founding fathers of Blood Leash experimentation—a former child prodigy. Ah, he's more handsome in person." Alexander blushed. "Why someone like him risked his life to become a Dreamer is beyond me. Just kidding, it's not. It's the gateway to divine power and millions of dollars. He wanted to be a god!" He palmed Sparrowhawk's cheek. "Darling, you already look like one."

"I'm seriously going to throw up everywhere," Lorelei said, gagging.

"Do it," Alexander said to her before he looked at Jericho. "I'm going to splash in her vomit, walk directly to your father's bed, and jump up and down on it with my shoes on."

"Alexander, you won already. You're literally unpacking your possessions into my home, and you've captured the Lynbrookians. I want to leave with dignity."

"Yes, yes. Like I said, my gripe isn't with you. It's with your father. I see those two helicopters over there. Let me guess; one's going to Meccanicville and the other to Kan. You Kites are so predictable because you think like neanderthals. But not so fast! Nobody's leaving until I get what I'm owed." Alexander stepped close to Jericho and looked up. He was shorter but equally imposing. "You think I don't understand what's happening here?"

"I'm sure you're aware, Alexander."

"I am, Jericho." He pointed to Sparrowhawk. "Who petrified him? Don't lie. Be a big boy and tell the truth."

Jericho cut his eyes away from Mikayla. "I did."

Alexander made the buzzer sound. "Petrification isn't a known power of the Equestrian."

"How many Pure-Blooded Equestrians have you encountered?"

Alexander glared at Jericho, then burst into laughter. He regained his composure and snapped his fingers. More of his uniformed men rallied behind him. His aggressive tone emerged. "You are dense, Jericho. Not dense as in unintelligent; dense as in incredibly hardheaded. Company, test Liam and those two." He split his fingers into a peace sign pointed at Mikayla and Isaiah.

One of the men approached Mikayla with a handheld wand sensor. A woman snatched Isaiah's index finger and pricked it with a small needle. She fed his blood into a different type of sensor. Meanwhile, the man hovered his wand over Mikayla's pelvis. It buzzed. He hovered it over her chest. It buzzed.

A third person pricked Mikayla's index finger and fed the blood into a sensor. The same was done to Sparrowhawk.

The man with the wand squinted at Mikayla doubtfully before he waved it around her skull. It beeped three times.

The woman who pricked Isaiah showed her sensor flashing a silhouette of a dog and the number 100%. The sensor for Sparrowhawk's results showed a silhouette of a hawk darkened a tenth of the way with a hawk and the number 9.3%. He also had less than a fourth of a horse filled, flashing 15.7%. The word NIL flashed at 75%.

"A Dreamer and a Pure Handler. Wait a sec, Jericho." Alexander pointed to Isaiah, whose eyes were comically bugging out his head. "Are you related to him?"

"I don't know," Jericho replied.

"Well…him being related to you through a Trembley is the only way his results would make sense. He looks nothing like you and Lorelei, and he's short. Who is this goofball? A distant cousin? Half cousin?"

"I don't know!" Jericho shouted.

Mikayla's brow furrowed. "Isaiah's not related to these people."

"No one's talking to you," Alexander said. He puzzled over things for a moment, and then he pointed at Lorelei, Jericho, Isaiah, Sparrowhawk, and Mikayla one by one. "Three Pure Blood Leashers! Two rare Capables. Jericho, you are a naughty, naughty boy. Caught you in another lie. You only told me about four. The Triad and two Dreamers! I could bankrupt Kan taking all five of you for myself!"

"No!" Jericho stomped the ground and grabbed Alexander's collar. "You promised not to mess with Meccanicville and Kan for three years. You got Lynbrook and the Lynbrookians."

"Oh, silly, silly boy." He slapped Jericho's hand away. "Stop calling it Lynbrook. This place is *New* Lynbrook now. Where is your father? I want to see his miserable face."

"He fled. You have me."

They both stuck their chests out and glared at each other.

"Alexander, look!" One of the women held up her sensor, showing Mikayla's results. The screen displayed the silhouettes of a dog, a hawk, and a horse, all filled a third of the way and flashing 33.3%. Alexander's twinkling eyes widened, and a grin stretched across his face.

"They say a Kite always gets what they want. Not this time. There will be no negotiating." Alexander smirked. "She's mine, and Liam will be too. And I'll take the Handler as well. Why not? I deserve restitution for taking all these Lynbrookians off your hands."

"What?" Jericho growled.

"I have to onboard and retrain them. Do you have any idea how expensive that will be? Of course you don't. You've never ran anything in your life, except through a carton of cigarettes." Jericho shifted his glare towards Alexander. "Yeah, I know about your pathetic habit."

"I thought you said your gripe was with my father."

"Collateral damage, Jericho. Collateral. It's a part of business."

Lorelei flashed her middle finger at Alexander. "Jericho, do you have any idea what you're giving up letting him take Mikayla and Isaiah? Don't let him have them. Take them both to Meccanicville with you. Anything but letting them go with *him*."

Jericho opened his mouth to speak, but his bottom lip hung slack. He had no idea what the significance of Mikayla's results meant. Judging from

Alexander's reaction, it meant a great deal. However, he felt overwhelmed with his family's enemy invading his one and only home. His gaze fixed back onto the continuous inbound flow of moving trucks imprinting the grass with deep tire marks. He closed his jaw and felt the lump in his throat.

"There's no perfect answer," Jericho whispered.

"Yeah, there is!" Lorelei lunged at Alexander. Her guard held her back. "You can have that petrified jerk! Mikayla and Isaiah stay with us!"

Alexander smiled at Lorelei. "You should shut your mouth and find out what your brother is before I do. Jericho, I spare you *only* because I think you facing your father once he finds out you've practically given away New Lynbrook to me is much, much more entertaining than anything I'd ever do. Besides, I have Liam Galton, his prized possession."

Jericho sighed. "Sure."

"Jericho, don't let him take Mikayla and Isaiah. Are you listening to me? Do you hear me?" Lorelei asked.

Alexander blocked Jericho's view of the workers hoisting a bronze statue of a rock star and his bass through the front doors. "Your father loved Liam more than you because you killed his beloved wife while she gave birth to you. To him, you were a disappointment from the second you were born. When you let that sink in, that's when you'll stop defending his interests."

Lorelei spat on Alexander's face. Her guard pulled her hair, jerking her away.

Alexander let the saliva smudge his black eyeliner. He held his hand up, signaling the guard to ease up on Lorelei. Then he snapped his fingers. Every uniformed worker who held a Lynbrookian retrieved a syringe full of blue substance from their pocket.

"You wish you were this well coordinated, Jericho, but your father held you back, allowing me to surpass you."

Jericho snapped out of it and looked around. "What's in those syringes?"

"This is a top-secret serum my family's scientist conjured in a lab in Switzerland. The American CIA wishes they could get their hands on something this efficient. The serum is designed to induce acute amnesia in the receiving individual's brain. They'll forget *all* events that occurred in the last ninety to one-hundred eighty days of their lives. Results may vary." He finally wiped the spit away, flicking droplets at Jericho and Lorelei. "I'm taking the Dreamers and the Handler because they're the last leverage you Kites have. You have three years before I come for what's left of the Trinity, Jericho Kite. On your mark. Get set. Go!"

The guards stabbed the arms of the Lynbrookians. Jericho and Lorelei watched in horror as everyone around them winced or cried in response to the sudden needle stick. Mikayla and Isaiah received a dosage as well.

Unfazed, Alexander returned to Sparrowhawk to caress his chin. "Jericho, relax. This is a good company merger that's happening here. Inside five to ten minutes, everyone here won't remember what happened. Their memory will simply reset to wherever they were three to six months ago, erasing all the trauma your family inflicted on them. The government won't poke their nose in, huh? See what I did there? It's like I pressed a big ol' reset button. Does that message get through to that thick, neanderthal skull of yours?"

"You're not helping them. You want to brainwash them into doing your will," Jericho said.

Alexander lightly chuckled. "Correct! You get a smiley face sticker. Now, go to Meccanicville and tell your daddy all about how you screwed him over. Take a picture of his expression for me."

One of Alexander's workers slapped a yellow smiley sticker on Jericho's cheek and walked away. Jericho snatched it off and ripped it into pieces.

Alexander winked at Jericho's and Lorelei's angry faces. "Say your goodbyes before the serum kicks in. Safe travels."

Blowing a kiss, Alexander walked alongside a guard who carried Sparrowhawk's petrified body. Lorelei fought to grab Alexander, but her guard snatched her back. She screamed. Jericho hushed her with a hug.

"I'm sorry, Lorelei," he said, tightening his embrace. "I wish I was a better cousin to you and Landon. Please tell him I'm sorry."

Lorelei cried on his shoulder.

Worried, Mikayla reached for Isaiah's hand. He took it, staring into her eyes.

Jericho let go of Lorelei and turned to Isaiah and Mikayla.

"Isaiah, I'll find out what I can about who you are. I'll find a way to get both of you out of Alexander's ownership."

Isaiah shook his head. "I don't want to be a dog handler. I just want to be a normal, boring person. I don't want to be saved by you and get sucked into whatever all this is. I want to forget."

Mikayla felt differently. "This weekend was the worst in my life, but I don't want to forget what happened to my dad, Naomi, and Mr. Rabbit. I don't want to forget what my mother did. I want answers." Mikayla squeezed Isaiah's hand and looked at a sniffling Lorelei. "There're people I don't want to forget."

Isaiah touched Mikayla's forehead with his. He had nothing to say.

"Mikayla, I'll keep all three of them safe from my father at Meccanicville. I promise."

She sighed.

"He'll do it, Mika. He'll find a way to fix all this mess," Lorelei said.

Jericho tensed up and nodded. "I will."

Mikayla nodded quietly and reached her other hand out. Jericho shook it firmly.

Two men suddenly loaded Mikayla onto a gurney. Another two did the same to Isaiah.

Lorelei's guard pulled her to the left helicopter for Kan. Jericho's guard pulled him right to the helicopter for Meccanicville.

Mikayla watched the helicopters ascend higher to depart Lynbrook's airspace. They became smaller, blending in with the gray clouds below the moon.

Onboard the helicopter, Lorelei buckled her seatbelt and hugged her bag, feeling parts of Mateo's stiff body against her fingertips through the fabric. She cried bittersweet tears. Soon she would be with her brother again, but they were destined for Kan.

Below Jericho's helicopter, more purple vans swarmed upon Lynbrook. Hundreds of Alexander's people roamed like ants invading an enemy colony. Jericho slouched into his seat, clenching the arms. His nails tore through the upholstery. His week was far from over. His journey was beginning.

Sharing an ambulance, Isaiah and Mikayla continued holding hands. They stared into each other's eyes until the moment their adoration for each other converted into unadulterated confusion.

Mikayla abruptly dropped Isaiah's hand and pulled away. "Don't touch me."

"You were the one touching me first!" he snapped, patting his eye patch. "What happened to my eye? Why am I in this cast?"

Mikayla rattled off multiple questions at the two men in lab coats riding alongside them. They marked notes on a clipboard, ignoring her. Isaiah barked questions at them. He was ignored too. They both continued beating the men down with questions until the men retreated behind a curtain.

Mikayla and Isaiah exchanged grins, blushed, and glanced elsewhere.

Mikayla beamed at Beau Heights out the back door of the ambulance. "Wow, that's a beautiful clocktower."

The moonlight reflected off the clocktower's crystal face at an angle making a glare so white she could barely read the hands stuck at 3:17. She had no idea how something so immense and powerful could become broken.

IV

Monday, November 10

Lunar phase: full moon
The Canine Moon

3:29AM

In the bal-chatri, five electric guitars plugged into amps blared heavy metal riffs. The players slammed on strings, dancing to the vibrato of the whammy bar. A drummer and a singer were stationed at the back, underneath the pristine stained glass of the baby kite. Ten heavily tattooed, robust men smashed sledgehammers into the other stained glass windows. Glass shards and gemstone projectiles flew everywhere, covering the carpet like pebbles.

Singing and headbanging, Alexander entered alongside an assistant whose name he didn't know. The players lowered the volume and continued strumming faintly. The assistant read the agenda off to Alexander as they gracefully avoided the debris in perfect tandem.

"Sir, at 4:00 AM, you will be defecating on the bed of Jericho Kite third in his name."

"Already did it. Twice. I pooped on his bed and on the pork rind-eating degenerate's. The bigot has a room full of taxidermy cardinals and squirrels."

She read from the clipboard. "I can move your 4:30 up. That is when you'll urinate on Matthew Jacob's computers."

"Did it. What's next?"

"Chelsea Sebring's quarters are available with paint buckets. Her blue, bedazzled furniture has been discarded, so you should have plenty of room. Jasmine Bellum's room is ready as well."

"I'm not in the mood to throw paint at their walls right now. Push that until the morning."

"It is the morning, sir."

"I mean when the sun comes up. The normal circumstances in which people say morning."

She made a deadpan face. "Of, course sir."

"I'm going to set the lawyer's office on fire at six. What's that old fart's name?"

"Gregory Mann. Sir, I advise that you refrain from arson until the leak in the western portion of New Lynbrook is mitigated."

"You've gotta be kidding me. The leak is way over yonder. No wonder the Kites didn't care about fixing it and just stayed on this side. The gas is like thirty minutes walking distance in that direction." He said, throwing his hand out.

"We shouldn't take chances, sir. Don't think like they did. That's how they got into this situation in the first place."

"Don't tell me how to think!"

"My apologies. We have personnel flying in right away to ventilate and remove the hazard and pipelines. The campus should be free of toxic gas inside a week."

Alexander palmed his forehead. "What's it going to cost?"

"Into the low billions of dollars to start, sir. Working underneath the clocktower is a delicate task. It made the cost higher."

"*Phew*! That's all?"

"Sir, you've spent well over half your budget tonight, figuring the cost of all those doses of Acute Amnesia Serum and *this*," she said, gesturing to the men bashing out the windows.

"*Ugh!* Whatever. This remodeling project is worth it. Everything happening is awesome. I knew taking the Trinity would be expensive."

"Your father said your budget was capped for assuming *all three* facilities of the Trinity. You've spent well over half capturing one."

"You're such a nag. My father supports me through and through. So what if it costs a few dollars more?"

"Yes, sir. My apologies again. We'll consult him for a budget revisal. Should we reactivate the clocktower once the work is complete?"

"Nah, let it stay on 3:17. I want the Kites to forever be reminded what time their legacy merged with mine."

Flashing a toothy grin, Alexander snatched a sledgehammer from the man standing closest to him. He bashed out what was left of Headmaster Kite's stained glass window and howled.

"You know, you are a very good assistant," he said, giving the sledgehammer back to the man. "Now, get me my rifle. I want to unload a magazine on Westley Hernandez's model airplane collection. Turn them into wooden Swiss cheese pieces. I want pictures of the whole mess sent to Meccanicville. The caption should read something like *New Lynbrook, Alabama's Up and Coming Hotel*. I don't know. You figure out how to phrase it."

"Of, course, sir. Will the 22LR be sufficient for the rifle?"

Alexander glared at her. "Don't make me take back your good assistant cookie."

"I'll ensure they bring in a heavier caliber."

He smiled. "Hey, before you go. Is Liam Galton awake?"

"Yes. He woke up fifteen minutes ago."

Alexander pumped his fist. "Tell them to play the guitars louder. I'd better feel this building shake like it's falling apart at the foundation! Tell them to play the song I wrote, Requiem of the Equestrian." He winked and pointed to the stained glass depicting the baby kite.

"As you wish."

Shortly thereafter, the heavy metal blared. Alexander made a sharp turn towards Sparrowhawk's quarters, grinning. He flung the door open and slammed it closed. The well-insulated room muffled the tremolo bar making a screech that sounded like a crying, neighing horse as he slowly trudged through Sparrowhawk's trashed quarters. The daggers Sparrowhawk had thrown in the wall earlier vibrated. Alexander walked by a blade lodged in a picture of a horse and snatched it. He kicked papers and torn curtains aside, approaching Sparrowhawk, who was chained to the wall upside down above his ripped bed. Alexander stuck the knife in the wall beside his face.

"Hey, Liam Galton. You awake, baby? Heads up, your name isn't Sparrowhawk anymore. I'm not a wannabe falconer like your former boss. We use government names over here, and you're lucky I care about knowing yours. You are—well, were—infamous in the eugenics community."

Liam glared at Alexander with his lips pursed. He was smug in the eyes, however.

"You knew I was coming. That's why you trashed your quarters, so that it wouldn't be me who gets to do it. You've got a ton of pictures of that Mikayla girl on your wall. Are you a predator or something?"

Liam smirked.

"Silent treatment? You've got fight in you. Tell me. Why did you choose to work for the Kites over us? Is it because they're stupid, easy to have your way with, and we're not? Yeah, it is, isn't it? C'mon…don't give me that face." Alexander gripped Liam's chin, digging in his nails. "You're being a bad, bad kitty-cat. You finally ended up with us now, so you have to be a good kitty-cat, right?" He forced Liam to nod. "That's right. You have a really, really special power, Liam. I know you know that." From his pocket, Alexander pulled out the key that would set him free. "I know you hate being humiliated. That's why you got kicked out of the eugenics community, isn't it? They weren't fond of you going out your way to get that surgery. You were trying to become a Dreamer with the 33.3 balance. I have a teensy-weensy bit of news for you: Mikayla Birdwing won that genetic lottery. It ended up that way. Darn those surgeons."

Liam's nostrils flared.

"I struck a nerve there, huh? I can tell. Your face is getting redder and redder. It's like you're blushing for me." Alexander kneeled, stooping down to eye level with Liam. He raised a cat-eared headband he pulled out from his other pocket. "I know a way to level the playing field so that you can be equal to that girl, maybe even better than her. You want to know what it is?"

Liam narrowed his eyes and nodded.

"Good. Listen to me closely. I may seem like a party guy, but don't be mistaken. I got eyes everywhere in the Electric Company, and my eyes showed me that you tried to harm the Triad and Mikayla. Unacceptable.

Jericho's goals align with mine. He isn't aware yet that Kite Express and Raven Dynamic should merge. Don't get in my way of making him realize that! You are not allowed to harm Jericho, Lorelei, Isaiah, and Mikayla or anyone they care about. Matter of fact, you can't go after them. New Lynbrook is your forever home."

"You mean my prison," Liam muttered.

"*Un-un-un.* That's a negative thought." Alexander wagged his finger. He paused, twirling the key and rocking his head to the guitar and drum duet. "You know where this is going, don't you, Liam? Sure, you do! All you have to do is leave them alone and be my—"

"I'll be your kitten," Liam muttered irritably.

"And now that you know what's in it for you, how are you going to be my kitten?"

Liam tried to pull his chains, but he was tightly restricted. He sighed, "With pleasure."

"Attaboy!" Alexander petted Liam and placed the cat ears on him. "You won't touch Mikayla, right?"

Liam glared.

Alexander grabbed him. "I need verbal confirmation."

"I won't touch her," he said, looking away.

"Good kitty-cat."

Afterword

Imagine this. You're a Texan growing up during the Great Depression in 1937. New London is your school. On 21 acres, the school is prestigious and well-built with steel and concrete, a major feat in its time. It resides in one of the richest towns in East Texas. The oil boom brings in lots of money to your town. Compared to other kids in the country, you're well off.

Here's what you don't know. The beginning factors that led to the explosion were created in 1932, years before you arrive at the campus. The building was built on sloping grounds with a large space of air between the basement and the foundation. Architects recommended the installation of gas boilers and a steam heating system throughout the building. The school board wanted to save money and instead chose to install multiple steam heaters in rooms throughout the building. The piping for the unrecommended installation ran through the basement, lacking proper ventilation for the gases to escape.

The school board signed a contract with United Gas Corporation for natural gas for the gas steam heaters; however, the contract was cancelled early in 1937. Saving more money, the school board opted to tap Parade Gasoline Company's pipeline for its residue gas. This was an unauthorized method of obtaining gas, but it was free. The school board hired a contractor who modified existing pipelines to allow for the siphoning of residual gas. However, the contractor was not a certified engineer. Gases began building up beneath the school afterwards. Back then, natural gas had no odor additives, which meant leaks went undetected.

It's March 18, 1937, and you have another headache this week, but you've gotten used to them. Nobody thinks much of it. This happens to everyone. Besides, the long weekend is coming up. Exciting times are ahead. It's after

3PM. You're walking down the hallway to the gymnasium for the afterschool event. Meanwhile, the shop instructor is in another room needing to use his electric sander. He turns it on, creating a spark that ignites. The boom is incredible. You fall, unaware what just happened. The roof jumped and everything came crashing down. Your ears are ringing as you blink, coming groggily into. The destruction all around is incomprehensible. Gazing to the left, through the haze, the lockers are ripped apart. Some hang off the wall dangling by its hinges. Down the hall a hand barely sticks out from a concrete slab. She's crushed, not moving.

A resident who lives near the school shifts through the rubble, pulling you out. You escape death as the emergency responders tend to your wounds. The rescue efforts eventually end. The reality of what happened sets in. Around 300 of your classmates and teachers are dead.

The investigation concludes that the pipeline connection to the residue gas line was improperly installed, releasing natural gas beneath the school in the crawlspace. Many lawsuits are brought against the school board and the gas company. But the court ruled neither party responsible due to the lack of physical evidence. Cases are dismissed.

Why?

The United States had no federal regulation for the mandatory odorization of natural gas on March 18, 1937. The school board and the Parade Gasoline Company had broken no laws because the laws did not exist at the time of the incident. Safety policies "are written in blood."

Germany notably had been using an additive in natural gases since the late 1800s. With lives lost and citizens demanding a solution, Texas legislation adopted and enforced the odorization of natural gases. Today when you smell gas you're smelling mercaptan, an odorous sulfuric mixture. May 28, 1937, Texas created the Engineering Registration Act, ensuring only contractors issued certification through the state of Texas were allowed to do engineering jobs on pipelines.

Throughout history, incidents like the one described above have happened over and over again. Some disturb communities locally. Others have become disasters garnering national attention. Safety policies "are written in blood."

In my opinion, both the school board and the Parade Gasoline Company failed to practice good business ethics and failed to uphold their social responsibility.

With all that said, one of the hardest battles of a safety professional is convincing the people in charge to invest money into fixing a known problem or the technology that prevents the development of a problem. In *Raptor Moon*, Headmaster Kite is irredeemable for demanding the execution of witnesses and putting lives of the Lynbrookians and his Raptor Administration in danger. The one right thing he does is listen to Edmund Rabbit, the Chemical Safety Board investigator. He shuts down Beau Heights to prevent a spark, saving lives. He puts his ego aside and exercises his social responsibility as a leader of a powerful conglomerate.

What would happen if powerful conglomerates like Kite Express and Raven Dynamic existed and were allowed to function lawlessly neglecting social responsibility? What if I were to tell you that the events in *Raptor Moon* are satirical in nature yet not too farfetched from what happens real world? Scary, huh?

Businesses have an ethical responsibility to uphold as they have potential to create damage socially to communities and to the environment on both a local and global scale. While greed and corporations taking shortcuts will always be an ongoing problem, you as an individual can prioritize safety and fight back using your voice and exercising your human rights. I challenge readers to research the business ethics of their favorite companies/busines ses. Do they align with your values? Do they pay their workers fairly and provide a workplace that cares for their wellbeing?

See something? Say something. Don't go about it alone. Team up with likeminded people to push your concerns from problem to solution. Citizens teamed up after the New London explosion, persuading lawmakers to create a positive change.

About the Author

KT Byrd lived most of her life in Alabama with her mother and sister after her parents divorced. She started writing at fourteen, striving to be a published author someday. In 2020, Byrd reunited with her father who she discovered was a retired aeronautical aviation analyst. Byrd worked as an air traffic controller in the United States Air Force before she changed careers to become an Occupational Safety and Health Specialist. She lives in Texas with her husband and pets. She enjoys cooking and makes the best pretzels ever on New Year's Eve.

You can connect with me on:
- https://ktbyrdtweets.com
- https://www.instagram.com/ktbyrdtweets

Also by KT Byrd

Canine Moon will be the next novella in the series!

Canine Moon

In pain and confused, seventeen-year-old Isaiah Marksman awakens in an ambulance with a broken wrist and a missing eye. At least there's a pretty girl next to him. But what is her name? He felt like he'd met her somewhere before. She's wearing his crescent moon necklace and a uniform matching his. Of course, they've met. When? The paramedic tells him it's November 9, and that they're in Alabama. Last time Isaiah checked, it was July 18th. What happened in the last three and a half months? The paramedic refuses to answer. The pretty girl is just like him but worse. She believes it's May. And yet, she somehow knows how he got injured.